THE LAST VIKINGS

S. P. Grey

First published in Great Britain in 2008
by
Hall Publishing

Copyright © 2008 S.P. Grey

A CIP Catalogue of this book is available from the British Library

ISBN 978-0-9558220-0-1

Cover illustration by Ben Baldwin.
Snickelway map by Mark Jones, author of 'A Walk Around the
Snickelways of York' and other interesting publications.
Text sketches by Peter Randall.

Printed and bound in
Great Britain by Biddles Ltd,
King's Lynn, Norfolk

CONTENTS

Prologue: The Legend of Sigurd the Dragon Slayer   1

Chapter 1:   Vikings in the Night   3

Chapter 2:   Sigurd the Dragon Slayer   15

Chapter 3:   The Last Vikings   23

Chapter 4:   The Viking Council   39

Chapter 5:   The Candle Chamber   53

Chapter 6:   The Quest   61

Chapter 7:   Learning to Fly   71

Chapter 8:   The Way Out of York   87

Chapter 9:   Attack in Ironwood   97

Chapter 10:   Race Across the Ice   113

Chapter 11:   Mimir's Well   127

Chapter 12:   Fast Flight Back Home   137

Chapter 13:   The Last Chance Café   149

Chapter 14:   After Dinner Surprises   163

Chapter 15:   After Dinner Guests   175

Chapter 16:   Race to the City Walls   191

Special thanks to

Pete, Colette, Jessica and Mark Jones
for all their help in producing this book
and the one to follow

Prologue

The Legend of Sigurd the Dragon Slayer

In the dark ages long ago, great stories were told of heroes and gods and the battles they fought with the fearsome creatures that stalked the earth.

Favourite amongst these was the tale of Sigurd, the greatest of the Viking warriors. None could match his strength and skill with the sword. His golden shield and helmet were emblazoned with a dragon so all who saw him knew that it was he who had killed the great dragon Fafnir.

Sigurd was no ordinary man. After eating the dragon's heart, he gained the ability to perform magic. He also possessed the gift of foresight, knowing events before they happened.

So it was that he foresaw his own death, though he was unable to avoid it. Treachery was his downfall. Consumed by jealousy, his own family plotted against him, stabbing him whilst he slept. But on his deathbed he vowed to return and fight again when the last Vikings face their most desperate peril.

For over a thousand years he has slept as the creatures of legend have retreated into the shadows, waiting for the final battle when all our fates will be decided. The world has changed and his story has almost been forgotten. But as fearful plans are being made far away in the Black Mountains, slowly Sigurd is beginning to stir.

Chapter 1

Vikings in the Night

The rain came down, tapping on the roof of their old estate car like a thousand drumming fingers, whilst Peter Thomas stared out of the misty back-seat window, watching his world slip away.

A silent tension hung in the air as Peter's mother drove through the puddles on the uneven country lane, pretending to be concentrating only on the road ahead. Her hands were clamped onto the top of the steering wheel so firmly that her knuckles were white, and her head was bent so far forward that her chin was resting on her wrists. Peter had seen her like this before. To anyone else, the fact that she was sad was only visible when she pretended to brush back her blond fringe whilst at the same time wiping a tear from the corner of her eye. But to him, her grief was as clear as the rain seeping down the windscreen.

Beside her in the front passenger seat was his grandmother. As still and stern as a rock-face, she was sitting bolt upright with a green scarf wrapped around her neck and a ridiculous purple furry hat perched on her head. Her hands were clutching a large black handbag in her lap. Without seeming to blink, her eyes as wide as a startled parrot's, she stared into the distance through her thick horn-rimmed glasses.

Peter sighed. Seeking distraction, he rolled up the sleeve of his baggy black jumper and rubbed a spy hole through the misty window. For perhaps a minute he watched the wet countryside roll by, then he craned his neck to look behind him. He could barely see their farmhouse now - a dark dot in the distance, tiny against the sweeping hills and valleys that surrounded it. It had been his home all his life and now he was leaving it, perhaps never to return. He knew that somewhere inside it, his father would be looking out of a window too as he watched them disappear into the distance. He sighed again, wondering what his life would be like now.

Throwing himself back into the seat, he thought about the past few months. Of course, he'd known something was wrong, no matter how much his parents had tried to hide it from him. Many nights he had lain awake listening to them arguing. But he never thought it would come to this – that he and his mother would be leaving his father and the home he had lived in all his life to live in York with his grandmother.

'Don't worry lad!' his father had said to him just a few minutes earlier, holding the car door open as he crawled into the backseat. 'Things will work out for the best. You'll see.'

His father had tried to smile to reassure him that everything was going to be alright, but Peter could tell he was just as worried as he was.

'You'll like York,' he'd said, smiling distantly, and for a moment there had been a sparkle in his eyes. 'Your mother and I first met there. It's a magical city!'

A *magical* city? For some reason that was the one thing that stuck in Peter's mind as his father waved a sad goodbye and they drove away. A magical city! A city full of magic!

Maybe because he needed something to distract him, a part of Peter clung to the idea of going somewhere magical. Somewhere he could walk down strange streets, not knowing what he would find around the next corner. Somewhere that would take away the pain of leaving his home and his father behind.

Lulled by the sound of the car's engine, he began to feel sleepy. As he felt his eyes slowly close, he made a silent resolution. If there truly was magic in York, he would find it. Then he slipped peacefully into dream filled slumber.

*

'Wake up Pete! We're nearly there! *Look!*'

Peter was awake in an instant, snapping out of the strange dream he was having of magical creatures flying through the night. Rubbing the drowsiness from his eyes, he peered through the windscreen in the direction his mother was indicating.

The first thing he noticed was that it was now dark outside, though the city was alive with hundreds of lights shining brightly.

Then he saw what his mother was pointing at. Soaring above them was the most enormous church he had ever seen in his life! The vast stained oval window closest to them was seemingly miles away from the identical twin towers that soared above its opposite end.

'That's York Minster Young Man!' his grandmother declared, catching his surprised expression as she turned stiffly in her seat to look at him. 'Marvellous isn't it? We're quite proud of it here. Biggest Cathedral north of the Alps, or so they tell me! Most beautiful too, in my opinion!'

Peter didn't speak. He was too busy staring at the enormous Cathedral. It seemed to shine with divine light that emanated from its every stone. Suddenly the hairs on the back of his neck rose. There was something mysterious about the great church - something he couldn't quite put his finger on. It carried a hint of danger – as if something powerful was hidden there.

Just as he was falling under the Minster's spell, they turned another corner and it slipped from view. Minutes later, they crossed an elegant bridge over a river then, turning again, they pulled into a narrow street and slowed. Passing between two brick pillars, they drove into a small car-park.

'Here we are!' his mother announced wearily as she pulled into a parking space and turned off the engine. 'Everybody out!'

They had rented the top floor flat of an old four-storied house. Unfortunately, this meant they had to heave their heavy luggage up three flights of stairs, and it took two journeys to and from the car before they finally stood outside the door to their flat with all their suitcases and bags piled up beside them. His mother retrieved a large golden key from her purse and opened the door.

'Welcome to your new home Pete!'

Stepping inside, she swung the key around her finger thoughtfully as she surveyed the interior of the flat.

Peter studied it too, and he didn't much like what he saw. The flat looked as dull as dull could possibly be. Small and cold, it was decorated with dreary brown wallpaper that was peeling where it met the ceiling. A threadbare green carpet containing a variety of dark stains covered the floor. It smelt of damp decay and mould. The only pleasant thing about it was the large windows. Hazy streetlight just penetrated the dirty net curtains which, judging by the expression on his mother's face, she was already itching to pull down.

Noting Peter's sour expression, she put her arm around his shoulders.

'Don't worry Pete. We'll soon get used to it! It's just that it's different, that's all. Things always seem strange when you're not used to them. It will be fun here once we've settled in. You'll see!'

Peter regarded her moodily. His life, it seemed, had changed even more than he thought.

*

That night, Peter lay on his bed with his hands behind his head, unable to fall asleep. As he pondered on what had happened during the day, he listened to the noises of the house: the faint sound of music coming from one of the flats downstairs, the occasional slamming of doors, the tapping of rain against the window and the slight flapping noise made by the swaying curtains as cold air seeped through from outside. Suddenly he threw back the blankets and punched the wooden headboard behind him in frustration. Why had his mother chosen such a horrible house to live in? Why hadn't they stayed on the farm where he'd been so happy? Eventually though, his eyes began to close. Moments later he was fast asleep.

In the dead of night he woke suddenly, jumping up so fast he almost fell out of bed. Blinking in shock, he peered into the darkness of his bedroom, his mind still dull with sleep. He could just make out the shadowy outline of his bed and the wardrobe with the door half open and his coat hanging inside. Nothing had changed. But though everything appeared to be the same, there was an undeniable tension in the air.

For almost a minute he stared into the darkness, wondering what had woken him. Then he noticed a faint glow coming from the window. At first he thought it must be from the street lamp in the car-park behind their house, but it seemed to be getting gradually brighter. Then, as he watched the window in alarm, the curtains suddenly leapt into the air and began dancing frantically in front of him! At the same time, the strange glow from outside dramatically increased in intensity, flooding his bedroom with light.

Too frightened to move, Peter could hear his heart racing in his chest. Finally summoning up enough courage, he slowly pushed the blankets aside and crawled to the end of his bed. Inch by inch, he lowered his feet onto the cold wooden floor and stood up. Immediately the curtains became still and the light vanished. Once more his bedroom was dark and silent.

Feeling confused and frightened in equal measure, he stood completely still beside his bed, wondering what could possibly be going on. He stared at the window again. The curtains were swaying gently as if beckoning him forward. Pausing for just a moment, he took a hesitant step forwards and slowly pulled back the curtains. His hands shaking, he undid the catch, opened the window and peered outside.

At first, all he could see was dense fog, giving the night a creepy, sinister feel. Only the street lamp in the car-park pierced it, dimly illuminating the eerie scene. All was quiet; all was still. Then he began to see more.

Almost hidden by the fog, something was moving through the air. For a moment he wasn't sure what it was, then he recognised it. It was snow. Flakes the size of golf balls were tumbling out of the sky, their small grey shadows briefly caught in the light of the street lamp as they drifted down to earth. As he watched them, a breeze came up from nowhere and whirled back and forth as if searching for something. Then, in response to the breeze, the fog began to roll back to reveal the cold grey world below.

The car-park appeared first, its white blemish-free surface marred by three large mounds where cars were parked, each of them indistinguishable beneath the snow. Just beyond the car-park was a low stone wall beside a row of tall trees. At the centre of the wall was an iron gate. The gate opened onto a narrow path that led through an overgrown graveyard to a small church. It looked incredibly old. The light cast by the street lamp in the car-park barely reached it but, like the Minster, it somehow generated its own light, and the whole church glowed faintly in the night.

As Peter gazed at it, the silence was suddenly ripped apart by a deep booming noise. It was so loud and sudden that he jumped in shock, banging the back of his head painfully against the bottom of the window frame. It only took him a moment to realise what it was. Rising from somewhere close by was the deep sound of men's voices, singing a strange song.

Overcoming his surprise quickly, he strained his ears to catch the words. But they sang in a foreign language and he could make nothing of it. Then movement caught his eye.

A tall figure appeared in the car-park, followed by another and another. Soon a dozen men were there, each slowly revealed as they stepped out of the receding fog. The light from the solitary street lamp glinted off their shields and swords as they sang. Peter immediately knew who they were. He had seen similar men in the books about York's history his mother had given him before they arrived. Beneath him, Viking warriors were marching through the night.

The Vikings passed through the iron gate onto the narrow path that led to the church. Peter could see them clearly now. They were dressed in dark tunics and chain mail. Each of them was bearded and wore a conical shaped silver helmet with a long thin nose-guard. Though they each held a sword and shield, something about the way they moved gave Peter the impression that they hadn't come to fight.

As he watched them, the Vikings formed a circle in the graveyard around a tall gravestone he hadn't noticed before. Then, as if in response to a silent command, they stopped singing.

All was ominously still once more except for the falling snow. The Vikings stood silently, their long blond hair flying up in the breeze beneath their helmets. Then, one by one, they bent down and laid their swords on the ground with the points touching the gravestone. Soon there was a circle of swords around it, each glinting faintly in the night.

After the last sword was laid, the Vikings stood perfectly still again. Then, in perfect unison, they held out their right arms with their fists clenched as if in salute and shouted a single word, their voices like thunder. Peter couldn't be absolutely certain, but he thought it was a name they called out.

As the sound of their cries faded, they began to sing again, their voices so deep and loud that Peter was sure they would wake everyone for miles around. Turning from the gravestone, they marched out of the graveyard, disappearing into the night as suddenly as they had come. Soon all Peter could see of them was a faint outline and the occasional glint of street-light off their helmets. Then they were gone, though he could still hear them singing. Eventually even their voices faded until he could only hear

VIKINGS IN THE NIGHT

the wind and the occasional creaking of swaying branches.

For perhaps a minute, Peter stood by the window in shock. A thousand unanswered questions came to him at once. What had he just seen? What were they doing in the graveyard? Why had they laid their swords at the gravestone? What had they called out? Why had no one else seen or heard them? He shivered with cold and excitement, his mind racing through the possibilities. Finally he breathed out, unaware that he had been holding his breath.

For the next hour Peter stood by the window, his eyes fixed upon the graveyard in case the Vikings returned. But everything remained quiet and still except for the constantly falling snow and the occasional creaking of trees in the wind. Eventually his hands and face became so numb with cold that he was forced inside. He closed the window and crept back into bed, though he left the curtains undrawn. But even though he wrapped the blankets tightly around him and was soon warm again, he didn't sleep. Every time he heard the slightest sound, he was at the window in an instant, peering through the darkness and chasing every shadow.

After jumping out of bed for the eighth or ninth time, Peter finally resolved to wait until dawn then creep downstairs to investigate the graveyard. He wanted to look upon the strange gravestone, feeling sure he would find some clue there to explain what had happened.

It was the longest night of his life! He couldn't believe how slowly the shadowy hands of the clock in his room crawled round! Finally, at 7.36, the first glow of dawn appeared and faint light seeped into his bedroom. Immediately he leapt out of bed, pulled on his worn jeans, black jumper and long black raincoat (which he had inherited from his father and was therefore several sizes too big), tripped into his trainers and tip-toed out of his bedroom into the living room.

He was thankful that his mother had taken to sleeping in recently, though he knew he might only have half an hour before she stirred. Glancing around the tiny flat, he searched for her keys, not wanting to waste a second of precious time. He finally spotted them on the kitchen table. As his hand closed around them, he felt a sudden pang of guilt, feeling like a thief in the night. But his curiosity was too strong. As quiet as a mouse, he stole across the living room, opened the door of the flat and stepped onto the landing. Despite his best efforts to be silent, he couldn't prevent the sharp *clunk!* of the door as it locked behind him. Freezing, he strained to catch any sound that would indicate his mother had heard him. But nothing stirred. Satisfied that she was still asleep, he ran lightly down the long winding staircase to the lobby, opened the front door with his mother's key and stepped into the freezing morning.

The snow was deeper than Peter thought. Immediately his feet sank so low he had to strain to pull them out, leaving deep footprints in the white landscape that was previously the car-park. Trying to ignore the cold dampness seeping through his trainers, he peered through the gently falling snow flakes towards the church and trudged towards it.

The first thing he noticed when he opened the gate and stepped into the graveyard was that it stopped snowing, though it was still falling in the car-park behind him. It was as if some unseen force prevented the snow from entering the church grounds. Even more peculiar was the graveyard itself. Despite the blizzard just beyond its boundary and the cold winter season, it was alive with springtime activity. The grass was lush, and several bright red flowers were dotted around the gravestones. As Peter slowly took in the strange scene, he noticed dozens of tiny yellow birds sitting in the branches of the trees beside the church wall, all huddled together and chirping merrily. He had never seen their kind before, though he recognised most birds from having lived in the countryside all his life. Like rows of tiny choirboys squashed together in a church pew, they sang their happy songs as if it was a warm spring morning and nothing could be finer.

Finally, he tore his eyes away from the strange birds to study the church. With its lopsided tower and sunken roof, it looked even older than he had first thought. Other than its great age, though, there appeared to be nothing unusual about it.

Remembering his task, he spotted the gravestone the Vikings had laid their swords beside. Almost black in colour, it towered above the smaller gravestones scattered around it. His heart beating faster, he jogged towards it. Once again though, he was disappointed. Pock marked and covered in moss, there appeared to be nothing peculiar about it, though it was clearly very old, perhaps as old as the church itself. He searched for the Viking swords but there was no sign of them, even when he crouched on his knees and ran his hands through the long grass. Feeling incredibly frustrated, he brushed the gravestone with his fingers. But if there was ever an inscription, the words had long since been erased by time.

Crestfallen, Peter wondered what he should do. In no rush to go back, he spotted a solitary wooden bench in front of the church and sat down to ponder the puzzle he had been set. What had he seen? Why was there no sign of the Vikings? What had happened to their swords?

As he struggled to find an explanation, the sun appeared for the first time, though it was still snowing beyond the church wall. At the same time, a rainbow appeared, arcing towards him. He followed its perfectly coloured bands as they curved down to the ground. Suddenly he jumped in shock. The rainbow was shining on the tall gravestone the Vikings had laid their swords beside!

His heart pounding, he leapt across the graveyard towards the stone. As he watched in disbelief, the gravestone slowly transformed. The moss faded away, the weather–worn pockmarks disappeared and it became smooth once more. Then, as he held his breath in amazement, an inscription appeared. As if written by an invisible finger, the letters emerged one by one, cut deeply into the stone.

HERE LIES SIGURD THE DRAGON SLAYER
VIKING KING OF KINGS

But just as he was pondering what the words could mean, they disappeared. Once again it was just a gravestone, old and covered with moss.

Blinking in surprise, he continued to stare at the stone. The rainbow was still shining upon it, as brightly as before. Then he saw something small and metallic catch the light. Resting on top of the gravestone was a golden talisman on a silver chain. It was fashioned in the shape of a dragon with its jaws agape. Its webbed wings were spread out as if in flight, and its eagle-like claws were outstretched, ready to rip and tear. A long reptilian tail trailed behind it. In the centre of its head, two red eyes seemed to regard him scornfully.

HERE LIES
SIGURD
THE DRAGON SLAYER

VIKING
KING OF KINGS

SIGURD'S GRAVESTONE

Instinctively he reached out to touch it. As soon as his hand closed around it, the rainbow disappeared and a deep voice spoke behind him.

'Hello Peter. I was hoping you would come. I have been waiting for you.'

Jumping in shock, Peter spun around.

Chapter 2

Sigurd the Dragon Slayer

An old man was standing in the middle of the graveyard. He appeared to have come out of nowhere! Peter had neither seen nor heard him until he had spoken, even though he was standing just a few feet away!

Without thinking, Peter dropped the talisman into the pocket of his jeans.

'H-How do you know my name?' he stammered, staring at the old man's wrinkled face and bright eyes that were shining with such fierce intensity that Peter barely dared meet them.

'*How?*' The old man pondered for a moment as if he hadn't expected the question. 'How? Let's just say that I need to know a lot of things in my line of work.'

Not sure what he meant, Peter tore his eyes away from the old man's face for a moment. He noticed he was leaning on an old garden hoe. The old man followed his gaze.

'Do not fear. I am just a simple gardener, that is all. I tend the church garden as best I can, though the work is getting too much for me I fear. I heard your name when you arrived with your mother and grandmother.'

Feeling slightly more comfortable with this explanation, Peter slowly recovered from his initial shock and studied the man more closely. Incredibly tall, he had long grey hair that reached his shoulders and a thick grey beard. His face was heavily lined with age and his skin had the rough texture of someone who had spent most of their life outdoors. He was dressed in a simple white woollen shirt with thick brown canvas trousers and peculiar shoes that had straps rather than laces and came up to his ankles. Despite his age, he leant on the hoe lightly as if he didn't really need it for support and he was far stronger than he pretended. Though it was only a garden tool, there was something about the way he held it that suggested he was used to handling tools of one kind or another and was skilled with his hands. Overall, though he was old, the impression he gave was one of hidden strength. He had an aura of quiet authority about him that demanded respect, and though there was kindness in his eyes, there was also a steely glint of unshakeable resolve.

The old man waited patiently as Peter regarded him. When he spoke again, his voice was deep and powerful.

'What brings you here so early in the morning? Do you seek to witness the dawn? If so, you are too late.'

Peter fiddled with the buttons on his coat nervously. The man's strange way of speaking and the utmost respect he commanded made him feel distinctly uneasy.

'I…I came to look at the graveyard. I…thought I saw something here last night and I wanted to check what it was.'

The old man nodded thoughtfully, as if pleased with the answer.

'You seek Sigurd then? I hoped it would be so.'

Peter almost choked. How did he know about Sigurd? Not sure how to reply, he simply nodded, avoiding the old man's eyes as they stared relentlessly down at him.

'Then your vigilance last night has not been wasted. You have found him. I am Sigurd, though I have not been called by that name for over a thousand years. I have come here to speak with you, Peter. Will you listen to me?'

Peter's mouth dropped open.

'But how can you be Sigurd? Isn't he…*dead?*'

The old man's eyes glinted beneath his thick grey eyebrows.

'Dead? You think death is the end? What do you know of death? Have *you* ever died?'

The question caught Peter by surprise.

'Err, no, I haven't. I haven't ever…died before.'

'Then why are you so certain about something you know so little about? You may find that the world is rather different than you think.'

Peter gaped stupidly, feeling like he was being told off by a wise old teacher, which only served to increase his nervousness still further. Meanwhile Sigurd calmly placed the hoe against the end of the bench and sat down, as if he was simply an old man in need of a rest. He gestured to the empty seat beside him.

'Sit down Peter. We have much to talk about, you and I.'

Feeling decidedly awkward, Peter sat down beside him. He longed to shuffle to the end of the bench, but feared Sigurd would be angered by such a gesture.

'Yes, I am Sigurd, or I once was,' continued the old man, his blue eyes staring intently into Peter's. 'I am the guardian of York until Ragnarok and the end of the world. But I am also a simple gardener, and this is my garden.' He gestured with his arm towards the graveyard, his posture erect and proud like a father pointing to his son. 'For many years I have worked here, though few have seen me. There is still so much to do. Now I must put aside gardening for a while. There are other matters I must attend to.'

Wondering what he meant by the sinister sounding 'Ragnarok', Peter risked a quick glance at the old man out of the corner of his eye. He half expected to be able to see through him to the church beyond, and was both disappointed and relieved to discover that he appeared to be as solid as himself. As if he could read his mind, Sigurd chuckled.

'Expecting to see a wraith? A terrifying ghoul? Have I disappointed you? Shouldn't you be scared of me, if you think me a creature from the grave?'

Reddening, Peter lowered his eyes and stared at his feet awkwardly. But though he was still nervous, he no longer felt scared, despite sitting next to a man who had been dead for hundreds of years. Shifting on the bench, he stared into the old man's eyes and found that he was watching him knowingly, as if he knew all about him and was waiting for him to ask a question.

'Why are you here?' Peter asked tentatively.

'Because of you. I wanted to meet you. You are a very important boy, though you do not know why yet.'

Peter stared at the old man in surprise. Was he making fun of him? Who did he think he was?

'What makes you think I am…*important?*'

The old man's eyes turned inward in silent contemplation. Raising his head, he took the hoe and passed it between his hands as he gazed across the dark graveyard.

'Because I have waited for you for many centuries. The time

has come. There have been signs. I am not wrong.'

'I…' Peter was lost for words. 'I don't understand! The time has come for *what?*'

'That is what I have come to speak to you about. You must listen carefully, for my time here is short. I have a long tale to tell that will seem wondrous beyond belief to you, but still it is the truth.'

Leaning the hoe back against the bench, Sigurd placed his enormous rough hands on his knees and bowed his head. His eyes went strangely blank as he relived distant memories.

'A long time ago, when even York was young, my kin came here. For hundreds of years we had searched for York and we crossed the sea many times in our longships before we found it. Your ancestors called us Vikings and feared us greatly. And rightly so, for many of us waged war upon them and took their lands. But most of us were explorers and settlers, seeking greater things than conquest. The reason we sought York was because of Yggdrasil.'

'What's *Yggdrasil?*' asked Peter immediately, determined to understand everything Sigurd told him.

'Yggdrasil is a tree, the tree of life. Its branches span the skies, enclosing the heavens within, though you cannot see them. It has three great roots that bind together the earth that forms this world. Two of them lie beyond the reach of men. The third rises almost to the surface where its sap can be drawn. That is what we were looking for, and after years of searching, we finally found it here in York, deep under the ground beneath the great church that is now called the Minster.

'The sap of Yggdrasil is a great treasure. Anyone who drinks even the smallest drop will gain great strength and power. We used the sap to begin the study of what you would call magic.' Sigurd stirred from the dreamlike state he had entered and stared deeply into Peter's eyes, smiling distantly. 'It was a great time for the Vikings in York. They became wise and strong. They built their villages by the river and lived in peace for many years. But Yggdrasil is a living thing and its sap is precious. It can only be taken in small doses for fear of harming the tree, and no Viking was allowed more than a single drop at a time.

'Then came Maledict. He was a powerful sorcerer. Many Vikings both feared and respected him, and because some craved for ever greater power, they listened to his counsel. But Maledict had his own dark purpose. He poisoned their minds, urging them to use the sap for conquest and destruction. Because of Maledict, many Vikings used the power of the sap to wage war, making them mighty foes who were feared greatly, for none could stand against them. Their conquests spread far across the seas.

'The Vikings did much mischief at Maledict's command. But in the end, the sap was their undoing. In their arrogance, they left York unguarded as they pursued conquests abroad, and the city was attacked by their enemies, who knew nothing of Yggdrasil yet were drawn to York for reasons they could not explain. Only those who retreated to the Viking Halls beneath the Minster to guard Yggdrasil survived. Later, other armies took the city: the Saxons and the Norman Conqueror. Though they fought to take it back, without the sap their strength was weakened and they were defeated.'

'What happened then?' asked Peter eagerly.

'Maledict saw his opportunity to strike. The Vikings were defeated and the Saxons and Normans knew nothing of Yggdrasil but rumour. He committed a terrible crime, almost the worst of all his foul deeds. He stole past the Vikings guarding Yggdrasil and set his axe to the root of tree. The precious sap poured from the wound and, in his greed, he drank deeply.'

'Why did he do that if the sap was so precious?'

'Why? For power of course! Power he would gain over others by drinking Yggdrasil's life-force. And to deny anyone else access to that power. But that was not all. Then he committed the worst sin of all.'

Sigurd paused, his eyes pained and distant.

'Yggdrasil had borne a single fruit within which was a stone – the Viking Stone - a single seed from which a sapling could be raised and a new tree grown. That stone was our great hope for the future. With it we could nurture a second tree that would one day spread its roots across the world, just as Yggdrasil had done when the world was created. Taking his knife, Maledict cut the stone from the wounded tree and took it for himself.

'Well he knew the significance of the Viking Stone: the concentrated power of Yggdrasil was within it. By taking it, he cheated death. Aided by its power, he has lived for over a thousand years. In his arrogance, he fashioned a steel crown to hold the stone. Now he wears the crown wherever he goes, and none dare challenge him.'

'But what about the Vikings who were guarding the tree?' said Peter. 'Didn't they try to stop him?'

Sigurd smiled grimly.

'They were fooled. Bitterly they have regretted their mistake in the years that have passed. Too late they realised the truth.'

'What happened then?' urged Peter, eager to hear the whole story.

'With the Vikings defeated, Maledict was free to pursue his dark aims. He set about poisoning the minds of men until they no longer believed in Yggdrasil and its powers. He knew that if men did not believe in magic, they would remain weak and corruptible, and none would ever rise to challenge him. At the same time, he destroyed any Vikings he found until they retreated to their hidden halls and did not dare leave them.'

Sigurd bowed his head, suddenly looking tired. A heavy atmosphere hung in the frosty air between them like a dark shadow. But Peter was desperate to learn more about the Vikings.

'You keep mentioning magic. Do you mean…*tricks?*'

Sigurd smiled and the heavy atmosphere was lifted instantly.

'No, I do not mean tricks. The power of Yggdrasil is strong. It allows men to access the power that lies sleeping within them so they can achieve what others believe impossible. But men no longer believe in magic. They live in a world of rules and laws that limit what they can achieve, little knowing that these limitations are of their own making. They do not believe that magic is possible. Now the last Vikings live in a world most men cannot see, as do other magical creatures, even Maledict himself. Men no longer see the magical world. They do not believe it exists and to them it is invisible. To them, I do not exist either.'

Peter frowned, confused by the prospect of a magical world.

'I don't understand. *I* can see you! Why can't other people?'

'There are still some children who can see the world as it truly is – children who can see through the illusion in which most men live to the magic that lies beyond.'

Peter's mind was racing as he tried to understand everything Sigurd was telling him.

'What about the Vikings who were guarding the tree? What happened to them?'

'They survived, though their number is greatly diminished. Even to this day they live in their halls beneath the streets of this city.'

Peter almost fell off the bench in astonishment.

'There are Vikings in York? Even now?'

'Indeed there are, though few realise it. Rarely do they venture above ground any more. They are a dying race, Peter.'

Suddenly Sigurd rose to his feet, towering over Peter. He gazed up at the sky, his brow furrowed as if he was listening to something.

'My time has almost come. I must go! There is much work to be done. Maledict has returned to finish what he began a thousand years ago and destroy the last Vikings. Even as we speak, his army is approaching York. Soon the city will be under siege. This is a battle the Vikings cannot win unaided. You will be needed Peter!'

'But...!' Peter leapt to his feet as he stared at Sigurd in bewilderment. 'I don't understand! Why me? What can I do?'

Sigurd turned to Peter and smiled briefly.

'Do not worry. Your place will become clear. I will be watching you.'

Then he started to stride across the graveyard. Peter trailed desperately in his wake.

'But what should I do? Will I see you again?'

Sigurd stopped and closed his eyes for a moment, as if searching for something in his mind's eye.

'Yes, I think you will. If all goes well and you prove your worth. When all seems lost, I will come. You will know how to summon me. In the meantime, return here at midnight tonight. You will meet someone - a friend. Your questions will be answered then.'

Sigurd began to walk again, his long strides taking him quickly through the graveyard towards the tall gravestone that bore his name. But as he passed his gravestone, he began to fade. In a moment, Peter could see through him to the wall beyond.

'Good luck my friend!' Sigurd called out, his voice sounding as if it was coming from far away. 'Until we meet again!'

Then he vanished completely.

Chapter 3

The Last Vikings

Peter crept back into the house. Quietly placing the keys on the kitchen table, he shut his bedroom door behind him and changed back into his night clothes. He had barely slipped into bed, however, when he heard a knocking noise on the front door of their flat that was gradually getting louder and louder.

Groaning, he crawled out of bed and shuffled wearily towards the door. He was halfway across the living room when the door of the second bedroom was flung open and his mother raced past him. As she ran, she wrapped her pink night-gown around her and tried to smooth her wayward hair. There were large black lines beneath her eyes and her skin was pale. She looked like she'd had a very bad night indeed.

Their visitor had launched into yet another round of insistent knocking by the time she reached the door, with Peter just a few steps behind. For a moment, he dared hope it would be his father come to take them home, but his heart sank when the door swung open to reveal his grandmother. She was looking very cross indeed. Several plastic supermarket bags were piled by her feet, overflowing with groceries.

'About time!' she protested, her eyes wide with recrimination beneath her ever present purple furry hat. 'Have you any idea how long you've kept me waiting? I was about to go home!'

Peter's expression clearly illustrated his disappointment at such a near miss. His mother, who seemed to have eyes in the back of her head, elbowed him in the ribs and flashed him a warning look. She reached for the bags and handed him one.

'I'm so sorry! We were still in bed, weren't we Pete? Haven't a clue what time it is. Late, I suppose?'

'It's almost nine o'clock, actually! Long past the hour when decent people should be up and about their business! You'll teach the boy bad habits! Fortunately, I've done some shopping for you both so at least you'll get a decent breakfast inside you.'

'Oh! You shouldn't have!' said his mother as she tried to usher her into the living room and deposit her on the settee so she could change clothes and straighten her hair.

But his grandmother refused to co-operate. Instead, she marched into the kitchen and immediately began unpacking the groceries and placing them in cupboards. She had a business-like, super-efficient air about her that was incredibly irritating when all they wanted to do was go back to bed.

'I didn't know what you'd like for your breakfast, Peter, so I've played safe and got plenty of cereals. There are *Cornflakes, Weetabix, Ready-Brek, Frosties, Coco Pops...*' She reeled them off one by one in her loud, super-efficient, tone of voice whilst producing an endless supply of small cereal boxes from one of the plastic bags and depositing them triumphantly on the kitchen table. 'So, which is it to be then young man?'

'Rice Crispies...please,' replied Peter after a moment's pause (which he'd used to think of the only cereal she hadn't bought).

His grandmother gave him a dangerous look, her nose twitching in irritation beneath her enormous glasses. She was about to point out the error of his ways when his mother quickly stepped in.

'Cornflakes will be just fine, thank you,' she said, kicking Peter under the cover of the kitchen table.

She pulled out a chair and forcefully pushed him into it. Meanwhile, his grandmother continued to unpack, mumbling incoherently to herself.

Twenty minutes later, they were all sitting around the kitchen table eating breakfast. His mother had finally managed to escape for long enough to change out of her night-clothes and comb her hair, and was now in a much better mood. As she chatted to his grandmother, Peter nibbled his toast in silence, thinking about Sigurd and wondering who he would meet in the graveyard that night. For a moment, he considered telling them what had happened, but then he changed his mind. Part of him feared they wouldn't believe him and would dismiss it all as just his imagination. But something else also held him back. He almost felt he would be breaking some secret pact he had unconsciously made if he told them about Sigurd.

Before long, his grandmother inevitably began to discuss the weather.

'Well, I simply *can't believe* this bad spell we've been having! It's not just in York mind. The weatherman on the tele said it's been like this over the *whole country!* Can you believe that? Apparently it's already the worst December on record! Pretty soon we'll be having floods, I shouldn't wonder! The river level's already so high that the *King's Arms* is practically underwater! It could be even worse than 1982!'

The *King's Arms,* she had previously explained, was an old pub next to the River Ouse (one of York's two rivers) which notoriously flooded several times a year - so often in fact that the pub's door proudly displayed flood levels going back almost seventy years. Peter's grandmother, who had lived in York all her life, could remember each one in excruciating detail.

'When this snow melts, it'll be the highest yet, you mark my words! They'll have to re-set the record books and put a new notch on the door - or maybe the roof even!' She laughed. It was a deep croaky laugh of someone who had smoked too many cigarettes. Then she stared at Peter and his mother in irritation, annoyed they weren't sharing her enthusiasm.

Happy to let them talk, Peter resumed his private contemplation on the events of the previous night, forming a hundred questions in his mind, none of which had an answer. He was just considering whether he would be able to sneak outside and look at Sigurd's gravestone again, when it suddenly became strangely quiet and he realised that his mother and grandmother were staring at him expectantly. As he gazed back at them, his mother asked him what he'd like to do that day, her voice sounding slightly irritated as if she had asked him once already. Fortunately, Peter had anticipated the question and prepared his answer. But when he told them he would like to go to some museums, particularly ones that concentrated on Viking history, they almost dropped their tea-cups in shock.

'But I thought you hated museums!' exclaimed his mother incredulously.

It was true. Peter generally hated stuffy old museums, particularly ones full of Victorian dresses or Roman floor tiles, but this time he had something specific in mind. He wanted to find out as much as he could about the Vikings, and the Vikings in York in particular, hoping to discover some clue that would explain what he had seen.

Once they got over their surprise, his mother and grandmother didn't waste any time, eager to make the most of his enthusiasm whilst it lasted. Within a few minutes, they had put on their coats and shoes and stepped outside into the cold snowy morning.

It was less than a week before Christmas and the streets were busy with shoppers, despite the biting cold and heavy snow. Countless people were slipping and sliding their way along the icy pavements and roads, their journeys made still more perilous by the numerous snow mounds that lined the streets where shopkeepers had swept the snow out of their doorways.

They spent all of the morning and much of the afternoon in two large museums. Desperate to learn as much as he could, Peter mercilessly led his mother and grandmother from exhibit to exhibit, asking a hundred questions about Vikings which they had no idea how to answer. Even the museum staff were left scratching their heads and reaching for their history books. By the middle of the afternoon, his grandmother could barely walk and they headed home, much to Peter's frustration. They had hardly walked through the door of their flat when his grandmother left them, complaining that her feet were sore and she needed a hot bath and an early night to recover.

As she left, Peter glanced at his watch. It was 4 o'clock – 8 hours until his mysterious appointment!

*

Two hours later, Peter was slumped on the sofa, prodding his spaghetti bolognese unenthusiastically with his fork. Usually they ate in the kitchen and discussed what had happened during the day, but tonight his mother had brought the food into the living room on a tray so they could sit in front of the television. His mother seemed distracted and they ate in silence, hardly watching the film that was showing.

Finally his mother rose to her feet and announced that she was going to bed early. Suddenly alert again, Peter glanced at his watch. It was past 9 o'clock – less than three hours to go until midnight and his appointment in the graveyard!

Within a minute, he was standing by his bedroom window again. Ignoring the pyjamas his mother had laid on the bed for him, he peered through the misty glass, wondering what the night would bring.

It was pitch black outside. The snow had finally stopped and there was an eerie stillness in the air as if the whole world was holding its breath, silently waiting for something incredible to happen.

Time moved slowly forwards.

At 10 minutes to midnight, Peter decided that he couldn't wait any longer. He grabbed his long black coat, put on his trainers and crept out of the flat, his heart pounding in anticipation.

It was every bit as cold and dark as the night before. Fastening the buttons of his coat, he jogged across the white car-park and stepped through the iron gate into the graveyard. His heart racing, he strode across the long grass past the gravestones, looking for any sign of the mysterious person he was due to meet. But there was no sign of anyone. Only slightly discouraged, he turned towards the church bench and sat down. Folding his arms underneath his coat and jumper to keep warm, he began to wait.

The graveyard was silent. All Peter could hear was his own breathing, each breath forming a wispy vapour cloud in front of him that drifted into the night. Suddenly the silence was shattered by a deep resonating sound. For a moment he had no idea what it was, then he recognised it. Across the city, the Minster bells were sounding out the hour. Twelve times the great bells rang whilst Peter waited anxiously, half expecting to see some ghostly form step out of the darkness. But once the echo of the bells finally faded, all was quiet and still once more.

12 o'clock had been and gone. He glanced at his watch, just making out the hands in the faint light. The Minster had been bang on time. A minute had now passed since midnight and still no one had appeared!

Shuffling uneasily on the bench, he peered across the dark graveyard towards Sigurd's gravestone, expecting to see a tall figure revealed behind it. Then he craned his neck around the corner of the church behind him in case someone was hidden there. But still he was disappointed. Shivering, he plunged his hands deeper into the pockets of his coat and wrapped it tightly around him as he huddled on the bench, grinding his teeth in frustration.

Time passed slowly and still he waited.

Seemingly an age later, the Minster bells rang out again, one long reverberating chime signalling the quarter hour. It was a quarter past 12! The person he was supposed to meet was *15 minutes late!*

The suspense was agony! Peter leapt to his feet and paced up and down beside the old church to fend off the cold, then walked briskly around the perimeter of the graveyard before flopping onto the bench again. But still no one appeared.

As if waiting with him, the graveyard remained eerily silent. There were no birds in the trees and no whisper of wind in the branches. An expectant intensity hung in the air, as if even the gravestones were holding their breath in suspense. He checked his watch again. Surely an hour at least had passed since midnight?

Just then the Minster bells rang out once more. Two great chimes echoed for several heartbeats, signalling the half-hour. It was 12.30! The person he was supposed to meet was now *half an hour late!*

For the first time, Peter began to seriously consider the possibility that Sigurd was mistaken and that no one would appear. Or perhaps Sigurd had told him the wrong time? Or maybe the person he was due to meet had forgotten? Or was he simply late? He hoped that was the explanation. The other alternatives were too depressing to contemplate.

Feeling the cold again, he hugged his enormous coat tightly around him once more and rubbed his hands against his jeans until the sensation returned. He resisted the temptation to check his watch. If he had to, he would stay all night, no matter how cold it got!

Seemingly hours later, in the midst of his worrying, the Minster bells rang out three times. It was now 12.45! *Forty-five minutes late!* In despair, he sank down the bench, wondering whether he should head back to his bedroom after all. He had never felt so deflated in his life.

At that moment, he heard a gentle rustling of leaves coming from somewhere at the back of the graveyard. Immediately he froze. There was silence for a moment, then a peculiar squeaky voice came out of the darkness.

'I say! I really am most *frightfully* late! Which way is it to the Viking Halls? I have urgent news for the Council, you know!'

To say that Peter was surprised would have been a gigantic understatement. He was so startled he practically jumped out of his skin! But it was nothing compared to the shock he got when he spun towards where the voice appeared to be coming from and discovered that there was no one there!

Leaping to his feet, he peered across the dark graveyard. He was almost positive the voice had come from somewhere near the church wall, but there was nothing there except the grass and trees. Was he going mad?

Despite his confusion, he was anxious not to appear rude. Just in case he'd not imagined the strange voice, he decided he'd better answer it.

'*Hello?*' he whispered, feeling a little foolish. 'Is anybody there?'

'Oh dear! Oh dear, dear, *dear!*' fretted the invisible person. 'I wonder what time it is? I really *must* get to the Viking Halls quickly or I'll be in no end of troublesome bother!'

There was no mistaking it! Someone was most definitely there! But where? Cursing the darkness, Peter raced to the back of the graveyard to examine the wall more closely.

He had just passed the part of the wall where he thought the voice had come from, when he saw something move out of the corner of his eye behind him. Immediately he spun around. There, gazing at him in surprise, was the strangest looking person he had ever seen!

The first thing that was peculiar was his size. Peter had expected to see an enormous Viking. Instead, the strange person was easily a foot shorter than he was! But this was no child. His dark hair was dotted with grey specks, and he had a large circular bald patch in the centre of his head. He was dressed in an old-fashioned brown blazer with a thick dark-green tie hung loosely around his neck. Beneath his blazer, he wore a matching green V-neck jumper and brown corduroy trousers that over-flowed onto his black boots. His head was large compared to the rest of his body, and his face was most unusual, with a long flat forehead and big green eyes that stared out through small circular silver glasses, making him look cross-eyed.

Something was clearly worrying the strange person. He stared at Peter for a moment then glanced past him to the church, his eyes wide with agitation.

'Oh dear! What have I done? I've come out at the wrong place again, haven't I? I really *must* get my spectacles fixed! Must! Must! *Must!* But where am I? I haven't got time to get lost again! I really am in such a dreadful hurry! If only I hadn't gone astray at the Walls! I hope I'm not too late! *Pleeeese* don't let me be too late!'

Peter didn't know whether he should be afraid or amused. Had it happened the previous day, he would have said it was the most bizarre thing he'd ever seen!

As Peter wondered what he should say, the strange looking person took off his glasses and cleaned them with a dirty looking white handkerchief he had pulled from his outside blazer-pocket. Putting them back on again, he squinted at Peter with a puzzled frown on his face, as if he'd just been set a particularly difficult problem.

'I say! Tell me. Are you a *human?*'

Peter was caught by surprise by the question.

'Err, yes I am. My name is Peter.'

Clearly this wasn't the answer the strange person was hoping for. Immediately he leapt into the air and started running frantically around the graveyard, pulling on his bright red ears in distress.

'Oh *deary, deary* me! This is *quite* dreadful! What will the Prince say? I really am in trouble now, you know! *Deep, deep* trouble!'

He came to an abrupt stop in front of Peter.

'Are you *sure* you're not an elf? A thin dwarf maybe, *mmm?* Are you *absolutely positive* you're not a pixie?'

'I am sure that I'm a boy, thank you!' replied Peter firmly, wondering what a pixie looked like.

Once again the strange person started running in circles around him, mumbling to himself and sounding most distressed.

'*What have I done? What have I done?* If only I hadn't taken a wrong turn at the Walls! If only they would put the signs a little lower so I could read them properly! If only I'd got my spectacles fixed! But what is to be done now, mmm? What is to be done now?'

Peter stared at him curiously, wondering what he meant by his gibberish. He was beginning to feel sorry for him.

'Is there anything I can do to help?'

Suddenly he stopped running and stared at Peter intently, as if trying to decide whether he could trust him. Making up his mind that he could, he ran over to the church bench and urgently gestured for Peter to sit beside him.

'Allow me to introduce myself. My name is Dunstable. I am on my way to the Viking Halls. I am a scout, well, more of a great explorer really! Lots of adventures, though I don't like leaving home as much as I used to! I have an urgent message for the Queen and the Prince, but I've rather lost my way! It really is *so* difficult to work out where you are going when you have to find the secret entrances and avoid City Dwellers all the time! And they do insist on putting the signs on the snickelway walls so high that I can't read them properly! It really is *most* inconsiderate!'

Sitting on the bench beside him, Peter gazed at him in bemusement as he tried to make sense of what he was saying. He assumed he must be a Viking, which was encouraging at least, though he didn't look anything like what he was expecting a Viking to look like!

'What are 'City Dwellers'? Why do you avoid them?'

Immediately Dunstable looked nervous again. He leant towards Peter and whispered behind his hand, his eyes darting from side to side as he scoured the graveyard to ensure they were alone.

'City Dwellers are *modern* people! That's what we call them. There were no big cities when we lived above ground – none at all! We're not allowed to speak to them, you see. None of us are! Normally, of course, it isn't a problem, as they can't see us – at least the adult ones can't anyway. They're too busy in their own little world to take any notice of ours, which is just as well really as they do rather make a mess of things these days!'

Peter was more puzzled than ever.

'But *I* can see you! You called out to me!'

Dunstable looked momentarily confused.

'I didn't call out to you! I was just…*talking* to myself, that's all! Perfectly normal! All the best people do it, you know! I didn't expect to find a City Dweller here so late. If I'd known you were here, I wouldn't have said a word!'

Suddenly he stared at Peter in a most peculiar way, his eyes big and round behind his glasses.

'You must be a very special boy to be able to see me, though these are strange times you know! Very strange times! I don't know what the Council is going to say about it! I really will be in trouble this time!' He shifted uncomfortably on the bench, his ears twitching as he imagined the trouble he would be in.

'Why aren't you allowed to speak to us?' asked Peter, trying not to stare at Dunstable's curiously twitching ears.

'*Why?* My dear boy, what do you think would happen if City Dwellers knew about us, *mmm?* They wouldn't be able to understand us at all! They would hunt us down or put us in a museum. Fortunately they don't believe Vikings still exist, and they certainly don't believe in magic, and you can't see what you don't believe in. Only a few of them know us now – the few who still believe. Children mostly, of course. They are laughed at by the rest. Modern people are such an unimaginative lot, you know!'

'But…*why* can some people see you, but not others?'

Dunstable smiled in knowing fashion, his glasses rising up his nose. As calm as could be, he settled himself more comfortably on the bench. Judging by his expression, 'City Dwellers' were a favourite subject of his. He seemed to have forgotten all about his urgent appointment.

'Well! It all depends on the City Dweller, you see. A few can see us, but not many, not any more. Of course, even those who *can* see us don't see us *properly*. They just see outlines or shadows that disappear when they turn around to look more closely! Usually they are children – very few adults can see us – almost none at all! Something happens to them when they grow up. When they get to about your age, they stop believing in magic altogether and can't see us anymore. No one knows why for sure. Some of us believe it is because they start thinking like their parents do, and adult City Dwellers think that magic is nonsense. Everything has to be logical and predictable in their world and there's no room for us – no room at all! What a dull life they must lead!'

'I don't understand! What do you mean by magic?' asked Peter, trying to sound calm, though he was barely able to control his mounting excitement.

Dunstable smiled knowingly again.

'Oh, it's all perfectly simple, once you know how. Or so they tell me. Anyone can do it. Well, almost anyone… '

By now Peter was so excited he could scarcely think properly. He had completely forgotten about the cold and the darkness, though he was vaguely aware of how silent the graveyard was as if even the gravestones were listening intently.

'Can you...*do* magic?'

'Me? Of course not!' snapped Dunstable, shuddering as if he'd just had a terrifying vision. 'I don't like magic! I don't like magic at all! Much too scary! All sorts of unpleasant things can happen if you don't know what you're doing! One minute you're minding your own business, the next you're suddenly flying through the air or bouncing on your head. No! Not for me! I like nice predictable things like tea and crumpets and a nice nap after lunch! But I am a special case, you see. I have a...err, *special* gift.'

Peter was about to ask what he meant, but Dunstable had simply paused for breath and quickly continued.

'Of course, it's the big Vikings who are the experts – the Queen and the Princess in particular. The knack, as I understand it, is simply *believing* that you can do it, then you can do almost anything! That's why City Dwellers are so hopeless at it. They don't believe in anything that doesn't fit into their predictable world. That's why they build machines that imitate magic: computers and airplanes for instance. Why build a machine if you're mad enough to want to fly? Quite ridiculous! Any other questions?'

Clearly Dunstable was enjoying his role as expert in the affairs of Vikings and seemed perfectly content to answer any question put to him. But there were so many things that Peter didn't understand, he didn't know what to ask next, though he was a little puzzled by Dunstable's remark about flying. Then he remembered Dunstable's boast earlier.

'You said you are an *explorer?*'

Dunstable nodded proudly. He took off his glasses with an exaggerated sweep of his arm and began cleaning them again with his dirty white handkerchief.

'Actually, I am the *greatest* Viking explorer! I am quite famous in fact! High in the affections of the Queen! She always asks for me personally! No one else will do for her, you know! Not many Vikings have travelled as far as I have – not for hundreds of years anyway! In fact, not many Vikings travel much at all these days. Much too dangerous! Most have never left York! You wouldn't believe the places I've been...' Suddenly he shuddered and his momentary air of arrogance disappeared in an instant. His eyes grew wide with fear as if he was re-living some dreadful memory.

Peter was so busy thinking of another question to ask before Dunstable remembered his urgent appointment that he didn't notice his discomfort.

'You said Vikings don't speak to…*City Dwellers*…and we don't believe you exist anymore. Why don't you speak to us, then we'd believe in you?'

Dunstable was still uneasy as he squirmed on the bench, peering through the darkness of the graveyard and twitching nervously.

'What did you say? Why don't we *speak* to you?' Relaxing slightly, he fixed Peter with an expression of mild irritation. 'Haven't you been listening? We'd scare the life out of City Dwellers if we spoke to them, even the children who believe in Vikings and magic! And even if we did speak to them and they heard us, all the other City Dwellers would think they were mad! Only a few can see us remember? Only the really special ones. But no City Dweller can see us properly. Well, except for you that is. That really is *most* peculiar!

'Of course, it hasn't always been like this, you know! One time, long ago, almost *all* children believed in magic and most of them still did when they became adults, particularly in York! But York is different from other places. There are more of us here than anywhere else. It's our capital city, you might say. In fact, in these dark times, it's almost the only place where there are any of us at all! It's the only place we're safe, you see. No enemy can break through the City Walls. There's powerful magic in them. Well, at least that's always been the case in the past. Who knows what will happen now *He* is coming?'

'*He*? You mean Maledict?' queried Peter, remembering what Sigurd had said.

Dunstable's jaw dropped as he stared at Peter in shock.

'M-*Maledict?* You've heard of Maledict?'

Peter nodded, anxious to hear more.

'Who is he? What's happening?'

But Dunstable was shrinking against the bench in terror. It took over a minute before he finally began to relax. Shuffling up closer to Peter, he peered nervously across the dark graveyard again as if expecting an army to break through the church wall at any moment.

'Maledict is a Necromancer! A *dark* sorcerer. He is totally evil!

The rumours are true after all. He has united the trolls and made them into an army!'

Peter stared at him in astonishment.

'*Trolls?* There are trolls? You mean real…live…trolls?'

But Dunstable didn't seem to have heard him.

'Long ago Maledict stole something – something very powerful. Since then he has been hunting us down. Now he is coming back to finish us off once and for all! But how can we defeat him when there are so few of us left?'

Peter just managed to regain his wits.

'He *stole* something? You mean the Viking Stone?'

Once again Dunstable stared at him in astonishment.

'But how did you…'

At that moment, the Minster bells rang out in one long resonating chime, signalling one o'clock. Immediately Dunstable leapt off the bench in panic, his ears flapping wildly.

'*Oh no!* It's one o'clock! I was expected at the Council at midnight! I must be off! Sorry! Haven't got time to talk now! I must be going! Goodbye!'

He raced across the graveyard at an incredible speed. Before Peter could say a word he was at the church wall where he paused and, rather oddly, began to press urgently on several of the bricks with his fingers. For a moment he stood there scratching his head with one hand whilst poking the bricks of the wall with the other. Then he turned towards Peter, who was jogging across the grass towards him.

'I say! You couldn't do me a favour, could you? I really would be most grateful! Which direction does the Minster lie in? Is it to the east or the west? They place the signs far too high for me, and if I go the wrong way again, I'll never get home!'

Peter thought quickly as he came to a halt in front of him. With the benefit of his greater height, he could just see the top of the Minster's twin towers over the roofs of the neighbouring houses. But he didn't want to let Dunstable go so easily.

'I'll only tell you on one condition.'

Dunstable regarded him warily.

'*Condition?* What condition?'

'That you take me with you.'

To Peter's alarm, Dunstable immediately began racing around

the graveyard again whilst pulling on his already painfully red ears. Coming abruptly to a stop, he stared up at him, his big green eyes pleading through his round spectacles.

'It's impossible! You don't understand what's at stake! If anyone finds out that I've even been *talking* to you, I'll be cast out forever! Forever, I say! Not a day less! Can't you forget you ever saw me? Pretend you had a funny dream or something, *mmm?*'

'No I can't!' replied Peter indignantly, determined to stand his ground despite Dunstable's obvious anxiety. 'Either you take me with you or I'll tell the next Viking I see all about meeting you!'

Dunstable was now absolutely frantic. Leaping into the air, he ran around in rapid circles again. Peter began to feel guilty and would have relented had he not been so eager to find out more about the Vikings. Sliding to a halt, Dunstable stared at him torturously.

'But…But *why* do you want to go with me? It's only a little Council, you know! No place for a boy, is it? No place at all!'

'Because I want to know all about magic and Vikings and…' Peter stammered, eager to mention everything he wanted answers to, '…and *Sigurd!*'

Immediately Dunstable's expression changed. He stood perfectly still on the grass and stared at Peter in absolute horror.

'*Sigurd?* You know about Sigurd?'

Peter was unsure how to react. Hoping for a change in Dunstable's attitude, he took a chance.

'Yes…I've seen him!'

'*YOU'VE SEEN HIM!!*' screeched Dunstable so loudly that Peter jumped in shock. 'When? Where? How? Tell me! *Quickly!*'

'Err…here! This morning! I saw him this morning!'

'*THIS MORNING!!!*' Dunstable was now running around in circles again, even faster than before, pulling on his ears and hair in panic. 'Oh dear! This is even worse than I thought! This is absolutely terrible! I must go! I must warn the Queen and the Prince! There's no time to waste! They must know about this immediately!' Suddenly he stopped and stared urgently at Peter. 'Quick! Tell me! Which way to the Minster?'

'But what about me? I want to come too!' demanded Peter firmly, stepping between Dunstable and the church wall.

As Dunstable's eyes widened in alarm again, Peter decided to take one more chance.

'Wouldn't it be better if I told them *myself*? If it's so important, after all?'

But Dunstable was looking utterly confused. He flopped down onto the grass and scratched his head frantically as he talked to himself.

'But City Dwellers aren't allowed in the Viking Halls! Who ever heard of such a thing? If I take him, I'll be in *big* trouble! But, then again, if Sigurd *has* returned, the Queen and Prince must know about it! What if I leave him here and they want to speak to him? Oh dear! This really is most difficult!'

'You must make up your mind quickly,' urged Peter, sensing his opportunity. 'You're already late, remember?'

Dunstable stared at him desperately as he fidgeted with his glasses, his hands shaking as he tried to place them back onto his nose. Suddenly he leapt into the air.

'OK! OK! You win! You can come with me! They'd never believe me on my own anyway! Now...*quickly!* Which way to the Minster?'

His manner was so urgent that Peter didn't hesitate. He pointed over the roof-tops towards the cathedral.

'It's there! Straight ahead!'

'Show me!'

To Peter's surprise (and considerable discomfort), Dunstable leapt onto his back and scrambled up his body as if he was a climbing frame until he was crouching on his shoulders.

'A-ha! *Now* I see it! Hold still – I need to make some calculations!'

Peter wobbled under his weight as he tried to lift Dunstable's foot, which was scraping painfully against his ear. He wondered what he was doing.

'*Hmmm.* Yes, I see. That must be two bricks down and two - no three to the right. Yes! That's it! *Put me down! Put me down!*'

Peter carefully knelt down, allowing Dunstable to leap off him and scamper across the graveyard to the wall.

'Come on! No time to lose! We're late! We're late for the Viking Council!'

Chapter 4

The Viking Council

Dunstable had set off at such a speed that Peter had to run as fast as he could to catch up with him. Fortunately, Dunstable came to an abrupt halt at the far end of the graveyard and peered up at the church wall.

'How are we going to get to the Council?' asked Peter, jogging up behind. 'I've been all around York, but I haven't seen anything that looked like a Viking Hall!'

Dunstable winked knowingly.

'Don't worry about that! We'll use the Magic Snickelways!'

Peter raised an enquiring eyebrow.

'The *Magic Snickelways?*'

'My dear boy, the Magic Snickelways are how we get around York and avoid City Dwellers,' explained Dunstable, grinning from ear to ear and looking very smug indeed about how many things he knew that Peter didn't. 'You don't think we simply walk down the high street do you? Goodness gracious no! The adult City Dwellers wouldn't see us, but some children might, and that would cause all sorts of troublesome bother! All sorts! This church is one of the principal station points, you see. All you have to do is find the invisible entrance, know the hidden way of getting in and speak the secret password. Couldn't be easier! Now, where *are* those bricks?'

He studied the wall again, rising up on his toes, as if looking for something hidden in the stonework.

'Hmm. Where *has* it gone? Two bricks down and three to the right! Or was it *three* bricks down and *two* to the right? Oh dear, this really is most confusing!' He tapped an ordinary looking brick twice with his right hand and his eyes suddenly lit up. '*A-Ha!* I knew it was here somewhere! Now I've got it!' Leaning towards Peter, he whispered mysteriously behind his hand, 'I would close my eyes if

I were you.'

As Peter nervously closed his eyes, he heard Dunstable mutter unintelligibly under his breath. When he opened them again, the wall, the graveyard and the church had all miraculously disappeared. To his astonishment, he found himself standing in a brightly lit alleyway!

'Where are we?' he gasped as Dunstable beamed at him triumphantly.

'*Where?* In a Magic Snickelway of course! This one runs straight through the church graveyard! No one can see us in here – not even children! They can hear us though, so we have to be very quiet!'

Peter barely heard him. He was staring at the snickelway walls in disbelief, wondering where he was and what had happened. On either side of them, the 'snickelway' snaked into the distance before disappearing around bends thirty yards from where they were standing. Above the walls, which were maybe twelve feet high and made out of dull red brick, heavy clouds were drifting across the night sky. It was the only thing that had remained unchanged.

As he turned slowly around, Peter suddenly noticed an elegant lamp-post behind him, its bright light flooding the narrow passageway. Above it was a sign. It read: '**VIKING GRAVEYARD EXIT. VIKING HALLS THIS WAY** →' in gold letters six inches high. Just beneath the sign where they had stepped into the snickelway was the white outline of a door, painted crudely onto the brickwork.

Dunstable was gazing up at the sign too, looking a little cross-eyed. He took off his glasses and cleaned them with his pocket handkerchief.

'I say! You couldn't read that out, could you? It's just a little too high for me!'

Peter read it out word for word and pointed in the direction of the arrow. Dunstable grinned at him in relief.

'Of course! Jolly good! Jolly good indeed! I know *exactly* where we're going! Follow me! Follow me!'

Immediately he dashed down the snickelway in the direction Peter had indicated. In seconds, he had disappeared around the bend.

'Come on!' he called out, already sounding far away. 'No time to waste, you know! Don't worry! We'll soon be there!'

Recovering quickly from his shock at being magically

transported into such an unusual place, Peter raced after him.

'Where are we going?'

'To the Viking Halls of course! Not far! Not far at all!'

Peter increased his speed to catch up to Dunstable, who was surprisingly fast despite his small stature. The snickelway meandered sharply and several times Peter bumped painfully into the walls, caught unawares by an unexpected bend. They had not gone far when he saw another bright lamp-post ahead and a second snickelway appeared, forking off to the right. High on the wall above the lamp was a sign displaying the snickelway's name. Beneath it was the white outline of a door painted onto the bricks. Within a few minutes, they had passed signs for '*BLACK HORSE PASSAGE*', '*CHEAT'S LANE*', '*LADY PECKETT'S YARD*' and '*SHAMBLES*', each illuminated by its own lamp-post. Where they all led to, Peter had no idea. He would have liked to have had the opportunity to explore them properly, but Dunstable was clearly in an enormous hurry and they only paused long enough for Peter to read out the names before racing ahead.

After a few short minutes, they turned into a strangely dark snickelway. Peter could just see the sign as they approached it. It read '*MINSTER GATES*' in bold gold letters. This time it was clearly a dead-end.

Almost immediately, Dunstable slid to a stop. Peter glanced above the snickelway walls, expecting to see the Cathedral, but there was no sign of it. All he could see was the night sky, full of dark cloud. He remembered what Sigurd had told him about the Vikings Halls being beneath the Minster. They presumably lay just ahead.

They walked a few yards further towards the end of the snickelway. A tall brick wall rose in front of them. In the corner was another lamp-post. Unlike the others it was barely lit, casting a faint orange glow that scarcely penetrated the darkness. Above it was another sign: '***VIKING HALLS. ENTRY ONLY ON AUTHORITY FROM THE QUEEN!***'

As they approached, there was a sudden flash of blinding light and the back wall vanished! In its place rose two tall golden gates, brilliantly lit by the now blazing snickelway lamp.

Dunstable reached up and tapped on the gate nearest to him three times with the knuckle of his fore-finger. He knocked so lightly that Peter was sure no one could possibly have heard, but almost immediately a woman's voice rang out into the narrow passageway.

Speak your name so I may decide
If I will let you come inside.
If a friend then do not fear
For you will find a welcome here.
But if a foe then please beware.
Viking magic guards this lair!

The words were sung as much as spoken, but there was no mistaking the warning. Peter dared not think what would happen if anyone didn't take it seriously.

Dunstable stood squarely in front of the gates and spoke to them as if they were living things.

'It's me - Dunstable! I got unavoidably delayed, you know! Let me in! I have urgent news for the Queen!'

For several seconds there was a deep expectant silence. Then, just when Peter thought that Dunstable hadn't been heard, the gates swung slowly open.

As soon as the gap was wide enough, Dunstable leapt inside like a schoolboy late for class. But Peter hesitated. The light from the lamp had dimmed again and he could see nothing beyond the gates. This was his last chance to turn back. As he wavered, he remembered what Sigurd had said and how he had emphasised the plight of the Vikings. It was too late to change his mind now. His heart pounding with excitement and trepidation, he stepped through the gates into the Viking Halls.

Immediately he was struck by bright light again, forcing him to screw his eyes tightly shut. When he opened them, he saw that he had entered what looked like a vast underground football stadium or, more accurately perhaps, a Roman amphitheatre brought back to life. All around him, countless stone tiers rose like huge steps towards the lofty ceiling, seemingly miles above him. Each of the tiers was fronted by golden railings to form a balcony. Behind the railings were rows of wooden chairs, all of them empty.

As Peter followed the tiers upwards, his attention was captured by the ceiling. It was absolutely covered with magnificent carvings,

THE VIKING HALLS

all displayed in glorious colour. There were incredible animals, some of which he'd never seen before and others, such as unicorns and dragons, which he'd only read about in stories. As he stared up at them, he gasped in shock. Some of them were moving! There was no doubt about it! Directly above him, a group of Vikings were fighting a black dragon, which was beating its wings in slow motion and roaring in fury! Behind them, a herd of unicorns were leaping elegantly through some far away forest, tossing their silvery manes! Suddenly he realised that a story was being told in picture form. There were terrible battle scenes in which Vikings fought enormous lolloping human-like creatures (possibly giants?), and then more peaceful scenes where a wise looking King and Queen sat on a throne watching over a great city.

Then a lump caught in his throat. Though it was clearly long ago, there was no doubt that the city was York! He could clearly see an earlier version of the Minster in the background between two meandering rivers, and the City Walls encircling regal looking buildings. To his surprise, one carving showed the church behind his house. A tall Viking warrior was standing there, his long blond hair caught in the wind. He was holding a great sword in his hand and gazing intently to the horizon as if standing guard against some unknown peril.

As Peter gazed across the vast hall, watching the carved stories unfold, his attention was caught by two enormous trees that rose to the ceiling from the centre of the floor. At first he thought they were real, but as he studied them more closely he realised they were made out of some kind of sparkling glass or crystal. They emitted a warm radiance that filled the hall with bright light. Where they met the centre of the roof they sprouted gold leafed branches that stretched out like a glowing web across the ceiling, merging with the carvings and forming part of the stories they illustrated.

It was some time before Peter could tear his eyes away from the crystal trees and the wonderful carvings to study the rest of the enormous hall. Beneath the lowest balconies on either side of the smooth marble floor were several stone archways, built onto the walls. They looked as if they should lead to other rooms, but in each case the wall beneath them was solid stone.

As his eyes followed them down the hall, he suddenly jumped in shock. In the distance beyond the trees, countless white faces were turned towards them! They were packed into a small section at the farthest corner of the hall. As he stared at them, Peter remembered what Sigurd had said about the Vikings being a dying race. Clearly there had once been so many of them they had filled the entire hall. But though they barely occupied one corner, the hall was so enormous that they still numbered in the hundreds.

Dunstable was already trotting towards them. Peter jogged behind him, painfully aware of the sharp clip of their feet against the hard marble floor as it echoed across the hall.

As they approached, the strange figures came slowly into view. Worryingly, every face was staring at them with startled expressions and angry frowns as they leant forward in their wooden chairs to get a better view. Peter would have liked to have stared back at them to see what they looked like, but he was too nervous to risk more than an occasional furtive glance. Despite this, it was clear that they were not at all what he was expecting. Like Dunstable, they each had large staring eyes and a long flat forehead, but that was where the similarity ended. Tall and elegant with long blond hair, they were dressed in white and grey robes and looked as strong and agile as gymnasts.

Now that they were closer, he could hear voices murmuring angrily.

'Isn't that a City Dweller?' asked a curious feminine voice.

'He's not a Viking, that's for sure! I've never heard of such a thing!' replied a male voice.

'This is an outrage! What on earth is Dunstable doing bringing him here?'

'I can't believe it! The Prince will have his head for sure this time!'

It seemed to take an age for Peter and Dunstable to cross the vast hall. Just after they passed between the two crystal trees, the voices stopped and it became so silent they could hear each other's breathing. Suddenly Dunstable froze. Pulling on his tie, he stared fearfully ahead. Feeling even more nervous himself, Peter followed his timid gaze.

At the back of the hall in the centre of the floor were two golden thrones. Their occupants were staring intently in their direction. There could be no doubting who they were. Directly facing them was the Viking Queen and her son, the Viking Prince.

Two such contrasting figures would be difficult to imagine.

The Prince was tall and upright, and had the arrogant bearing of someone who was used to having his orders obeyed without question. Though he was probably only a few years older than Peter, he had the manner of someone far older and wiser. He was dressed in an elegant robe tied at the waist which, at first glance, appeared white, but when he moved it shimmered with dozens of vibrant colours. His face was pale, with a long chin that almost came to a point and long blond hair that fell to his shoulders. His wide eyes studied Peter sternly, as if weighing him up and not at all sure he liked what he saw. On his head was a crown fashioned out of golden leaves that shone like the leaves of the crystal trees. Ominously, a large sword in a silver scabbard was at his side and his right hand was resting on the hilt.

Whereas the Prince appeared stern and arrogant, and was the embodiment of strength and grace, the Queen could not have been more different. Short and dumpy, she reminded Peter of his aunt who loved to bake cakes and mother him. Sitting slightly slouched with her hands crossed in her lap, she was wearing a simple white dress. Unlike the other Vikings, her hair was short and dark, though her eyes were piercingly blue. Though she looked ordinary, there was something about her that gave the impression of strength of will and a power far greater than that of the Prince beside her. As she gazed at Peter, he felt as if she was looking *into* him and reading his mind. Held by her eyes, he felt as if there was nothing he could hide from her; no hidden desire or wish that she could not discover.

For a few seconds he stood rooted to the spot by the Queen's eyes. Then she smiled and beckoned them forward.

Apprehensively, they shuffled towards her. Peter noticed that Dunstable was quivering beside him. His anxiety was contagious and soon Peter began to feel more nervous than he'd ever felt in his life. He had a sudden urge to turn around and run back through the gates into the snickelways, not stopping until he reached the safety of his mother's flat. But somehow he kept walking, his legs seeming to have a will of their own.

When they were about ten yards from the two thrones, they came to a stop. All around them hundreds of Vikings were peering at them over the golden railings of the balconies. As Peter stared ahead, determinedly avoiding eye contact with the Queen or Prince, he was uncomfortably aware that Dunstable had stepped backwards and was now standing directly behind him.

There was a long awkward silence as the Queen and Prince studied Peter. Finally the Queen raised her hand. Immediately Peter felt a wave of calm descend upon him. All his fear and apprehension vanished and he felt as relaxed as if he was walking through the woods on a fine summer's day.

Dunstable visibly relaxed too. He pushed past Peter and strode forward in a confident, most un-Dunstable-like manner. Standing just in front of the two thrones, he bowed exaggeratedly, took a deep breath and drew himself up like a cockerel about to announce the dawn. Then, in a very matter-of-fact kind of way, he began to speak, pronouncing his words so precisely he sounded like a reporter on the six o'clock news.

'Your Highnesses! I have returned from a *perilous* journey beyond the City Walls to bring you my report! I regret that the rumours are true! I have seen trolls! A great army of them is approaching. Trolls from the Black Mountains lead them. They are very big and they are very strong. More are coming. I barely escaped with my life! On my return, I met this City Dweller. His name is *Peter*.'

Suddenly his voice became quieter and almost Dunstable-like again as he whispered behind his hand.

'He, err, caught me unawares in the Viking Graveyard, you see. I thought I'd better bring him here so that…'

'Yes, Yes! Come on! We haven't got all day!' interrupted the Prince, drumming his fingers impatiently on the golden armrest of his throne. 'Let's not get side-tracked eh? What of the troll army? How many are they? Where are they gathering? When can we expect the attack? Has *HE* come yet, or does he command from afar? Come on! Quick, quick!'

Dunstable turned to the Prince. His previous calm demeanour appeared to be evaporating and he was beginning to fidget. He pulled on his green jumper then prodded his glasses up his nose with the middle-finger of his right hand, almost poking himself in the eye in the process.

'Well…err, the *main* troll army is gathering a few miles outside the Walls on the northern side, but smaller bands are patrolling around the outskirts of the city to ensure no one escapes! There are more than a thousand of them already and more are coming! I think they are waiting for something before they attack, maybe

M-Maledict himself? But it can't be long before he arrives, I think – not long at all!'

'Dammit!' swore the Prince. He leapt to his feet and glared at the Vikings peering down at him from the balconies, his fists clenched in fury. 'There is no time to waste! To arms! To arms, I say! We must repel the enemy before they make plans against us! We have a battle to fight!'

There was a roar of approval from hundreds of voices followed by the deafening sound of chairs being pushed backwards as all the Vikings rose to their feet at the same time.

'STOP!' commanded the Queen.

Instantly there was silence. Slightly sheepishly, the Vikings returned to their seats. The Prince, with a rueful sideways glance at his mother, sat back down on his throne. The Queen waited until everyone was settled before continuing.

'Let us hear what Peter has to say! He can help us I believe, or Dunstable would not have brought him here.' Turning to Peter, she beckoned him towards her, smiling at him encouragingly. 'Don't be afraid. Step forward so we can see you better!'

She spoke with a voice that was both calm and friendly, as if she had known him all his life. There was a strange power in it – something he'd only experienced when Sigurd had spoken to him - and when her eyes fell upon him, his whole body froze. He felt as if she had complete faith in him, as if she believed that he was capable of incredible things, and he was terrified that he might disappoint her if she learnt the truth.

'Stop dawdling boy! Step forward as you have been commanded!' barked the Prince, drumming on the arm-rest of his throne again. 'Come on! Chop-chop! We haven't got all day you know!'

Reluctantly Peter inched forward until he was standing beside Dunstable just a few feet in front of the two thrones.

'*Hmmm*,' pondered the Prince, rubbing his chin as he stared at him critically, noting Peter's oversized clothes and unkempt dark hair. 'He's a little *young*, don't you think?'

The Queen watched Peter closely, but didn't speak. Once more he felt the weight of her eyes upon him.

'So! Let's see what you're made of then, eh boy?' said the Prince in a tone of voice made all the more irritating by the fact that he was probably only two or three years older than Peter. 'How many dragons have you fought?'

The question caught Peter completely by surprise.

'Err, none...your highness.'

There was a faint murmuring from the balconies above as several voices whispered disapprovingly.

'None, eh? Thought as much! How many trolls have you slain then?'

'None at all...your highness,' replied Peter quietly, beginning to feel very inadequate indeed.

The murmuring got steadily louder.

'Not even any trolls?' bellowed the Prince, pushing down on the sculptured arm-rests of his throne so hard that his body swung into the air. He glanced at the Queen as if to say *'told you so!'* and scanned the faces peering over the railings above, his expression clearly showing his disgust at such pitiful achievements. Dropping down onto the seat of his throne with a disgruntled *'huff!'*, he asked his next question, his voice laced with cynicism.

'What about magic then? I trust you at least know a *little* magic? What level of skill have you reached – practitioner or master?'

'But I don't know how to do any magic, your highness,' whispered Peter, wishing he was far, far away.

The murmuring intensified still further.

'*DON'T KNOW ANY MAGIC?!!!!*' roared the Prince, positively spinning on the arm-rests of his throne. Red faced, he struggled to contain himself as he plopped back down onto the cushioned seat. 'Surely you can at least fly? I assume that even an ordinary boy like you can fly?'

Peter shook his head, not daring to speak.

'So,' continued the Prince, sounding extremely pompous, 'if you haven't fought any dragons or killed any trolls, and you don't know any magic or even how to fly, how are you going to help us defeat Maledict, eh? Answer me that!'

The murmuring, which had briefly subsided when the Prince had spoken, grew quickly louder again as hundreds of Vikings whispered to one another, nodding their heads vigorously. They clearly thought the Prince had made an excellent point.

For his part, Peter couldn't recall offering his help, not that he thought he had any to give. Unsure how to reply, he stood uneasily before the two daunting thrones with his head bowed in embarrassment. He was aware of Dunstable hiding behind him again, hopping nervously from one foot to the other. Meanwhile, the voices continued to rise in volume as hundreds of Vikings talked at once, each expressing their disgust at his pathetic level of achievement.

Suddenly the Queen spoke, her voice rising above the commotion and silencing them instantly.

'Let Peter speak!'

She raised her hand and Peter felt a calm reassurance surge through him once more.

'Peter! Tell us what you have seen. Don't be afraid! You are welcome here.'

Without thinking, Peter spoke calmly.

'I have seen Sigurd.'

If he thought it had been loud before, it was nothing compared to the reaction his words caused. Immediately the hall erupted as hundreds of horrified voices all shouted at once. In amongst them, Peter could just make out the voice of the Prince.

'Impossible! I don't believe it! The boy must be mistaken! Mistaken I tell you!'

The Queen alone remained calm. With the slightest gesture of her hand, every Viking in the hall fell silent.

'When did you see him Peter?'

'This morning, in the graveyard behind our flat.'

Once more the silence was shattered as countless Vikings leapt to their feet and cried out in alarm. Glaring up at them, the Prince just managed to make himself heard.

'Are you *sure* boy? Are you *absolutely positive* it was Sigurd? How do you know it was him, eh? Tell me that! How do you *know* it was Sigurd?'

Peter, still completely calm, felt mildly annoyed at the Prince's insinuation.

'Because I spoke with him and he told me, that's why!' he replied, a little louder than he'd intended. 'I also saw his gravestone with his name on it. It read: *'Here lies Sigurd the Dragon Slayer, Viking King of Kings.'* Last night twelve Vikings laid their swords by his grave. I saw it all from my bedroom window! This morning Sigurd told me that Maledict is going to attack York. He told me to go to the graveyard at midnight and that I would meet someone there. That's how I met Dunstable.'

By the time he had finished speaking, complete silence had fallen in the vast hall. When the Prince eventually spoke, his voice was barely a whisper.

'Do you realise the importance of what you are saying, boy?'

Peter glanced at the Queen, who was watching him silently, then returned his attention to the Prince.

'Who is Sigurd? Why has he come back?'

The Prince glared at him incredulously.

'You haven't heard of Sigurd?'

Peter shook his head.

The Prince gripped his throne as if he barely had patience for Peter's ignorance.

'Sigurd was a great warrior – the greatest of the Viking heroes. He was the mightiest man that ever lived! He slayed the great dragon Fafnir when he was little more than a boy your age. Long ago he was killed by treachery, but before he died, he promised to return when our need is the greatest. If you have seen him, then it seems that time is upon us. But why now, after all these years? Will he fight with us again?'

There was intense silence again as the Vikings stared at one another, their faces long and their expressions uncomprehending. The Queen was still studying Peter intently.

'We have much to think about it seems,' she declared finally. Her eyes left Peter and drifted across the rows of anxious Viking faces in the balconies above her. 'We must discuss the news Dunstable and Peter have brought us and decide what action is to be taken.'

She turned to Peter.

'Will you be our guest whilst we hold our debate? We may need to call upon you again. There is clearly some connection between Sigurd and yourself, and I believe you have come to us for a reason. But we will have a short break first, I think. Perhaps you would like to be shown the Viking Halls before we resume?'

Peter almost leapt in excitement. Not trusting his voice, he merely nodded his head in agreement.

'Good! The Queen rose to her feet and addressed the assembly. "The Council is suspended! We will return to the Debating Hall in one hour!"

There was a disappointed sigh as the heads peering over the golden railings withdrew, immediately followed by the sound of shuffling feet and muffled voices as the Vikings rose to their feet. The Queen approached Peter and put her arm around his shoulders.

'Come with me,' she said softly. 'There is something I want to show you.'

Chapter 5

The Candle Chamber

The Queen led Peter to the back of the Debating Hall. Behind the two thrones, a large semi-circular arch was built onto the wall beneath the lowest balcony. Just like the other arches, it looked as if there should be a passageway beneath it, but the wall was solid stone. Despite this, the Queen strode purposefully towards it. Peter hesitated, assuming that at any moment she would stop or turn. Much to his alarm though, she did neither. He was about to shout a warning when the wall suddenly became transparent, briefly revealing a dark chamber beyond as she walked through to the other side. A moment later, the Queen was gone.

Peter had seen so many incredible things in the past day that he quickly recovered from his surprise. Closing his eyes and wincing in anticipation of striking solid stone, he stepped through the wall exactly as the Queen had done.

When he opened his eyes again, he was standing in a colossal oval chamber, far larger even than the Debating Hall. But whereas the Debating Hall had been warm and bright, here it was dark and cold. The only light was provided by tiny pin-pricks of light that cast flickering shadows on the grey ceiling high above them. It took him a moment before he realised that they were candles. Thousands upon thousands of white candles were strewn across the stone floor as far as he could see. Strangely, only a few of them were lit - so few that the light they shed barely illuminated the vast chamber.

Standing just in front of him, the Queen studied the burning candles for a moment as if counting them, her eyes flitting across the sweeping floor. Then she sighed sadly as if she had just heard bad news. Peter looked at her questioningly, but she offered no explanation. Gazing ahead, her face expressionless, she stepped down three wide stone steps onto a narrow pathway that weaved through the ocean of candles into the heart of the vast chamber.

As he walked behind her, Peter felt a heavy, almost sacred, atmosphere in the air. It reminded him of an old church or cathedral. He instinctively knew that he shouldn't speak, though he burned with questions.

For almost half an hour they followed the pathway as it lead them deeper and deeper into the cavernous chamber. Then, just when Peter was wondering whether the path would go on forever, it suddenly came to an end. Ahead of them was a large circular area completely free of candles. At its centre was a wide altar, raised several feet above the ground. Steps led to the top where, to Peter's astonishment, a tall blue flame was burning brightly. At least seven feet high, it swayed gently, occasionally rising and sparking, then falling again as if resting. Strangely it generated no heat despite its great size. But Peter instinctively knew that the flame was real, and if he touched it he would be severely burned.

Without looking up, the Queen crossed the empty floor and mounted the steps. When she reached the top of the altar, the flame suddenly reared to twice its height as if in greeting, then settled down and swayed contentedly from side to side.

For a moment she stood beside it, gazing into its depths as if reading some sign hidden there. Then she turned towards Peter as he hesitated at the bottom of the steps.

'This is the Eternal Flame of the Vikings! Let us hope it is never extinguished! Come up Peter! It will not harm you if you do not touch it.'

Expecting to be scorched at any moment, Peter nervously climbed the steps. When he reached the top of the altar, he stood close to the edge, trying to keep as far away from the flame as possible. But even though he was now just a few feet away, he still didn't feel any heat.

The Queen smiled at him reassuringly and placed her arm around his shoulders. Turning around, they gazed across the candle strewn floor stretching in every direction. For several minutes they stood silently, then Peter asked the two questions that had been on his lips almost from the moment they had entered the strange chamber.

'Your...*Highness*,' he stammered, unsure how to address the Queen. 'What are all the candles for? Why are only a few of them lit?'

The Queen turned towards him, her deep blue eyes staring intently into his. For a moment he saw the same intensity as the Eternal Flame burning deep within them.

'I brought you here so you might better understand the position we are in. The candles represent the lives of every Viking in York. Every Viking has a candle. When they are born, it is lit. When they die, it is extinguished forever. When the last candle is put out, the Eternal Flame itself will die and the race of Vikings will come to an end.'

Peter stared at her in shock. Tearing his eyes away from her face, he gazed across the chamber again. He estimated that less than one in a hundred candles was lit.

'We are a dying race, Peter! Soon we will no longer exist! One by one Maledict has hunted us down. Now there are few of us left and we are forced to hide here in York, deep beneath the ground.'

Peter's mind was spinning as the terrible reality of the Vikings' plight became clear. He tried to think of something appropriate to say but couldn't think of anything. Perhaps a minute passed in silence. Finally the Queen spoke again.

'There is one more thing I want to show you, though it pains me to do so. Follow me!'

She turned and walked back down the steps, then led him around the Eternal Flame. At the base of the altar, previously hidden by the flame, were the remains of what was once the root of a gigantic tree.

'I am showing you now what no one outside these halls has seen since the days of Maledict. This is why we built our home here. This is the root of Yggdrasil!'

Peter stared at the root in astonishment, trying to recall what Sigurd had told him. Clearly a calamity had struck it in its prime as it was now no more than a withered hollow stump. Across the top of what remained of its thick trunk was a hideous black scar. About eight feet long, it cut deep into the heart of the dead wood.

The Queen approached the stump slowly, her head bowed. She ran her fingers over the scar as if to heal it, then drew back in disgust.

'This is the mark of Maledict! Long ago he took his axe to the sacred root and drank its precious sap. In his greed, he took the power of the tree from us and consumed it for his own ends. What was meant for good was turned to evil.'

A shadow seemed to descend over them and Peter shivered, suddenly feeling cold. A momentary vision crossed his mind of a sinister dark figure cutting into the tree with a sharp-bladed axe. He glanced at the Queen. A single tear was trickling down her cheek. When she spoke again, her voice was quiet as if she was talking to herself.

'Never again will we let ourselves be so misled! Now he is returning it seems. But this time we will be ready!'

Peter forced his eyes away from the terrible cut, but as he turned his head he noticed something strange. In the middle of the great stump was a slender branch. It arched wearily upwards then sagged at the end, as if it had once carried something heavy.

The Queen followed his gaze.

'Before Maledict came, a single fruit hung from that branch - the only fruit she has ever born. At its centre was the seed of Yggdrasil - the Viking Stone – our only chance to grow another tree. We thought it was safe here, but we were wrong…' She paused for a moment and swallowed hard, brushing the tear from her cheek. 'After Maledict drank from the root, he cut the fruit and took the stone. Now he wears it in his crown in defiance of us.'

Together they stared at the decaying stump and the single lonely branch. A thousand thoughts raced through Peter's mind, and through his confusion his intention became clear. The Queen was right. He had come to the Vikings for a reason and, as incomprehensible as it seemed, he must try to help them, though he had no idea what he could possibly do.

At that moment, the Queen placed her hand upon his shoulder once more and gazed into his eyes, all trace of her former anguish gone.

'Come Peter! Let us return! The Council is about to re-convene.'

*

The Queen led Peter back down the path through the candles. Neither of them spoke. When they finally reached the front of the chamber, he tentatively followed her through the magical stone archway. But this time they didn't emerge in the Debating Hall. Instead, Peter found himself standing in a small stone room with a large gushing fountain in the middle. Around the rim of the fountain was a raised stone seat. The Queen turned towards him.

'Wait here until I send for you. I must return to the debate. We have much to discuss due to the news you and Dunstable have brought us.'

She turned away and disappeared through the archway again. This time it was clear that she had stepped into the Debating Hall as, for a fraction of a second, Peter heard hundreds of voices talking at once. Then there was silence again.

Peter sat on the stone rim beside the fountain and gazed into the leaping water as he contemplated what the Queen had told him. But after everything that had happened in the past few hours, he found it impossible to simply sit and wait. Jumping to his feet, he started to pace up and down impatiently, hoping that the Council would finish their debate quickly. He wanted to see the Vikings again, ask more questions, wander through the mysterious halls, learn about magic – anything but sit in a room alone with nothing to do! He glanced at his watch. It was 3 o'clock in the morning. He wondered when Vikings went to bed. Surely they wouldn't be long?

Once again, time seemed to creep forward, each minute lasting an eternity. After about half an hour, he flopped onto the stone rim again in frustration. Without thinking, he dug his hands into the pockets of his jeans. His right hand closed around Sigurd's talisman. He had almost forgotten about it in all the excitement! Lifting it out, he held it in front of him on its silver chain and stared at the strange golden dragon once more. Should he tell the Queen about it? His first thought was that he should. After all, she knew so much and it was probably something important. But then he changed his mind. Something inside him told him that Sigurd had intended it for him and him alone. He quickly dropped it back into his pocket again.

As he listened to the soothing sound of running water, he suddenly felt incredibly tired. Despite the discomfort of the cold seat, his head began to nod. Before he realised it, he slumped onto the rim and crumpled onto his side. Almost immediately he fell into a deep sleep.

*

Peter was woken suddenly by the sound of footsteps. In an instant he was alert again. Turning around so quickly he almost fell over, he was surprised to see a girl dressed immaculately in a long blue shimmering dress walking confidently towards him from the magical archway.

'You must be the City Boy called Peter!' she said precisely, as if she had just completed an elocution course. 'I am Princess Eleanor, daughter of the Queen. You can call me 'Princess' or 'Highness', I do not mind which. Move over please!'

Recovering quickly from his surprise, Peter shuffled awkwardly across the rim of the fountain to allow the Princess room to sit beside him, though he was not at all sure he wanted to share the seat with her, even if she was a Princess. The tone of her voice and the expression on her face were so irritatingly superior, he disliked her already. Remembering his manners, he waited until she was seated then made an attempt at polite conversation.

'It's…*nice* to meet you. Why aren't you at the Council? Are you too young?'

Clearly he had unwittingly said the wrong thing. Instantly the Princess stiffened in outrage, her eyes wide as she glared at him furiously.

'*Too young?* I am the daughter of *the Queen!* I am most certainly *not* too young to attend the Council, thank you very much! I simply decided to leave early, that is all!'

Slightly bemused by her reaction, Peter hesitated for a moment, unsure whether to risk another question. Meanwhile, the Princess turned her back to him and ran her hands through her long blond hair, ignoring him completely. He got the distinct impression that she had been forced to talk to him against her will and would much rather be somewhere else. She seemed far more interested in her hair than she was in him. For a moment he considered ignoring her, but then decided he should probably at least try to speak with her. She was a Viking after all, and the daughter of the Queen, even if she was incredibly annoying.

'Why did you leave early?' he asked tentatively.

The Princess paused in her endless hair brushing to briefly glance at him over her shoulder.

'Well! If you really *must* know, I have already made up my mind, that is why! I do not need to sit and discuss the matter for hours on end like they do! When I stood up and told them that I was bored with their endless debating, my mother...*suggested*...that I come here and speak to you. As I had nothing interesting to do, I agreed. You are very lucky. I do not suppose you have ever met a Princess before.'

'Of course I have. I've met lots of Princesses,' lied Peter, unable to resist the temptation of being rude to her. 'The Queen of England is a close friend of mine actually.'

The Princess's eyes narrowed as she stared at him, unsure whether he was making fun of her. She tossed her head petulantly, her long blond hair swishing behind her.

'So, what do you think they will decide to do?' asked Peter quickly.

'They will announce a Quest of course! They always announce a Quest when there is something really important that has to be done.'

'A *Quest?*'

'Yes, a Quest! To stop Maledict? You are rather dim, but I suppose that is to be expected. You are only a City Boy after all.'

Peter bit his lip to stop himself saying something very rude indeed.

'It will be highly dangerous of course,' continued the Princess matter-of-factly, barely glancing at him as she brushed her hands through her long hair again. 'They will need to choose a strong leader who is an expert in magic. *I* am the obvious choice.'

But Peter was no longer listening to her. As soon as she'd said the word 'Quest', he had begun to dream of heroic adventures and journeys to mysterious, far-away places. Suddenly he wanted to ride off into the sunset with the Vikings - to learn magic and battle with the mysterious Maledict.

The Princess regarded him loftily.

'Do not worry. I do not suppose the Queen will choose a weak City Boy like you. It is *far* too important for that!'

Peter's dreams of adventure were shattered in an instant. Flushed with sudden anger, he glared at the Princess. She was easily the rudest, most irritating person he'd ever met! It wasn't as if she was older than him. He guessed that she was at least a year younger than he was. She was skinny too, and he was several inches taller than her. She had no right to be so rude to him, even if she was a Princess! He drew himself up to his full height and glared down at her.

'Actually, *your highness*, I am not 'weak' or 'dim'! And, unlike *some* people, I am also not rude or arrogant!'

For a moment, the Princess simply gaped at him in shock, unable to believe that he'd dared insult her. Then she leapt to her feet, her face bright red with fury. Immediately Peter leapt up also. He raised himself onto the tips of his toes to emphasise his height advantage and stared at her defiantly. Their eyes locked together, each unwilling to give an inch. For ten long seconds they stood toe to toe, Peter's face set determinedly and the Princess's eyes flaring with rage. Finally she turned her back on him and stomped to the other side of the room.

'I should have known you were not worth speaking to!' She crossed her arms and glared at the far wall.

Peter was about to answer in kind when a tall, official looking Viking suddenly appeared through the magical archway behind them and coughed politely to gain their attention. Facing the Princess, he bowed very low, completely ignoring Peter.

'The debate has ended your Highness,' he declared, sounding like a butler announcing that dinner was served. 'Your presence is requested.'

The Princess gave Peter an arrogant glance as if to say '*I told you how important I am - my presence is requested and yours is not, so there!*' But her expression changed to one of absolute disgust when the Viking then turned to Peter.

'City Dweller called Peter! Your presence is *also* requested - by order of the Queen!'

Peter beamed at the Princess triumphantly. She turned away from him and strode towards the archway with a decidedly irritated '*humph!*'

Fortunately Peter was so angry with the Princess that he forgot to be worried about facing the ordeal of the Council again and, in particular, the Queen and the Prince. In any case, he would rather die than show any fear in front of her.

Trying to look as casual as possible, he followed her through the magical archway back into the Debating Hall.

Chapter 6

The Quest

They entered the hall just behind the Queen's throne, in full view of the Vikings in the balconies. Clearly the debate had been heated as they were instantly greeted by a cacophony of voices. The Vikings were yelling and arguing, making as much noise as a dozen rowdy classrooms put together. The Queen and the Prince were sitting on their thrones. The Queen looked serene, but the Prince's expression was like thunder. He was muttering to himself as if he'd just been over-ruled and was decidedly unhappy about it.

As soon as she saw them, the Queen beckoned them forward. The Princess swaggered towards her, tossing her hair pompously, whilst Peter jogged behind, beginning to feel uncomfortable again. He glanced around the hall, looking for Dunstable, but there was no sign of him. The Queen gestured for them to sit in the lowest balcony just a few yards from her throne, then rose to her feet and waited patiently for silence before addressing the assembly.

But the Vikings didn't seem to notice her as they continued their heated discussions with one another, the volume rising ever higher. The Queen continued to wait for the din to subside, looking as composed as ever. Somewhat less patiently, however, the Prince began to tap his fingers on the golden arm-rests of his throne whilst glaring at the chattering Vikings, his face turning an ever brighter shade of red. Suddenly he leapt to his feet in fury.

'AHH HUMMMMM!! IF YOU'VE *QUITE* FINISHED, PERHAPS *WE* MAY BE HEARD?'

Instantly there was complete silence. Hundreds of faces peered down over the golden railings, blinking guiltily. After a quick sideways glance at the Prince, the Queen addressed the assembly.

'We have debated long and hard on this issue over the past few hours. A course of action must now be taken. I will now declare a Quest!'

Immediately several Vikings behind Peter and the Princess cried out in excitement. *'A Quest! She's declaring a Quest!'*; *'About time too! Now we can fight at last!'* The Prince glared at them, silencing them immediately. Beside him, Peter could feel the Princess grinning at him smugly as if to say *'I told you so!'* He pretended to ignore her.

The Queen continued.

'We have learned a great deal in the past few hours. First, Dunstable told us that a troll army is gathering outside York, then Peter told us that Sigurd has risen again. We have agreed that these two events must be linked and we are therefore in desperate peril. The long peace has come to an end. Maledict has returned!'

There was subdued murmuring as the Vikings glanced at one another apprehensively.

'The time has come to decide what must be done. York will shortly be under siege. The magic that runs through the City Walls is strong, and even Maledict will not find it easy to breach them. But if we do nothing, eventually he will break through and we will be over-run.

'We face a cruel dilemma. If we march to battle outside the protection of the Walls, we will be no match for his troll army and our defeat will be swift. If we stay here, Maledict will eventually break through and seek us in our halls. Our choices therefore are few and desperate, but we will not let Maledict defeat us without a fight! We have debated long enough! Now is the time for action!'

There was a roar and a deafening pounding noise as hundreds of Vikings stamped on the floor to demonstrate their approval. The Queen regarded them regally.

'I will now declare the nature of the Quest!'

A hushed silence fell. An intense expectancy filled the hall as everyone wondered what the Queen would say. Peter noticed that the face of the Princess was glowing with anticipation.

'Our choices are all bad. We cannot hope to defeat Maledict when there are so few of us and his power has grown so great. Never before have we faced such a challenge! We must therefore seek help before it is too late. I propose that a party of Vikings should leave York before the siege begins and travel to the mountains beyond Ironwood. There they will consult Mimir's Well of Wisdom…'

Immediately hundreds of voices cried out in alarm. *'Mimir's*

Well of Wisdom? Does it exist?'; 'I thought it was a myth!'; 'But what about Ironwood?'; 'I'd rather take my chances with the trolls than the Frost Giants! They're thirty feet tall and eat rocks for breakfast!'

Peter took the opportunity caused by the commotion to whisper in the Princess's ear.

'Who is Mimir? What are Frost Giants?'

The Princess gazed at him contemptuously as if he'd just asked the most stupid question she had ever heard.

'Mimir is the keeper of the Well of Wisdom of course! Do you not know *any*thing? The Well lies in a cavern in the mountains. Mimir has put an enchantment on the Well. Anyone who looks into the water drawn from it can ask any question and receive the wisest answer! But to get to the Well you need to go through Ironwood and it is a dangerous journey! The wood is full of dangerous animals, or so the old Vikings say. Frost Giants guard the Well and won't let anyone near it. No one has ever dared to go there – not for hundreds of years anyway! And even then, no one ever came back!'

'But…'

Peter was about to ask why Mimir would want to live in such a terrifying place, but he didn't have time to finish his question. The Queen was ready to speak again, silencing the arguing Vikings with a single glance.

'For the Quest to succeed we must hold off Maledict's army and stop his entry into the city until we have heard the wisdom of Mimir and learnt how best to defend ourselves against this threat. Maledict must not be allowed to break through or all we do will be in vain!'

Once again, hundreds of voices immediately rose up in protest. The Prince leapt to his feet.

'But this is *folly!* Absolute *folly* I tell you! The journey to Mimir's Cavern is full of danger! Only an army of the strongest Vikings could hope to reach it! And how can we defend York if we send half our army to the mountains? We are too few! This plan cannot succeed I tell you! Absolutely impossible!'

'*Hear! Hear!*' cried several voices at once whilst many of the heads that were peering over the railings nodded sagely. The Prince acknowledged them with an arrogant toss of his head and sat back down on his throne again, sinking into the cushioned seat.

The Queen waited patiently for silence.

'We will *not* leave York undefended. Nor would a great army have any hope of success. It would only arouse the attention of Maledict and would be crushed by his trolls before it reached the mountains.' She paused for a moment, her eyes scanning the faces peering down at her. 'I propose that a small party should attempt this Quest, small enough to creep through the troll patrols and walk the dangerous path to Mimir's Cavern unnoticed. I propose that this party should consist of just three travellers.'

There was a collective gasp of disbelief.

'Three travellers? They'll be eaten alive!'; 'If Maledict doesn't get them, the Frost Giants will, even if they make it through Ironwood!'

'I will now announce who I propose should attempt this Quest, should they be brave enough.'

Instantly there was silence again, though this time it was filled with nervous suspense rather than eager anticipation.

'The leader will be Princess Eleanor. She is brave and skilled in magic. This will be her first great task!'

There was an immediate roar of approval combined with raucous stamping of feet as every Viking expressed their approval of the Queen's choice. The Princess rose to her feet, took one step forward and bowed, basking in her moment of glory and looking very smug indeed. She nodded to the Queen then turned around and made a somewhat false appeal for quiet to the applauding Vikings, looking like an arrogant film star who had just won an award.

The Queen waited for the applause to die down before continuing.

'I have thought long and hard about who should go with the Princess and I have now reached my decision.' She paused briefly. Once again, there was not a whisper in the hall. 'With her will go Peter, for I believe he is linked to these events and has a great part to play, though I cannot foresee what it is.'

Peter practically leapt out of his skin in shock. He wasn't alone in his reaction. After a moment's silent incomprehension, there was a deafening roar of protest from the Vikings around him. The Prince, who had been trying to look regal and wise after making his earlier comment, leapt up from his throne in outrage.

'*A City Dweller?* You would send a *City Dweller* on a Quest? This is madness, I say! *Utter…utter madness!* He doesn't even know any magic! He's never seen a troll in his life! He can't even *fly*, for goodness sake! You need a strong warrior, not a half grown boy! The trolls will make mincemeat of him! And even if he escapes the trolls, the Frost Giants will crush him *Absolute...utter...mad-ness!!!'*

The Queen turned her head slightly and stared at her son. Such was the power of her eyes that even the Prince sat down, though he continued to mumble angrily to himself under his breath. She addressed the Vikings again, silencing them as quickly as she had the Prince.

'Are not City Dwellers involved in this affair also? That is why Sigurd has returned. Viking blood has worn thin, but it still exists in this city and beyond. I believe that Peter has come to us for a reason and his fate is woven into this Quest. Remember that it was *he* who saw Sigurd. But I will not send him completely unprepared. The Princess will instruct him in the art of magic. He will have one night to learn how to fly, for before the Quest is over, I fear he will have need of speed!'

Beside her the Prince mumbled to himself as he slouched on his throne.

'One night to teach a City Dweller how to fly! Impossible, I tell you! Absolutely impossible!' But a raised eyebrow from the Queen quickly silenced him.

Peter was still reeling from the shock of being picked when he suddenly realised that the hall had fallen deathly silent and hundreds of eyes were peering down at him expectantly. The Queen was also watching him intently. But the worst was the Princess. Standing just in front of him, she was repeatedly glancing over her shoulder and whispering something urgently under her breath. He gazed at her blankly, unable to understand what it was she wanted.

Seeing his confusion, the Queen spoke to him directly.

'Do you accept this Quest? If so, you must take a step forward and stand next to the Princess. I will not send you against your will. Neither will I lie to you. This will be a perilous task and you may not survive it. You will face many dangers and many evil creatures. No one would blame you if you refused. We will return you to your home and you will go with our gratitude and blessings. Do you refuse?'

Peter squirmed under the intense scrutiny of every Viking in the hall. The Queen's description didn't exactly make the Quest sound appealing! But despite (or was it because of?) the apparent dangers, something within him longed for adventure. He had never seen trolls before. What would they look like? Would he be brave enough to face them? And what about Maledict? He couldn't imagine such a powerful sorcerer! Still he hesitated. There was so much at stake! The fate of the Vikings depended upon the Quest's success. If it failed, Maledict would surely be victorious, and he dreaded to think what would happen then.

The Princess was still staring angrily at him over her shoulder, mouthing to him exaggeratedly, demanding that he make up his mind and *'stop messing about!'* Suddenly he realised that there was one more thing he was worried about. Could he stand going on a Quest with the Princess? He'd only known her a few minutes and she already irritated him more than anyone he'd ever met!

Wavering between his yearning for adventure and his fear, Peter dropped his hands into the pockets of his jeans self-consciously and his right hand touched Sigurd's talisman. Instantly he relaxed. What was he so worried about? After all, Sigurd himself had chosen him, hadn't he? Rising to his feet, he took a step forward so he was standing alongside the Princess and met the Queen's eyes confidently.

'I accept the Quest,' he said simply.

To his surprise, there was an immediate sigh of relief from several of the Vikings, followed by subdued cheering and stamping of feet. The Prince slumped back into his throne with a dismissive *'phah!'*

'So be it!' said the Queen 'The Quest will leave at dawn tomorrow. Before then I will prepare gifts to help the travellers on their journey.'

Whilst the Vikings on the balconies speculated excitedly on what gifts she would prepare, the Queen turned to Peter and spoke to him quietly so that no one other than himself and the Princess could hear.

'Soon it will be dawn. The Quest will leave in one day's time. For now you should rest. You have already had a long night. Tomorrow we will show you our halls. Then, at sunset, the Princess will teach you how to fly. Be brave, Peter, and do not give in to doubt! The Princess will do all she can to help you!'

Peter glanced at the Princess and let go of the talisman in his pocket. Suddenly the enormity of what he had agreed to struck him like a thunderbolt. But despite his fears, his heart was racing with excitement at the prospect of learning how to fly. Could Vikings *really* fly? And even if they could, could he learn in just one night?

The Queen held his eyes for a moment and smiled. He felt as if she was reassuring him of her belief in his abilities and felt a little confidence return. Finally she turned away and addressed the assembly once more.

'There is one further companion I would send. This has been the most difficult choice. The Quest party will need a guide - someone who has walked paths others have not. Only one of us has ventured beyond the Walls of York. Therefore the last of the three companions will be Dunstable!'

Once again there was stunned silence for a long second before hundreds of voices screamed in disbelief as the Queen's decision sunk in. The Prince was out of his seat in an instant, his face bright red again as he shrieked in protest. But even his voice was lost amongst the racket.

'What is the problem with Dunstable?' Peter shouted in the Princess's ear, struggling to be heard above the yelling voices.

The Princess gave him one of her superior sidelong glances.

'Two years ago he was captured by Maledict and tortured! He managed to escape from his dungeons, but he has never been the same since. Before then he went everywhere – tracking troll movements, searching for the last dragons. Then Maledict caught him! Ever since he returned, he has been scared of his own shadow. Magic terrifies him! He will not try it himself and hides whenever someone else does. He is useless now. Nobody thinks very much of him, except the Queen for some reason. She still sends him to spy on trolls every now and then, though he does not dare get close to them.'

Peter was shocked.

'How did he escape from Maledict?'

'No one knows! Maybe that is why the Queen chose him. He is certainly no use as a guide anymore! He can barely find the Viking Halls without getting hopelessly lost!'

But before Peter could ask another question, the Queen spoke again and the Vikings were hushed to silence.

'Now the three companions must join together. Summon Dunstable!'

A shrill bell rang from somewhere nearby and Peter instinctively turned towards the archway through which he had entered earlier. Suddenly it flashed and Dunstable appeared. Looking lost, he took two hesitant steps forward then stopped and cleaned his glasses with his handkerchief. He gazed around the hall in blurred confusion.

'Goodness gracious! The Debating Hall! How on earth did I end up here? I thought it was the way out!'

Suddenly he froze. Placing his glasses back on his nose, he stared at the Queen and Prince in alarm then slowly took in the hundreds of faces turned towards him. As terrified comprehension dawned on his face, he let out a high-pitched whimper of fear.

'*Oh no!* Not a Quest! *Pleease* not a Quest! I'm not going! Count me out! No! No! *NO!!!*'

He shrunk underneath his brown blazer until his head disappeared beneath the collar, except for a few tufts of hair that sprang up like little antenna on his balding head.

'Dunstable?' called out the Queen.

There was barely a movement beneath his blazer.

'Dunstable?' called the Queen again, a little more insistently.

'Who? He's not here! I don't know where he is – maybe he's gone - far away I expect!'

'Dunstable!' repeated the Queen a third time. This time her voice was a command, not a question.

'Leave me alone!' cried Dunstable, shaking under his blazer.

'We need your help Dunstable. Now come out of there immediately! We do not have much time!'

The Queen made a curious gesture with her hands as if pulling on a string and Dunstable's head slowly re-appeared above his blazer.

'*Ouch!*' he squeaked, his eyes tightly shut.

He opened one eye and then the other. Realising that everyone was staring at him, he glanced nervously at the Queen, noting her serious expression. Licking his lips in apprehension, he decided upon an alternative approach.

'I say! I, err, heard that you needed my help? Always glad to be of assistance you know, so long as there's no danger involved of course!'

The Queen held him in her eyes.

'Dunstable. There is something very important I must ask

you to do for us. You must listen carefully. We need your help on a perilous Quest.'

'A, err, *perilous* Quest?' squeaked Dunstable, somehow managing to look even more terrified.

'Yes. You may not survive it. But if you do your honour will be restored. All Vikings will hold you in high esteem forever.'

Dunstable started to whimper again. He wiped his nose on his blazer and began pulling on his tie, his head bowed towards the ground.

'What do you want me to do?' he asked quietly, sounding as if he was dreading the answer.

'Your role is simple. You must lead the Princess and Peter to Mimir's Cavern in the mountains. Then you must lead them back again safely.'

For a second, Dunstable gaped at the Queen in wide-eyed astonishment as her words slowly sunk in. Then he shrieked in fear and tried to duck underneath his blazer again. But some force prevented him from raising it above his chin.

'But...the city is surrounded! There are trolls...*everywhere!* Terrible, nasty trolls that are just *looking* for a Viking to squash! We'll never get past them!! And even if we do, there are all sorts of wicked creatures in Ironwood! And then there's the Frost Giants! Nasty big giants with long icy beards! They *hate* Vikings! Oh dear! I don't feel very well! I don't feel very well at all!!'

The Queen regarded him sympathetically.

'You are the only Viking to have travelled that far since the City Dwellers built their roads and cities. Only you can help us. Without your help we will be lost.'

'But what if we get caught? Maledict...he has such terrible torture machines! I know – I've seen them!'

'Your job is to ensure that you do not get caught.'

'Oh dear! This really is not very good! Not very good at all!'

'Do you refuse the Quest?'

There was an audible intake of breath as everyone in the hall inhaled at the same time, waiting for Dunstable's answer. His eyes wide in alarm, he stared at the Queen, then at the Prince (who frowned back at him) and then at the countless faces peering down at him from the balconies. Finally his eyes rested upon Peter. Peter tried to smile reassuringly, though he only managed a worried grimace. Dunstable seemed to understand his intention, though, and smiled back weakly. He turned nervously to the Queen.

'You said that all Vikings will hold me in *'high esteem'*?'

'All Vikings will hold you in the highest regard for ever,' replied the Queen.

'And if I refuse?'

'Then we will be lost and Maledict will be victorious. He will take York and we will become a forgotten race. Do you refuse?'

Dunstable glanced at Peter again in a curious way as if he was asking him for guidance. *'We'll be alright'* Peter mouthed hesitantly. *'We've got the Princess to help us. I'm sure we won't get caught!'*

Strangely, Dunstable appeared to relax slightly.

'Oh dear! What a dilemma!' he whispered to himself as he fiddled with his tie. 'If Maledict doesn't get me, I'll either be squashed by trolls or slaughtered by Frost Giants!'

Perhaps a minute passed in silence, his expression constantly alternating between terror and thoughtful calculation, as if he was weighing up the odds of living through such an ordeal and gaining respect from the Vikings again. Finally he glanced at the Queen apprehensively.

'Ok! I'll...*I'll go!* Though don't expect me to do any fighting! If we meet any trolls I will be running away you know! When do we leave?'

There was a collective out-take of breath as several hundred Vikings all exhaled at precisely the same time.

'Then it is decided!' announced the Queen in obvious relief. 'The three companions will set out at dawn, one day from now, and all our hopes rest with them!'

Chapter 7

Learning To Fly

'Come on Peter! It is *ee-see*! *Any*one can do it!' whined the Princess, as she hovered miraculously in the air ten feet above the river, seemingly without effort.

Peter swayed on the narrow wooden jetty that jutted out from the riverbank like a diving board. Steadying himself, he stared apprehensively at the murky water just a few feet below him and tried yet again.

Using all his powers of concentration, he pictured himself rising gracefully into the air as the Princess had taught him. But after a few minutes, he gave up. He just couldn't do it. No matter how hard he tried or how much the Princess reassured him, he simply couldn't believe he could fly. Utterly deflated, he leapt down onto the grassy riverbank and glared up at the Princess.

'It's hopeless! This is a complete waste of time! Who ever heard of anyone being able to fly anyway?'

Slumping down onto the wet grass in frustration, he stared across the night sky towards the city. His mood darkened still further when he saw the Princess whizz past him, twisting and turning in mid air as if flying was the simplest and most joyful thing in the world.

Peter's day, which started off so well, had turned dramatically for the worse.

After the Council he had been led by the Princess to another magical archway, half way down the Debating Hall. Without a word, she had indicated that he should go inside, then left him to prepare for the Quest. Slightly bemused, Peter had closed his eyes and stepped through the solid stone.

When he opened them again, he had found himself in a small square room, the walls of which were glowing dimly, providing just enough light for him to see. In the centre of the room was a wooden bed. Upon it was a thick mattress, two pillows and a quilt, all of which had appeared to be made out of thousands of tiny leaves sewn together. Pausing just long enough to throw off his clothes, he had pulled the quilt aside and climbed wearily into the bed. Immediately, he had fallen into a deep dreamless sleep.

The following day, he had been woken in the early afternoon by the Princess. After a wonderful few hours spent exploring the Viking Halls, she had led him back into the city after nightfall. They had walked through a number of oddly named snickelways (*MUCKY PEG LANE, POPE'S HEAD ALLEY, FISH LANDING* and *ST GEORGE'S FIELD*). At the end of *ST GEORGE'S FIELD*, they had stepped through the white outline of a door on the snickelway wall and magically emerged amongst some trees by the river. From there, the Princess had led him a short distance along the riverbank to a place where the river bent sharply to the south. At the apex of the bend where the river was at its widest, someone had built a short jetty, presumably for fishermen, that stretched ten feet across the water like a half finished bridge. It was here that she had begun to instruct him in the art of flying.

For almost an hour, the Princess had painstakingly explained the fundamentals of flight, emphasising that it would only be possible if Peter truly believed he could fly. But soon his attention had wavered. It was impossible for him to imagine someone flying, despite all the incredible things he'd seen since meeting the Vikings. Then, to his utter amazement, the Princess had risen effortlessly into the air and performed several astonishing acrobatic feats in front of him before finally landing on the riverbank with a spinning pirouette. Unfortunately, Peter's amazement was so great that he then found it impossible to concentrate on what she was telling him. Eventually though, he almost began to believe that he too could fly. At first he'd been excited - so excited that he'd been willing to put up with the Princess's endless bragging about how wonderful and talented she was and how everybody loved her. He'd even pretended to be interested when she told him how she'd learned to fly before she could walk, and could fly backwards when she was just two years old. But, after almost five hours of endless failures, his enthusiasm had begun to wane. To make matters worse, it had started to rain. He was cold, wet and tired, and he was beginning to get very irritable indeed.

'Why do we have to do this in the dark, anyway?' he whinged sulkily after his latest failure. He glared at the narrow jetty and the dark river just a few feet below it. 'I can hardly see what I'm doing!'

'Because someone might see us if we did it in the day, stupid,' explained the Princess with false patience whilst hovering a few feet above him in a reclined pose, as if she was lying on a bed.

'I thought City Dwellers couldn't see Vikings?'

The Princess tutted, clearly annoyed at having to explain *everything* to such a stupid boy. She flew down until she was level with Peter's head and crossed her arms as she hung in the air in front of him like a genie.

'*Most* City Dwellers cannot see us. But there might be *some* that can – anyone who still believes in magic. Children for instance? Now, try harder. I do not want to be here all night!'

Peter rose to his feet and paced up and down the narrow jetty like a boxer preparing for a fight. He finally positioned himself a few inches from the end and gazed across the water to the tree-lined bank opposite.

The Princess followed him from the air, now flying on her back and doing some weird kind of air-backstroke. He shot her an envious glance and tried to focus as she had taught him. But, after a few minutes, he gave up once more and flopped onto the grass. He was tired and cold, and so much had happened over the past twenty-four hours that he found it impossible to concentrate. He gazed up at the Princess and saw that she was grinning at him infuriatingly.

'It's alright for you! You've been surrounded by flying Vikings and magic all your life. I've never seen anyone fly before, unless they've been in an aeroplane!' He kicked a stone into the river. 'It's impossible! I'll *never* learn how to fly!'

The Princess drifted down until she was hovering just a foot above the river in front of him.

'You do talk a lot of nonsense. What kind of poor excuse is that? Do you think that simply because you have not seen anyone do something, it must be impossible? *City Dwellers!* You are all the same! No imagination! You think that if you cannot understand something, it must be impossible! Can you explain how an enormous tree grows from a tiny seed? How a bird hatches from an egg? Can you explain how you breathe without thinking about it? All these things happen without you knowing why or how. City Dwellers are so narrow-minded!'

'Excuse me! *I'm* a City Dweller you know!' It may have been the cold, his tiredness or simply because she was annoying him so much, but Peter suddenly decided he'd had enough. He threw a stone into the water sullenly. 'I don't think you can teach me to fly anyway. I don't think you're good enough!'

The Princess's mouth gaped open in shock at being spoken to so bluntly.

'*Really!*' was all she managed to say, too furious to express anything more. Red faced, she flew to the opposite bank and glared at him across the water, her arms tightly crossed in temper.

Peter felt absolutely no remorse. The thrill of learning how to fly had long since faded. He seriously doubted he could ever succeed anyway. Now, more than anything, he just wanted to go to bed.

As he lay on the grass, he gazed moodily over the dark trees towards the city. Towering above the rooftops in the distance was the Minster, perfectly illuminated against the night sky. Suddenly he thought of the Viking Halls and the Queen. Somewhere beneath that great church she was waiting for them to return, hoping he had succeeded. She had such faith in him! He had never experienced anything like it. She had barely met him, yet she was willing to trust him with a vital Quest. He dreaded to think what she would say if he failed. Suddenly he felt horribly guilty that he had given up so easily. For her sake, if nothing else, he decided to try one final time.

First though, he would have to persuade the Princess to stop sulking and speak to him. He glanced across the river. She was still hovering above the opposite bank. The moment she realised he was watching her, she turned her back on him theatrically and crossed her arms even more tightly than before. He was sorely tempted to try again without her, but he knew he would never succeed without her help, much though he hated to admit it.

He waited the minimum amount of time his pride insisted, then called out to her across the water.

'Your Highness?'

She turned her head briefly in his direction, surprised that he had addressed her so politely. Turning away again, she drifted further down the river, pretending to be interested in some bushes that grew beside the water.

'Your Highness?' Peter repeated, slightly louder than before. 'Come back and teach me to fly!' He thought for a moment and decided to try some flattery. 'If anyone can teach a City Dweller how to fly, I bet you can! I bet you're the only Viking who is good enough to teach me!'

This seemed to strike a chord with the Princess. Dropping the leaves she had plucked from the bushes, she flew slowly across the river towards him.

'Yes, you are right of course. If anyone can teach a mere City Dweller how to fly, it surely must be me! After all, I do fly rather well, do I not?' She was just a few yards away from him now and beaming enthusiastically, all trace of her former sulkiness gone. 'In fact, though I do not like to boast, I think I am probably the best flyer of all the Vikings. That is probably why my mother chose me to teach you.'

'That must be true,' agreed Peter, resisting the urge to react to her incredible arrogance. 'And imagine what all the Vikings will say if you teach me - a *'mere'* City Dweller - to fly! They'll say that only the best flyer who ever lived could have done that!'

The Princess glowed visibly.

'You know, that is probably true! After all, no one has *ever* taught a City Dweller to fly before!'

A far away look fell across her face as she imagined the acclaim she would receive if she succeeded. In the space of a few seconds, what had previously been a chore to her became a unique opportunity to show off, something she had never been able to resist.

'Right then! Get up! Get up!' she suddenly insisted after basking in her anticipated glory. 'We have not got all night you know!'

She was now hovering about six feet in front of him. Without a word, Peter resumed his position at the end of the narrow jetty and awaited her instructions.

'Let us start again, but this time we will do it *properly!* Listen to me *very* carefully. Are you ready? Right then...' She rolled up the sleeves of her blue dress as if she was a doctor about to perform a complex operation. 'First, I want you to stand at the end of the jetty and raise your arms like a scarecrow!'

Forcing himself to remember the Queen again, Peter suppressed his surprise at this peculiar suggestion (and annoyance at the Princess's irritating school-teacher like tone) and did exactly what he was told. For once he was glad that it was dark and they were far away from the city. He glanced at the gloomy looking water just a few feet below him, remembering how he'd learnt to swim by falling into the deep end of the swimming pool and not relishing a similar experience.

'You're not going to tell me to jump off or something are you?'

'Of course not!' snapped the Princess. 'That is the *worst* way to learn! You have to understand how lift works first! Now…shut-up and listen to what I am about to tell you!'

Suppressing a sudden desire to haul her down and throw her into the river, Peter closed his eyes to concentrate.

'First, you must reach out with your senses. Feel the air against the palms of your hands. Feel it against your fingers. Feel how it moves. Got it? Now, slowly extend your senses with your mind until you can feel the air against your arms, then against your body, your legs and your face. Feel the wind in your hair. You need to feel it against every part of your body. Can you feel it?'

Peter nodded, deep in concentration.

'Good! Now I want you to imagine that you are incredibly light – as light as a feather drifting on the breeze. Feel how the air lifts and carries you.'

Peter concentrated even harder. A strange tingling sensation was developing in the pit of his stomach. He felt as if he had no weight at all. It was like being in a car speeding downhill, or in a diving roller-coaster. He was tempted to open his eyes to see if his feet were still on the ground.

'Do not open your eyes yet!' warned the Princess, reading his mind. 'Now, this is the most important part! Imagine yourself rising off the ground, inch by inch. Keep thinking of the feather! Remember how light you are – lighter than the air. Feel yourself floating upwards, slowly rising higher.'

Peter did exactly as he was told. The strange sensation in his stomach was getting stronger and he was beginning to feel queasy. He desperately wanted to open his eyes to see if it was working.

'Good!' continued the Princess. There was a strange tone in her voice that sounded like excitement. 'When I tell you, I want you to open your eyes – not a moment before! When you open them, you must *not* look down! This is *really* important! Whatever you do, you must *not* look down! Look straight ahead at me – I am right in front of you. Are you ready? Right! Open your eyes!'

Peter opened his eyes and blinked in surprise. He knew immediately that he was in the air, and could tell from the position of the trees on the opposite bank that he must be several feet above the ground. Hovering in front of him with a triumphant smile on her face was the Princess. It was incredible! But then the excitement overcame him and the inevitable happened. He couldn't help it. He looked down.

For a moment, he marvelled at the sight of the river several feet below him, then he stared in bemusement at his feet dangling in mid air without any means of support. What on earth was keeping him in the air he wondered? Then he fell. With an enormous *splash!* he was suddenly immersed in freezing cold water.

Furious with himself, he managed to half-swim, half-wade onto the bank, then hauled himself out of the river using a branch that was hanging over the water. He was covered from head to toe in mud. As he leant against a tree, exhausted and shivering with cold, he heard the Princess almost sobbing with laughter above him.

'I *told* you! 'Do not look down', I said! What did you do as soon as you opened your eyes? You looked down!'

Peter was livid. The Princess was acting as if it was the funniest thing she had ever seen, but he was freezing cold, filthy and, as he sniffed his mud-covered arms in disgust, he smelt absolutely terrible!

'Look at me! I'm *covered* in mud!' He tried to wipe the dirt from his face with his equally muddy coat sleeve, but only succeeded in smearing it across his mouth and nose. 'Why do we have to do this over the river anyway?'

'Because,' explained the Princess, managing to subdue her laughter just long enough to adopt her *'all City Dwellers are stupid'* tone of voice, 'if we did it above the ground and you fell, you would break every bone in your body! I deliberately chose this part of the river because it is not too deep. This way you just get very dirty – and I get to have a good laugh!'

Peter frowned, failing to see the funny side. He was beginning to wonder whether the second reason wasn't more important to the Princess than the first.

'Let us try again, shall we?' she urged, a little too enthusiastically for his liking.

She really seemed to be enjoying herself now. She flew down until she was hovering just above the river in front of him.

Wiping his hands on the grass, Peter took up position at the end of the jetty again. The fall hadn't put him off. On the contrary, he knew that for a moment he had actually been flying - or remaining in the air at least. Now he was more determined than ever to learn how to fly, if only to wipe the smirk off the Princess's face. He certainly wasn't going to give her the pleasure of watching him fall into the river again!

Once more he closed his eyes and concentrated. Holding out his arms as the Princess had taught him, he felt the wind brushing against his skin and hair. He imagined he was incredibly light - lighter even than air. In his mind's eye, he pictured a balloon floating on the breeze. Almost immediately, he felt a tingling sensation in his stomach, but this time it passed quickly. Suddenly he felt strangely warm, as if he had just drunk something delightfully hot that was coursing through his body.

Meanwhile, the Princess directed him as before.

'Good! Now this time, when you open your eyes, look only at my face. Ready? Open your eyes!'

Hesitating just for a moment, Peter opened his eyes. Once again, he knew immediately that he was in the air. The Princess was hovering a few feet in front of him. A wave of excitement rushed through his body and he felt a strong desire to look down, but this time he just managed to suppress it. Instead, he concentrated solely on the Princess's face.

'Very good!' she exclaimed, clapping her hands together, almost as excited as he was.

He allowed himself a brief self-congratulatory smile but kept staring at her face, focusing on her nose.

'Do not get cocky!' she warned, instantly sounding like her usual condescending self again. 'You are only floating, not flying. Floating is the easy part!'

She cleared her throat as if in preparation for making an important speech.

'Now, flying is *easy* – much easier than you think it is. The most important thing is to *believe* that you can do it. As soon as you stop believing, you fall. You are only floating now because you have convinced yourself that you are lighter than air. Do you understand so far?'

'Yes, thank you,' replied Peter irritably. He just wanted to get on with it now, and the Princess's superior tone was starting to annoy him again.

'Good!' she continued, ignoring the obvious irritation in his voice. 'What you need to do is picture yourself flying in your mind. As soon as you feel yourself move, focus on where you want to go and imagine yourself flying towards it. Got that?'

'I think so,' replied Peter through gritted teeth.

The Princess drifted backwards and positioned herself about forty yards away, above the opposite bank of the river.

'Right!' she called out enthusiastically. 'When I say 'go', I want you to fly towards me. Remember what I said. Picture yourself flying, and as soon as you feel you are moving, focus on where you want to go. Ready? Go!'

Peter closed his eyes and was about to concentrate once more when the Princess yelled at him.

'Do *not* close your eyes! How will you see where you are going if your eyes are shut? You could fly straight into a tree and that would be the end of you! Now – do it *properly* please!'

Trying to ignore her, he began to concentrate again (though this time with his eyes wide open). He stared straight ahead at the Princess and tried to imagine himself flying towards her. Again, he felt a sudden rush of warmth through his body, but he forced himself to focus until he was oblivious to everything except her face. He had never concentrated so hard on anything in his life! But when he expected to feel himself shoot towards her, nothing happened. He simply hung in the air like a tethered balloon.

Undeterred, he paused for a few seconds then concentrated again, picturing himself gliding effortlessly through the air.

Still nothing happened.

For a moment he felt utterly deflated. His elation at learning how to hover was replaced by complete frustration at not being able to move. However, he was not about to give up so easily. Immediately he tried again.

And then again.

And again…

For the next 30 minutes he hung in the air, concentrating as hard as he could, but not moving an inch.

Meanwhile the Princess was getting bored by his lack of progress. Instead of giving him something to focus on, she decided to do some more aerobatics, just to demonstrate how much better she was than he. Round and round she flew, looping the loop, flying feet first, doing air walks, flying vertically upwards whilst hanging upside-down as if she was being pulled up by her feet. She looked like she was born in the air.

Despite his best efforts to ignore her, Peter began to feel more and more irritated by her antics. To make matters worse, the intense concentration was giving him an enormous headache.

'You are still not moving!' the Princess called out unnecessarily, as she whizzed past him after completing yet another repertoire of complex aeronautical manoeuvres.

'I know!' he yelled back, absolutely infuriated. 'You're meant to be helping me, not doing silly tricks!' He glanced up and saw her grinning at him as she raced past, flying backwards. 'And stop smirking! This isn't easy you know!'

She flew towards him until she was hovering just above his head, then pulled her legs up and 'sat' in the air.

'Go away! I'm trying to concentrate!' He tried to push her away but immediately withdrew his arms as he wobbled in the air. The Princess gazed at him, an irritatingly superior grin on her face.

'Do you have a bicycle?'

He glared at her, furious at having his concentration broken yet again.

'What's that got to do with anything?'

'I had one when I was younger. Mother thought that a City Dwellers' machine might help educate me, though I cannot think why. You see, flying is very similar to riding a bicycle. Do you remember how difficult it was to keep your balance and how terrified you were of falling off? But then, when you learned how to ride properly, you found that it was really easy and you did not need to concentrate at all? Well, flying is just the same. You just need to relax.'

'So you're saying I'm trying too hard, is that it?'

The Princess nodded, grinning smugly.

'Exactly! It is really *very* easy. You do not need to think about it – just *feel* it. A bird does not have to think about flying – it just flies! Simply picture yourself flying through the air to where you want to go and *expect* to move. And *do not* close your eyes!'

Peter thought this sounded too good to be true, but he was cold and tired. His clothes were baked in mud and, with the possible exception of wiping the superior smile off the Princess's face by soaring like an eagle, his greatest desire was to curl up in a nice warm bed.

His mind dulled by fatigue, he imagined himself flying, this time without concentrating on anything. In his mind's eye, he simply pictured a bird flying effortlessly through the air. But he soon gave up. Birds clearly had wings. He simply couldn't picture himself flying so easily. Eventually, without really thinking about it, he pictured a leaf carried by the breeze, slowly drifting through the air.

He moved a yard forward then juddered to a halt.

He was so startled he almost cried out in joy! Finally he had the encouragement he'd been looking for! Suddenly his head stopped aching and he felt fresh and alert once more. Trying to subdue the whirl of excitement rising from his stomach, he tried again. This time, he imagined a kite soaring through the air, completely under control.

Like a faltering car, he jolted forward about five yards then drifted slightly to the left before coming to a complete stop.

'Do not stop now!' shouted the Princess excitedly. She darted down and resumed her previous position above the opposite bank of the river. 'You have almost got it!'

Encouraged, Peter conjured up his mental image of a kite again, using his imagination to make it glide smoothly towards the Princess. Immediately he began to move, but this time more quickly and easily. Almost before he realised it, he was by her side above the trees on the opposite bank. Hardly able to control his excitement, he made the kite stop in his mind's eye and came to a halt behind her.

'I can fly! I can *REALLY FLY!*'

'Not bad for a City Dweller,' said the Princess, trying to sound casual but grinning as much as he. 'Of course, you do have an excellent teacher.'

Peter was too happy to take offence and simply beamed stupidly at her.

'I can fly! I can *flyyyyy!*' was all he managed to say, repeating it over and over again.

The Princess allowed him a moment's glory before reverting to her usual self.

'Yes…yes. Very good. Now, let us do some *real* flying, shall we? See if you can follow me!'

She dived down to the river, only levelling out again when she was a few feet above the surface. Feeling confident now, Peter followed her without thinking. To his delight, he flew as effortlessly as the Princess had done. In fact, he dropped faster than he expected and only levelled out at the last moment. Just beneath him, the river sparkled as he raced over its surface, so close he could have reached down and touched the water.

The Princess was waiting for him fifty yards down the river.

'Not bad. You *might* be getting the hang of it,' she admitted grudgingly. 'You were a little slow in the descent though, in my opinion. Now, let us see if you can manage something a bit more complicated, shall we?'

Turning, she briefly glanced over her shoulder to ensure he was following her then dived down again until she was just inches above the river. Levelling out, she placed her hands by her sides and gradually increased her speed, following the river's course towards the city. Peter dived after her, exulting in the thrill of flight as he skimmed over the glistening water, almost crying out in joy. Faster and faster they sped side by side, the wind roaring in their ears. Peter glanced at the bank and saw the trees race by. He could hardly believe how fast they were going! He had never felt so excited in his life!

'This is *brilliant! This is absolutely brilliant!!!*' he shouted, struggling to make himself heard above the rushing wind.

The Princess grinned back at him.

'Let us have some fun! Do *exactly* what I do!'

Immediately she began to sway from side to side, zigzagging like a skier on a slalom course. Peter was right behind her, following her easily as confidence surged through him.

They were now flying so quickly that the surface of the water below them was a blur. Up ahead, the city was fast approaching.

Four hundred yards away, an elegant bridge spanned the river. It was supported by three graceful arches - a larger middle one with a smaller one on either side - and formed part of a busy road into the city centre. As Peter glanced ahead, he could clearly see the bright lights of car headlamps as they flashed across it.

The Princess saw the bridge too, but she didn't slow down. Glancing at him with a mischievous glint in her eye, she raced towards it even faster than before. She was about fifty yards from the bridge when, to Peter's horror, she suddenly veered sharply to the right. Instead of flying through the larger middle arch, she was now aiming to pass through the much narrower arch to the right! She turned her head and grinned back at him, daring him to follow her.

For a fraction of a second, Peter hesitated. The semi-circular archway was no more than six feet wide at water-level and its highest point was barely four feet above the water. There was no room for error. But the excitement of his first flight was too strong. He picked up speed until he was hot on her heals again. The bridge was almost upon them.

'Keep close behind me!' the Princess shouted. 'We are going through!'

There was a rush of wind, a splash of water, the sound of a car horn then momentary darkness before they shot out the other side like a cork from a bottle, screaming in delight.

They were now fast approaching the city centre. After the excitement of the race to the bridge, the Princess began to slow down and, side by side, they climbed until they were a hundred yards or so above the ground. Catching his breath, Peter gazed down to the city below, feeling a sudden stab of fear at being so high. But it only lasted a moment before he suppressed it, his confidence in his new found abilities renewed.

Beneath them, the city stretched to every horizon. Thousands and thousands of houses and buildings were lit up in the night. Everything looked so small and peaceful. The houses in particular looked like little toys, and it was hard to think of them as real. But he knew that in each of them, people would be sitting on their sofas watching television or lying in their beds asleep, little realising the incredible things that were happening just beyond their windows.

They flew on until they were above the centre of the city.

FLYING OVER YORK

Beneath them, York Minster glowed in the darkness. It looked so grand and regal, like a wise old monarch quietly watching over the city.

'Doesn't the Minster look incredible from up here!' said Peter, feeling strangely drawn to it.

'There is Viking magic in it, though the City Dwellers do not realise of course,' replied the Princess. 'It would have turned to rubble hundreds of years ago if it had not been for us. Follow me! Let us go down to the streets!'

Like a high board diver above a swimming pool, she ducked her head down, put her arms by her sides and dropped down to earth. Peter dived behind her, and together they fell out of the sky with the wind roaring in their ears.

They came to a sudden stop about fifteen feet above one of York's medieval streets, close to the Minster. Both sides of the narrow walkway were lined with shops, their window displays lit up in the night. As they flew slowly along it, Peter's heart was in his mouth with excitement and trepidation. Despite the late hour, there were several people walking just beneath them. If they looked up, they would surely be seen.

'Do not worry,' whispered the Princess, noticing his uneasiness. 'Hardly any adult City Dwellers can see us, and the children are all in bed.'

She appeared to be right as no one took any notice of them, even when they dipped lower so they were flying just a few feet above the ground.

They were almost at the end of the street when suddenly a group of drunken men staggered out of a narrow passageway just as they were passing. The Princess immediately darted away, but Peter wasn't so quick and, as he leapt in the air, he knocked the baseball cap off the head of one of the men with his foot. The man turned and stared blankly around him, sure that something had touched him. Peter held his breath as the man gazed up, staring right through him. But then he shrugged his shoulders and jogged after his friends.

'We must be more careful,' whispered the Princess when he flew up to join her. 'Though they cannot see us, they can feel us if we touch them and hear us if we speak. Come on! Let us fly some more!'

Rising higher above the streets, they began to explore the city from the air. Soon the Minster rose in front of them, beckoning them forward. The vast church was gloriously bright, every stone seeming to glow radiantly. Climbing almost vertically, they dashed between its twin towers before racing across the gardens behind it and over the City Walls. Turning around, they skimmed over a main road, passing just a few yards above the cars, then darted through an ancient stone gateway back into the narrow streets.

For more than an hour they flew over the city, sometimes climbing high into the sky, other times skirting close to the ground, unseen by those below. To Peter, it was like a gloriously vivid dream and the time seemed to pass in minutes. When the Princess finally said they should head back, he begged her for another ten minutes, fearing that if he stopped now, he might never experience such a wonderful feeling again. But the Princess was insistent. Her job well done, she was anxious to rest and prepare for the Quest.

As they headed back down the river, the thrill of learning to fly slowly receded as Peter began to worry about what the morning would bring. In just a few hours, the Quest would begin. So far, he felt as if he'd been on an incredible adventure. He had met the Vikings, seen the wonderful underground chambers in the Viking Halls, spoken to the Queen and learnt how to fly. But soon he would leave York on a dangerous journey with strange people he had only just met – a journey from which he might never return.

As he landed on the riverbank and followed the Princess into the *ST GEORGE'S FIELD* snickelway, he suddenly felt very cold and alone once more.

Chapter 8

The Way Out of York

As soon as they returned to the Viking Halls, the Princess led Peter to the bedroom he had slept in the previous night then marched off to 'discuss his progress' with the Queen, making him feel like a struggling schoolboy.

It was another late night. Peter immediately crawled into the bed, barely pausing to throw off his muddy clothes. He had hardly closed his eyes when he began to dream. Once again, he was flying with the wind blasting against his face and the ground far below, looking so peaceful in the night. This time he was alone. For hours he flew, relishing the wonderful feeling of freedom he felt. Suddenly he froze in fear. As if aware of it for the first time, he realised that he was hundreds of feet up in the air, completely unsupported! Surely it was impossible for someone to fly? As soon as the thought occurred to him, he began to fall. He tried to react – to remember what the Princess had taught him - but he couldn't stop himself! Down he fell, the wind screaming in his ears as the ground rushed up to meet him. Down. Down. Then there was darkness.

He woke up with a start, sweat pouring off his brow. It was dark. The Princess was leaning over him, shaking him vigorously. Behind her, Dunstable was fidgeting nervously.

'Come on! Get up! Get up! It is almost dawn! Time to get ready!'

Groggily, he staggered out of bed and began to dress, vaguely aware that his muddy clothes had been cleaned in the night. Feeling distinctly troubled by his dream, he followed the Princess and Dunstable into the Debating Hall.

*

The Debating Hall was almost empty. No Vikings peered down from the lofty balconies as they jogged to the back of the vast chamber. There, sitting on her throne alone, the Queen was waiting for them. On the floor in front of her was a golden casket.

As they approached, she watched them closely, following their progress across the hall until they stood before her. Peter stared at his feet to avoid her eyes, whilst beside him Dunstable fiddled with his glasses nervously. There was an uncomfortable silence for several long seconds as she regarded each of them in turn before she finally spoke.

'The Princess has told me of your success last night, Peter. You have done well, as I thought you would. But the journey to Mimir's Well will be a difficult one and you will face many dangers. Do you still wish to go?'

Peter raised his head and nodded.

'I do.'

'Good. The Princess and Dunstable will go with you. The Princess is skilled in magic and Dunstable will be your guide, as only he has travelled beyond the Walls of York.' Out of the corner of his eye, Peter could see Dunstable pulling on his tie, his ears twitching. 'But I want to help you further, if I can. I have therefore prepared three gifts to aid you in times of danger.'

As the Queen bent down to open the golden casket at her feet, Peter's heart began to race in anticipation of what the wonderful gifts might be, hoping they would be magical. Dunstable shuffled up closer beside him, his curiosity overcoming his fear of magic, whilst the Princess regarded them both loftily. She was pretending to be uninterested, though Peter could tell from her eyes that she was as curious as he was.

As Peter and Dunstable leant forward expectantly, the Queen rose up. She was holding what looked like a thin multi-coloured mask. As it moved in her hands, the colours changed chameleon-like to blend into the background, making it almost invisible. Only its grey outline could be seen clearly, glinting in the light from the crystal trees.

'I say! A *transformation mask!*' gasped Dunstable, practically falling over Peter in excitement. 'That'll be jolly useful!'

The Queen handed the mask to Peter.

'Take care of this rare gift. It took a powerful spell to make it!

It will turn you into whatever living thing you ask of it. Be warned though! You can only wear the mask three times before the spell will break, so think carefully before you use it!'

Peter took the mask gingerly and stared at it in wonder, gazing at its changing colours. He resisted the urge to try it on, just to see if it worked. Meanwhile, the Queen had reached into the casket once more. She emerged with a tiny glass bottle with a miniature cork in the top which contained a dark green liquid.

'Goodness gracious! *Speed Potion!*' whispered Dunstable in amazement. 'Never know when you might need some of that!'

The Queen passed the bottle to Peter.

'A few drops of this potion will give you the speed of a falcon. Your pursuers will fall far behind you, and those you pursue you will surely catch. But the liquid is precious. Use it only in the utmost urgency!'

The Queen reached into the casket for the final time.

'And now for the greatest gift of all…'

There was a sharp intake of breath beside Peter as Dunstable sucked his teeth, his eyes glued to the Queen. Peter felt his pulse racing with excitement. Even the Princess gave up pretending to be uninterested and leant over Dunstable, desperate to see what the last gift would be.

After several painstakingly long seconds, the Queen stood up again and the casket clicked shut. She held out her hand to Peter. In her palm was what looked like a very small bar of chocolate, wrapped in silver foil.

'*Eh?*' said Dunstable. 'What's that then?'

'This,' said the Queen in a commanding voice, 'is Viking chocolate. It contains pure essence of joy. Whoever eats it will feel unlimited pleasure. He will cease any wrongdoing, shed his fears and experience pure bliss. Even the cruellest heart will be gladdened!'

'I say!' said Dunstable. 'Can I have some too?'

Peter took it gratefully, though he couldn't imagine when he would need it. The Queen turned to all three of them.

'Now the Quest to find Mimir's Well must begin, and the hopes of all Vikings go with you! Use the gifts I have given you wisely. Many perils lie ahead and each of you will be sorely tested. Be brave! Mimir is the wisest of all Vikings. There is no question he cannot answer. His wisdom lies in the enchanted water from the mountains. Look into the water drawn from his Well and you will find the answer to how we can defeat Maledict. It is our only hope. Go now with the blessings of all Vikings, and may our next meeting be a joyful one!'

*

It was another two hours before they were ready to leave. During that time, Peter struggled to keep awake as the Princess tried on an endless selection of brightly coloured clothes, tirelessly assisted by three stressed looking female Vikings. Finally, she settled on a thick yellow coat and pale blue trousers, though it was clear by the way she constantly adjusted her hair and picked at the coat with her fingers that her appearance would require her constant attention.

When she was finally satisfied, one of the three Vikings handed Peter a large brown pouch attached to a belt by thick string. Peter immediately knew what to do with it. Lifting his jumper, he tied it around his waist above his own belt then carefully placed the Queen's magical gifts inside. They fitted perfectly. Relieved, he pulled his jumper over the pouch to conceal it.

They were about to leave when Peter suddenly thought of his mother. He'd barely given her a moment's thought since he'd arrived in the Viking Halls! She would be going frantic with worry wondering where he was! A wave of guilt rose from the bottom of his stomach. But what could he do? He could hardly go back and explain that he was helping the Vikings overcome a powerful sorcerer and his troll army. He'd get locked up in a hospital before he could say 'And I can fly too!' His only option was a message.

He reached into his deep coat pocket for a pen and scribbled a message on the back of a museum guide he found there: 'Mum. Don't worry about me. Gone on a very important journey. Will be back as soon as I can. Love Peter.'

He passed the message to the Viking girl who had given him the pouch and tried to explain to her where his mother's flat was. Somewhat bemused, she nodded and promised to deliver it. Feeling marginally happier, Peter was ready for the journey ahead.

A few minutes later, they finally left the Viking Halls. Much to Peter's disappointment, the Princess announced that they weren't going to fly.

'Why did I learn how to fly if we're going to walk all the way?' he complained when she told him.

'We cannot fly because we would be spotted!' replied the Princess dismissively. 'As well as the risk of being seen by children, the troll army would immediately know we are Vikings and would try to find us. In any case, Dunstable cannot fly.'

'You can't fly?' Peter asked Dunstable in surprise.

'No, of course I can't fly!' replied Dunstable irritably. 'I never told you I could fly, did I? I *hate* heights! I have two feet so I can walk!'

'But I thought all Vikings in York could fly?'

'Not *all* of us! Whatever gave you that idea? Not even all birds can fly!'

Their journey from the Viking Halls through the magic snickelways was as entertaining as ever. As they followed the secret passageways through York, Peter recognised some of the snickelway names from streets he had seen with his mother and grandmother. Clearly the snickelways ran along similar paths to the streets that lay beyond their invisible walls. But the Princess quickly led them to parts of the city he had not visited before, and soon he was completely lost.

After about ten minutes, she stopped beside the snickelway lamp-post beneath the sign for *STRAKERS PASSAGE* and gestured for Peter and Dunstable to come closer to her.

'We are about to emerge into the city. We are not far from the City Walls. Once we pass through them, we are going to have to creep past the troll army. We should be all right as the trolls have not all arrived yet, but we cannot be too careful! If we are spotted, they will attack us immediately, so pay attention to me and do exactly what I say!'

Dunstable, who was already looking worried, began to pull on his tie again.

'Oh dear! Why did I agree to go on this dreadful Quest? If they see us, they'll squash us! They'll squash us all!'

The Princess glanced at him scornfully.

'Do not be silly! I am not going to let any ugly troll squash me, but I do not want us to be seen either! Where is a good place to pass through the troll patrols without being spotted?'

Dunstable thought carefully, his mind struggling with fear as he recalled his hurried journey back to the city.

'By the river, I think,' he whispered finally, scratching his bald head nervously. 'Trolls don't like water very much, you see. That's why they smell so bad! I don't think there will be many of them there!'

'Good! That is what I thought too. Follow me!'

They turned towards the white outline of a door on the wall. Immediately the snickelway disappeared and they found themselves standing in bright daylight beside a tall house on an ordinary looking city street. It was mid morning, after everyone had left for work or school but before the earliest lunch, and the streets were quiet. Once again, it was raining heavily.

The Princess led them quickly past shops and houses. A few minutes later, they turned a corner and the City Walls loomed up ahead. Set on top of a steep grass embankment, they stretched into the distance as they encircled the city. Peter gazed at them in surprise. The Walls looked strangely different from the last time he'd seen them with his mother and grandmother. The most obvious change was their size. Now they were much taller - almost twice the height they had been before. But it wasn't just their size. They also looked thicker and stronger, as if they had been restored to a former glory.

The Princess stopped and turned to see what was delaying him. Realising what he was staring at, she dug her hands into her hips and glared at him impatiently.

'This is what the Walls *really* look like silly! City Dwellers just see the stones – they do not see the *real* Walls and all the magic that is in them. You do not think we could keep trolls out with just a few old rocks piled on top of one another, do you?'

Peter continued to stare at the Walls, ignoring the sarcasm in her voice.

'So, things look *different* in your world?'

'Only *magical* things. City Dwellers' things like cars and houses look exactly the same. City Dwellers cannot see magic, remember?'

Peter looked at the imposing looking Walls in a new light. Suddenly they appeared strong and full of magic. Perhaps the Vikings would hold out against Maledict and the trolls after all.

Ahead of him, the Princess had already scaled the grass embankment and was examining the stones in the Wall, running her hands over them as if searching for something. Peter scrambled after her with Dunstable, watching her curiously. Whatever she was looking for was clearly difficult to find as her eyes were closed in concentration. A minute later, she smiled triumphantly and stepped back. Glancing at them to make sure they were watching, she nodded towards the section of the Walls in front of her. Suddenly two parallel cracks appeared. About three feet apart, they snaked up from the ground to a height of about six feet then joined together at the top to form a door-shape. As soon as they met, the whole Wall enclosed within the cracks swung open as if it was on a hinge. The Princess grinned at them smugly.

'This is one of the secret ways out of York. No one has used it for hundreds of years!'

Dunstable, who had practically jumped out of his skin when the 'wall door' had opened, gazed at her sulkily.

'No one bothered to tell *me* about it! I've always had to *climb* the Walls! And jolly painful it can be too, you know!'

'You are not important enough,' said the Princess matter-of-factly, as if she either didn't know or didn't care that she was being rude. She glanced through the wall-door to ensure there were no trolls on the other side.

'Now, remember what I said before. We must get past the trolls without being seen, so do *exactly* what I tell you! Is that clear?'

Ignoring their somewhat cold reaction to her instructions, the Princess stepped through the wall-door, quickly followed by Peter and Dunstable. They emerged on top of the grass embankment on the other side. Below them was a very normal looking city street. There was no sign of any trolls. In fact, everything looked exactly the same as it did on any other morning, though it was a little quieter than usual due to the heavy rain.

As quickly as they could, they slid down the muddy embankment and raced into a narrow street between two rows of terraced houses. Darting across another road, they cautiously made their way through the outskirts of York. After about ten minutes they came to a halt behind a large pub. In front of them was a puddle-strewn sports field containing several rugby pitches, their tall white goalposts leaning slightly askew. Just beyond the fields they could see a large boat on the river as it drifted casually by.

The Princess was uneasy. The field was several hundred yards wide and there was no cover. If any trolls were about, they would easily be spotted.

'We must cross this field! It is the only way out of York that is close to the river! Hopefully we are near enough to the water to avoid any trolls.' She leant out from behind the wall of the pub and peered across the field. 'When I say go, we will make a run for it! Ready? *Go!*'

Without waiting for a response, she sprang out from behind the wall and dashed towards the field with an amazing turn of pace. Peter and Dunstable immediately raced after her. Peter considered himself to be a fast runner and had won several school races in Wales, but the Princess was quicker. The gap between her and Dunstable and himself grew and grew. Soon she had reached the other side of the field and was frantically urging them on from behind the garden wall of a large house.

'Come on! Why are you so slow? *Hurry up!*'

With one final effort, Peter and Dunstable sprinted to the end of the field and slid to a halt beside her. Peter was so exhausted he flopped against the garden wall, breathing heavily as sweat poured off his brow despite the cold weather. Dunstable crouched beside him, his face bright red. The Princess, though, looked pleased.

'Good! We are almost out of the city now.' She glanced thoughtfully at Dunstable. 'I wonder whether you were exaggerating when you said an enormous troll army was gathering outside York? We have not seen anything at all!'

But she had barely finished speaking when suddenly they heard the sound of heavy marching feet in the distance. Dunstable's eyes immediately grew wide with terror. The sound quickly became louder. As they peered around the corner of the garden wall, a troll battalion appeared, heading across the field towards them.

Peter stared at them in horror. But before he had the chance to study them properly, the Princess hauled him back. Suddenly a deep voice rang out.

'LEYYYYFT-RIGHT! LEYYYYFT-RIGHT! COME ON YOU 'ORRIBLE TROLLS! I'M GONNA EAT YOU FOR MY DINNER!!'

Dunstable fell onto the pavement beside Peter, shaking in terror. As the Princess tried to calm him, Peter's fear fought with his curiosity. His curiosity won. Slowly, inch by inch, he stretched forward and peered over the wall.

Though he had often imagined what trolls might look like since he had first entered the Vikings' magical world, he was still totally unprepared for what he saw. Two hundred yards from where they were hiding, fifty or more trolls were marching four abreast behind a leader. Each was carrying a long spear and had a brutal-looking wooden club fastened to their belts. But it was their size that shocked him the most. They were absolutely gigantic - easily two feet taller than any man! With enormous muscles rippling beneath their grey chain-mail and brown tunics, they reminded him of rugby players, only much taller and even broader.

As they got closer, his attention turned to their faces. They were, quite simply, the most hideous creatures he had ever seen! With tiny squinting eyes, large lopsided mouths and flat noses complete with nose rings, their features were so squashed and twisted they looked like something very heavy had been dropped on their faces. Each of them had thick black eyebrows and a long flat forehead, with a few greasy strands of hair on their otherwise bald heads. Their skin was a sickly shade of pale green, except for their flabby cheeks which were bright red with exertion as they marched in quick time across the field, travelling as fast as a man could run.

By far the most fearsome, though, was the leader who marched in front of them, occasionally turning and shaking a black whip threateningly as he barked out orders. If the other trolls were enormous, he was absolutely colossal! Dressed in battle armour, he stood at least another foot taller and was somehow even broader than the others. As Peter watched him, he slowed and stepped to one side to let the other trolls march past him, then jogged up the line, shouting insults in his deep thunderous voice.

'LEYYYYFT-RIGHT! LEYYYYFT-RIGHT! COME ON YOU 'ORRIBLE LOT! MY GRANNY MARCHES FASTER THAN YOU DO!'

Though the smaller trolls kept their eyes focused ahead and betrayed barely a hint of emotion, it was clear that they were terrified of their ferocious leader.

As Peter continued to watch them, the Princess crept beside him and peered over the wall.

'Dunstable was right after all! The trolls have never come so far south! Maledict must have united them somehow!'

Peter couldn't take his eyes off them.

'Why is the leader so much bigger than the others?'

'He is a Mountain Troll. They are the real fighters. They come from the Black Mountains far away in the north. They eat raw meat and become enormous. The smaller trolls are the Wood Trolls. They are cousins to the Mountain Trolls, but less ferocious. Normally they just hide behind trees and jump out on people stupid enough not to see them. There are hundreds of them – far more than there are Mountain Trolls.'

But then they fell silent. The trolls were approaching them at an alarming rate. They were now so close that Peter could hear their heavy breathing and the metallic clinking of the leader's armour. Dunstable ducked his head underneath his jumper, whilst the Princess's eyes narrowed in concentration as she contemplated whether they should run or hide. The trolls were less than thirty yards away now. If they came any closer, the three of them would be in clear view.

But just when it seemed certain that they were about to be discovered, the trolls veered away and continued their patrol across the centre of the field, moving swiftly away from them.

Dunstable sighed in relief. His head cautiously re-emerged above his jumper.

'That was *much* too close! We could have been squashed!'

The Princess also looked alarmed.

'They must be preparing for an attack. They are trying to stop any of us leaving! We must hurry!'

As soon as the trolls were far enough away, she darted out from behind the garden wall and raced along the street away from the city, running as though the whole troll army was after her.

'Hurry up! We have not got much time!' she called out over her shoulder as they raced after her. 'The trolls will attack in days, and if Maledict is with them, the Walls will not keep them out for long! Come on! *We must hurry!*'

Chapter 9

Attack in Ironwood

Peter sank against a tree trunk to catch his breath and gazed across the rain swept fields. He had never felt so exhausted in his life! Ever since they had narrowly avoided been captured by the trolls, they had been sprinting between hiding places and darting across streets and parks, constantly on the look-out for trolls. Even when they had left the city outskirts and emerged into puddle-strewn farmland, the Princess hadn't slowed down. She had led them relentlessly onwards until Peter felt his lungs would burst. Only now, when they were miles out of the city and daylight was fading, did she finally decide that they were behind any scouting trolls and could rest for a while.

As Peter regained his breath, he tried to gather his bearings. As far as he could tell, they were still close to the River Ouse, though he could no longer see it. All around them, open fields stretched for miles, the landscape almost completely flat. In the distance he could see grey mountains rising boldly over the horizon. Beneath them, he could just make out something darker than the surrounding land. He studied it for a moment, wondering what it could be

Leaning against the tree trunk beside him, Dunstable was staring into the distance too, his mouth wide open and his tongue hanging out like a dog's.

'Ironwood!' he said simply.

The Princess, who was standing a few yards in front of them beneath the outstretched branches of the tree, turned and nodded, satisfied for the moment that they had made good progress.

'We should be there by midnight. Then we will need to find some shelter. It is going to be cold and wet again tonight!'

Peter's heart sank. He hadn't realised they would be spending the night outside. Suddenly the Quest didn't feel like the magical adventure he had first imagined, and he briefly wondered whether he had made the right decision to come. He could have been sitting in front of the tv, eating his tea with his mother. But he quickly dismissed his doubts. He had made a promise to the Queen.

Shivering, he watched the rain lashing down beyond the protection of the tree's outstretched branches, forming puddles the size of lakes in the darkening fields around them. He hoped the Princess and Dunstable knew where they were going and that they would find some proper shelter. The thought of spending the night huddled up against a tree was too depressing to contemplate.

Glancing up at the sky, he brushed his soaking wet hair away from his face.

'This rain! It never stops!'

'It's not as bad as the cold! I'm absolutely freezing!' moaned Dunstable, wrapping his blazer tightly around him.

'You had better get used to it,' said the Princess distractedly, as she brushed her coat with her fingers and frowned at the muddy stains on the bottom of her pale blue trousers. 'It's going to get a lot colder when we get to the mountains! We have a long journey ahead of us!'

Peter glared at her. He got the distinct impression that this was what she'd wanted to do all her life and she was loving every minute of it, except perhaps the effect trekking through muddy fields was having on her fine clothes. Still, if she could stand the cold and wet, then he certainly could!

'Right!' said the Princess brightly, turning towards them. 'Are we all properly rested? Good! Dunstable! What is the best way to Ironwood? Straight across the fields?'

Dunstable jumped, his mind far away.

'Ironwood? Right! Oh dear! Are you *sure* you want to go there?'

'Yes, I am!' replied the Princess indignantly. 'It is the quickest way to get to Mimir's Well. I do not believe all those silly stories that are told about it anyway. Childish nonsense!'

'I do! I've *been* there!' said Dunstable, his big ears twitching. 'It's full of scary things, you know! Lots and lots of scary things! Monsters, witches – all sorts of horrible animals, I shouldn't wonder! I don't want to go there! Couldn't we could go *around* it, maybe? If we approach Mimir's Well from the west where the mountains start, we could avoid Ironwood altogether! It's much safer that way, you know!'

'No time!' replied the Princess firmly. 'It will take an extra day at least to walk around it. By then, Maledict could have launched his attack and we will be too late. Do not worry! I promise I will not let any 'monsters' harm you!'

As far as the Princess was concerned, the debate was over. Without bothering to ask them if they were ready to leave, she turned towards the wet fields.

'Come on you two! No time to lose!' she called out as she ran in the direction of the distant wood. 'We *have* got rather a long journey ahead of us after all!'

Peter glanced skywards and gave Dunstable a pained grin. Reluctantly, they stepped out from the cover of the tree and jogged after the ever-energetic Princess as she raced into the murky distance.

*

Darkness fell alarmingly quickly and the weather became even worse. Exposed in the wide open fields, the wind howled and gusted around them, throwing armfuls of icy rain into their faces as they trudged forwards, their heads hung low.

For another six hours they made their way across endless muddy fields, occasionally crossing deserted country roads. By then, Peter's legs were numb with fatigue, and his feet were so heavy with mud he could barely lift them. Beside him, Dunstable was faring even worse. He was constantly mumbling to himself under his breath, clearly regretting the promise he had made the Queen. Even the Princess was wilting, though she would never have admitted it. Earlier she had tried to urge them on, but now she simply traipsed silently beside them, looking frustrated and tired in equal measure.

Finally it was clear they could go no further. Dunstable was totally drenched and had turned a worrying shade of blue, and Peter's legs were aching so much he could scarcely move. Wearily, they gazed ahead. They were close to the edge of Ironwood now and the first trees were just a stone throw away. Suddenly Peter noticed how eerily silent it was. There were no birds singing in the trees, despite their closeness to the wood. Even the wind had fallen to barely a murmur. The only sound came from the rain pounding the muddy ground all around them.

He was not the only one to feel uneasy by the wood. Beside him, Dunstable was staring anxiously at the dark trees ahead.

'There is something very nasty in there looking at us! I can sense it!' he whispered. 'I have a very good nose for scary things, you know! I don't want to spend the night in the wood!'

Peter stared at the sinister looking trees.

'Is there any shelter nearby?' he asked hopefully.

Dunstable looked blank for a moment then suddenly jumped.

'I say! I think there is! Goodness gracious! Why didn't I think of it before? There's a cave! We can go there! It's quite small, but it's nice and clean. It will be dry there too, you know!'

The Princess was as relieved as Peter at Dunstable's suggestion, and they immediately trudged away from the wood, following Dunstable's eager lead.

Fortunately they didn't have to go far. A few minutes later, Dunstable gave an eager shout and pointed ahead. There, almost hidden in the darkness, a grey cave was cut into a sloping wall of rock on a small hill, about half a mile from the edge of the wood. Despite their fatigue, all three of them raced forward, desperate to escape from the wind and rain.

As Dunstable predicted, the cave wasn't big - barely ten feet deep and eight feet wide - but it was still large enough to provide welcome shelter for all three of them. Once inside, Peter wearily took off his coat. It was so wet it clung stubbornly to his body and it took him several seconds to peel it away. Underneath it, his clothes were absolutely soaking. He pulled off his jumper and wrung the collar, creating a large black puddle around his feet that snaked its way towards the cave entrance.

The Princess was scarcely any better. She looked particularly bad tempered as she examined her mud stained clothes in disgust. Meanwhile, Dunstable sat in the furthest corner of the cave. The last dash through the rain had affected him badly. He was shivering and rocking back and forth.

'I'm *so* cold and w-wet!' he stuttered through chattering teeth. 'Does anyone have any m-matches to start a f-fire? We'll n-never get dry without a f-fire, you know!'

'Do not be silly!' snorted the Princess, staring at him through the long strands of wet hair that were hanging over her face. 'We cannot make a fire here! What if we are seen?'

'Seen? Goodness g-gracious! Who on earth would 'see' us on a n-night like this? We simply *m-must* get dry, I t-tell you! We'll *freeeeze* to death if we d-don't!!'

'He's right you know,' said Peter, shaking his dripping shirt sleeves and sending tiny water droplets flying all around him. 'Anyway, we won't be able to rest properly if we're all soaking wet.'

The Princess regarded them both irritably.

'Oh, all right then! But only a small one. Dunstable! Turn around and face the cave wall please!'

Dunstable looked confused. After a moment's contemplation, he shrugged his shoulders and turned around. As soon as he wasn't looking, the Princess made a small gesture with her hands and immediately a fire leapt up on a small pile of twigs in the middle of the cave.

Peter was astonished.

'How did you do that?'

'Oh, it is really very easy! Just a simple spell, that is all. Dunstable! You can turn around now!'

Dunstable turned around and stared at the fire and the Princess suspiciously, clearly afraid that a magical act had been committed whilst he wasn't looking. For a moment, he looked as if he was about to ask how it had suddenly appeared, but then he thought better of it, clearly deciding that it was best he didn't know after all. Grateful for the warmth, he sprang forward and stood a few inches away from the rising flames, rubbing his hands together vigorously in-between feeding various twigs and leaves from the cave floor into the fire. Within a few minutes, the colour returned to his cheeks. It wasn't long before he curled up into a ball and fell fast asleep with a contented smile on his face.

Peter was glad of the fire too, not just for its warmth but also for the light it gave. He was still worried about the nearby wood and decided he would be far happier when daylight returned. He determined to stay awake until dawn in case something happened during the night, and sat on the rocky ground on the opposite side of the fire from Dunstable. But soon the heat became irresistible. As soothing warmth seeped through his body, the hard cave floor began to feel like the softest mattress. He closed his eyes and within seconds he was fast asleep.

*

Peter woke with a start. It was still dark. Dunstable was at the back of the cave, snoring contentedly. Beside him, the Princess was also fast asleep. The fire was burning low, almost extinguished.

Feeling strangely uneasy, he stared out of the cave mouth. But it was so dark outside, he couldn't see a thing. Then he heard it again – the sound that had woken him. A strange rasping noise was coming from somewhere hidden in the darkness outside the cave. He had lived on a farm all of his life and was used to strange noises in the night, but he had never heard a sound like this before.

As he held his breath, the sound changed. Outside the cave, something was definitely moving. He could distinctly hear footfalls - heavy but precise like a hunter's. The creature was cautious, pausing every few seconds. Then there was silence.

The whole episode only lasted a few seconds. Peter was beginning to wonder whether it was just his over-active imagination when he heard the sound of something moving once more, this time much more clearly. It sounded like a dog, but its footfalls were much louder. Whatever creature it was, it was now bold enough to not worry about being heard. The footfalls were approaching the cave. Then they stopped. He heard a sniffing noise just beyond the cave's entrance.

Slowly, Peter sat up, his eyes fixed on the cave entrance. Fortunately the fire still gave off enough light for him to see inside the cave, though beyond it everything was pitch black. As quietly as he could, he rose to his feet and stepped past the sleeping Princess.

Immediately the sniffing stopped and was replaced by a faint growling noise. Peter froze. It sounded horribly close. His heart pounding, he searched the cave floor for a weapon. Just in front of him was a short broken branch. Not daring to take his eyes off the cave entrance, he stepped towards it and groped blindly on the ground.

The growling got louder.

Finally his fingers touched the branch. He grasped it firmly.

The growling stopped. Once again, it was silent.

Now, if anything, Peter felt even worse. Had the creature left or was it simply waiting to pounce? He stood completely still, his ears straining to catch the faintest sound. But all he could hear was Dunstable's snoring, the Princess's light breathing and the soft patter of rain from beyond the cave. For a moment, he considered stepping outside, but then thought better of it. Whatever was out there could almost certainly see better in the dark than he could. He decided to wait.

For what seemed like an eternity, he stood completely still with the branch clasped in his hand, wondering whether the creature was still outside the cave. He dared not close his eyes, though he felt so tired he could have slept where he was standing. But he didn't hear another sound.

Eventually, to his immense relief, faint light began to filter into the cave-mouth as dawn finally arrived. Slowly the darkness outside faded and daylight returned, filling the fields and the distant wood with glorious radiance. For an agonising half-hour Peter waited until it was bright enough to feel safe, then he finally relaxed and returned to the side of the cave where he had previously been sleeping. Whatever creature it was, it had long since disappeared into the night.

He had barely closed his eyes when the Princess sprang out of her resting-place and began shaking him vigorously.

'Wake up sleepy-head! We have a Quest to complete, remember? Come on! Get up!'

Wearily, he staggered back to his feet, longing for a nice warm bed and a night of undisturbed sleep.

After a hurried breakfast of Viking biscuits, which the Princess retrieved from the depths of her coat pocket (Peter nibbled on one experimentally – it tasted like oatmeal but was so hard he could barely chew it), they gathered their belongings and stepped outside into the damp morning. The Princess immediately began jogging across the sodden fields towards Ironwood.

'Come on!' she called out enthusiastically. 'No time to lose! We should reach Mimir's Cavern today if we get a move on and do not dawdle!'

As Dunstable trotted wearily past him, Peter stepped out of the cave and gazed up at the sky. It was still raining, though not quite as heavily as it had been the night before. After the long tense night though, he was simply glad that it was daylight again.

He was about to follow the Princess and Dunstable when he saw something that made his heart miss a beat. Deeply imprinted in the mud in front of him were the footprints of a large animal. They led from the wood directly to the entrance of the cave, then backtracked towards the wood again. Whatever creature had made them had stood just a few feet from the cave's entrance.

For a moment, he considered mentioning it to the Princess and Dunstable, but then he changed his mind. He had no idea what animal had made the tracks, and there was no evidence that it was anything sinister. The last thing he wanted to do was worry Dunstable unnecessarily when they were about to enter the wood. Forcing it from his mind, he jogged after them.

*

It was another cold wet day, and by the time they reached the first trees, they were thoroughly drenched again. The Princess set a fast pace as they followed a narrow trail that led into the heart of the wood.

Now that they were inside it, Ironwood looked even more forbidding than it had from a distance. Immediately the dark trees closed around them, their leafless branches reaching down to them like grasping skeletal arms. Beneath their feet, the boggy undergrowth was dense with stinging nettles and full of unseen stumps and sharp thorns that could penetrate any clothing. Once again, Peter had the unpleasant feeling that unfriendly eyes were watching them and that, hidden amongst the trees, evil creatures were lurking.

'I don't like the look of this wood,' he whispered gloomily to Dunstable as he scratched his ankles, which were itching like crazy where he had been repeatedly stung. 'And I'm sure we're being watched.'

'Do not be so silly!' said the Princess, glancing over her shoulder as she waded through the nettles ahead of them, seemingly impervious to their stings. 'It is just a sleepy old wood, that is all! There is absolutely nothing to be worried about!'

'There jolly well is, you know!' protested Dunstable. 'We're getting scratched and stung to death! We'll have no skin left by the time we reach Mimir's Cavern!'

The Princess stopped on the narrow trail and regarded them both critically.

'Do not be such babies! It is only a few nettles! Hardly the end of the world, is it?'

She had barely finished speaking when a deep growling noise suddenly rose from somewhere close by, hidden in the trees. Peter recognised it immediately. It was identical to the sound he had heard the previous night.

Dunstable froze. Only his eyes moved as they swept from one side of his face to the other.

'What's *that?* It doesn't sound like *'nothing to be worried about'* to me!'

'Oh, it is probably just a fox or something!' replied the Princess nonchalantly, barely glancing over her shoulder as she marched ahead again.

As if to prove her point, the growling stopped almost immediately and the wood became silent once more, so silent that Peter winced at the sound of a leaf being crushed beneath his foot. The feeling that they were being watched grew even more intense.

They continued cautiously, tip-toeing along the winding trail through the trees behind the Princess. But the growling followed by the intense silence had a profound effect on Dunstable. Ducking his head so low that his blazer rose almost to his ears, he peered through the trees like a startled rabbit, looking as if he was ready to bolt at any moment. Peter was feeling anxious too. His heart was racing as he gazed around him, half expecting to catch a glimpse of some sinister creature prowling through the undergrowth. But all he could see was dark trees stretching for miles in every direction. He wondered how big the wood was and how long it would be until they reached Mimir's Cavern. They were heading uphill, which comforted him slightly, knowing that their destination was the mountains beyond Ironwood. At least they appeared to be going in the right direction.

The further they walked into the wood, the denser the trees became. Soon the trail was barely visible as the trees packed closely together as if they were guarding something behind them. At the same time it became gradually darker, the faint daylight unable to pierce the canopy of branches above them, and they were plunged into an eerie twilight. It became so quiet that the sound of their breathing seemed to echo around them, alerting whatever might be lurking nearby to their presence.

By the time they reached the welcome relief of a small treeless glade three hours later, it was clear that they were completely lost. Predictably, the Princess blamed it entirely on Dunstable.

'I cannot believe you do not know where we are! I thought you had been here before? You are supposed to be our guide!'

'It's not my fault!' whined Dunstable. 'I told you we should have gone *around* the wood, didn't I? But did you listen? No one ever listens to me!'

'I cannot do *everything!* You are meant to be the great explorer after all, not me!' Turning away from him, she prodded Peter with her forefinger. 'It looks like *we* are going to have to get us out of this mess! We are going to have to fly above the trees to see where we are, otherwise we will never get out of this horrible wood!'

To Dunstable's dismay, she rose into the air until she was hovering six feet above them, staring down at Peter impatiently.

'Come on! Once we get above the trees, we should be able to see where Mimir's Cavern is!'

Barely suppressing his excitement, Peter ignored Dunstable's whimpers at such blatant use of magic and leapt into the air. Together, they rose up the tall trees surrounding the glade until they had climbed above the wood into the gloriously clear light of the day. For a moment they simply hung in the air, relishing being out in the open and being able to see properly again after spending so long in the oppressive darkness of the wood, but then a cold breeze threw icy rain into their faces and they were stirred into action. Side by side, they climbed higher until the trees merged into a dark canopy beneath them. They were now so high that Peter began to feel giddy, and it was several seconds before he had the courage to peer down to the world below.

Beneath them, the wood stretched for miles in every direction. Only from this height could its size be truly appreciated. They were now so high they could see beyond its boundaries. Far away, Peter could see the field through which they had walked before they entered Ironwood. But it was in the other direction that his attention was ultimately drawn. There, looming in the distance, were the mountains. They looked enormous – cold grey shapes standing boldly against the horizon. As he gazed towards them, he noticed something odd. At the top of the nearest mountain beyond Ironwood was a strange rocky mound. It looked as if a small mountain had collapsed upon itself.

'Mimir's Cavern!' confirmed the Princess.

Tugging on his billowing coat, she pointed down. Flowing from the mountains past the strange rocky formation was a shining river. From their great height, it looked like a tiny silver thread. As they followed its course, it wound its way through Ironwood towards them. They had found what they were looking for. If they could find the river, it would lead them through Ironwood to Mimir's Cavern.

Having now obtained all the information they needed, they dived back down to the ground. But neither of them was in a hurry to return, enjoying the brightness of the sky compared to the darkness of the wood below. Peter in particular was intoxicated by the thrill of flying and the peacefulness he felt high above the world with the cold wind brushing against his face.

They were so high that it was some time before they could see Dunstable sitting in the glade waiting for them, and when they did he was a tiny speck amongst the ocean of trees. Then, with one final glance at the sky, they dropped reluctantly beneath the tree-tops into the gloomy wood.

As they slowly descended, the figure of Dunstable gradually became clearer. Suddenly a movement in the wood a quarter of a mile away caught Peter's eye. Unsure what it was, he called out to the Princess and pointed. For a moment they hung in mid-air. Then they froze in horror. A pack of gigantic wolves were making their way through the trees, their heads low to the ground as they followed a scent. They were heading straight for the glade!

'Black Wolves from the mountains!' gasped the Princess in horror. 'Usually they never stray from their own lands. Something must have stirred them! Quick! We must get back to Dunstable before they attack!'

They didn't wait a moment longer. Side by side, they dived down to the ground, weaving precariously through the trees, oblivious to the numerous cuts they received from the sharp branches, until they landed with a resounding thump in the middle of the glade. Dunstable almost jumped out of his skin in shock.

'*Hurry!*' screamed the Princess. 'Wolves! There are wolves about to attack!'

But they had no time to prepare. As soon as she spoke, the wolves appeared. In a moment, six at least surrounded them, growling and baring their sharp white teeth as they circled the perimeter of the glade to ensure there was no escape.

Immediately Peter and the Princess leapt back to back on either side of Dunstable. The wolves snapped and snarled at them, trying to draw them out. Then the wolf circle parted and into the gap stalked their leader. As large as a pony and as black as the night, he studied them for a moment, a look of scorn in his evil red eyes as if he was amused by their attempts to defend themselves. Then, from all sides at once, the wolves attacked.

Before Peter had time to defend himself, the Wolf Chieftain leapt forward, knocking him over and pinning him to the ground. With a snarl of triumph, he lowered his jaws to bite.

At that moment, something very strange happened. As the Wolf Chieftain's jaws descended upon him, time seemed to dramatically slow as if someone had pressed a slow motion button. With terrified fascination, Peter watched the wolf's massive jaws gape wider. It was so slow he could count the teeth in his mouth and see his red tongue curling in anticipation. He glanced across the glade and saw the Princess make a motion with her hands and watched in bemusement as one of the wolves she was facing flew languidly backwards. Her head turned slowly towards him, an expression of fear and urgency on her face.

Then, when the Wolf Chieftain's jaws were just a few inches from his neck, Peter felt a sudden rush of energy through his body. At the same time, something in his pocket burned against his skin.

'GO!' he commanded mentally, the powerful voice in his head sounding foreign to him.

In an instant, time returned to its normal speed. The Wolf Chieftain flew off him as if he had been hit by a juggernaut and landed twenty feet away, his fall broken only by the trees. Outraged, he immediately sprang to his feet. His red eyes burning in fury, he gathered himself on his haunches then leapt towards Peter again, seeking to tear him limb from limb. He was almost upon him when suddenly he lurched backwards as if he had struck an invisible wall. The Princess raced forwards, her hands moving furiously. Yelping in pain, the Wolf Chieftain crashed to the ground, scrambled desperately for a moment, then turned and sprinted back into the

THE WOLVES ATTACK

wood without a backward glance, howling as he ran.

With their great Chieftain gone, the other wolves turned tail and fled. In a moment the glade was almost quiet again, the only sound the howls of the wolves, slowly receding into the distance.

Peter rose slowly to his feet. Breathing heavily, he glanced at the others. Dunstable was lying on the ground, his head buried beneath his jumper. He was shaking from head to foot, but appeared to be unharmed. Then Peter's eyes locked with the Princess's. She was looking at him in a most peculiar way. Dusting herself off, she approached him curiously.

'How did you do that? I thought you said you did not know any magic?'

Peter stared at her in confusion. He reached into his pocket where he had felt the burning sensation and his fingers closed around Sigurd's talisman. It was still warm, though not nearly as hot as it had been moments earlier when the wolf had attacked him.

The Princess continued to gaze at him with an expression on her face he'd never seen before. It almost looked like respect. Receiving no answer to her question, she helped Dunstable to his feet.

'We will figure this out later. Let us find Mimir's Cavern first.'

Peter sighed. Utterly confused by what had just happened, he followed the Princess and Dunstable back into the wood.

*

The Princess raced through the trees in the direction of the river they had seen from the air, desperate to leave Ironwood before nightfall in case the wolves attacked again. As he jogged behind her, Peter noticed that Dunstable kept glancing at him anxiously, as if he was not sure what to make of him. When the Princess had told Dunstable what had happened in the glade, he'd insisted the Wolf Chieftain had simply slipped. *Don't be ridiculous! Everyone knows a City Dweller can't perform magic! There's always a perfectly good explanation for these things if you look hard enough you know!* The thought of Peter performing magic clearly upset Dunstable greatly, and he appeared to have decided to give Peter a wide berth until he was sure that he wasn't going to do anything really scary when he was least expecting it.

But Peter had more to worry about than Dunstable's sullenness.

He had a great deal of thinking to do. In his mind's eye, he kept replaying the Wolf Chieftain being flung into the air after he had commanded him to '*Go!*' How had he done it? *Had* he done it at all, or was there some other explanation? Had Sigurd's talisman somehow helped him? He reached into his pocket again. It was cold now, but during the attack it had been red hot. If the talisman had been the cause, had it somehow acted *through* him?

Then there were other considerations. If he *had* somehow performed magic, could he do it again? Suddenly he felt the same thrill of excitement he'd felt when he'd learnt to fly. If he could perform magic, what other fantastic things could he do?

But before he had time to consider what had happened properly, he became aware of a more immediate concern. Once again, the wood had fallen eerily silent. As the trees closed in around them, the feeling that unfriendly eyes were watching them returned as strongly as before.

The afternoon seemed to drag on forever. Finally, they heard the faint sound of running water filtering through the wood. After a moment's frantic searching, they saw it. Fifty yards away, the glorious river was rushing through the dense trees into the distance. All they had to do was follow it and it would lead them to Mimir's Cavern and the last stage of their dangerous journey.

Chapter 10

Race Across the Ice

As the daylight faded, the trees began to thin. At the same time, the heavy atmosphere and uncomfortable feeling that they were being watched diminished. Soon they entered grassy fields with only occasional trees. In the distance, the mountains loomed, their cold grey peaks towering into the sky. At the top of the highest one nearest to them was the strange rocky formation Peter and the Princess had seen from the air. Still several miles away, it looked like a crumbling crown on top of the mountain. Peter remembered what the Prince had said about the Frost Giants guarding Mimir's Cavern, but there was no sign of them. For once he was glad that night-time was falling. Perhaps they would reach the cavern without being seen now that it was dark. But despite being faced by a steep climb and the possibility of facing even more sinister creatures than wolves, he was relieved to be out of the wood and in open fields again.

With their goal in sight, they rested for a few minutes. The Princess gave Peter and Dunstable one of her strange biscuits, which they ate in silence, oblivious to the constant rain. They were just about to set off again when they heard a cold lonely cry. At first, Peter thought it was simply the wind, but then he heard it again, clearer and louder. It was answered by another more distant call. He strained his ears to hear it more clearly, almost sure that some message was being passed. But just as he thought he could hear high-pitched words, it stopped and an eerie silence descended, punctuated by the occasional blast of icy wind.

'Probably just a bird or something,' he said as Dunstable stared at him, his eyes wide with fear behind his glasses.

'Robin I expect,' agreed Dunstable, nodding vehemently as if trying to convince himself as much as Peter. 'They like the cold, you know!'

Immediately they raced after the Princess who, oblivious to everything but their Quest, was jogging towards the distant mountains as if nothing in the world could stop her.

Three hours later, they had almost reached the rocky mound. Peter stopped to gaze around him and massage his legs, which were aching after climbing for so long. They were now high above the world. He could just make out Ironwood far below, barely distinguishable in the darkness against the grey landscape. As he turned around, he saw grey wispy clouds hanging in the air ahead of them. He could scarcely believe how high up they were! For a moment, he felt dizzy and almost fell over. Recovering quickly, he jogged after the Princess.

Up ahead, the rocky mound rose still higher above them. As they approached it, the landscape changed dramatically. Suddenly they found themselves tripping down endless rocky pits then struggling up the sharp inclines on the other sides. The going also became more perilous as they had to dodge enormous boulders that littered the ground. Every few minutes they passed great mounds of them, piled on top of one another as if there had been a landslide.

As they were scrambling out of yet another pit, a strange sight confronted them. Just ahead, a bright light lit up the dark horizon. Curious, they clambered a few feet higher. Lying in a deep valley beneath them was a vast frozen lake. It was like nothing any of them had ever seen before. The ice on the surface of the lake was shining with countless colours that sparkled vibrantly, dazzling them with their intensity.

The lake stretched several miles across the valley in front of them, but it was only about a mile wide. The rocky mound lay on the opposite bank.

Side by side, they stared at the strange scene. Peter couldn't take his eyes off the dazzling lights on the lake's frozen surface, thinking he'd never seen anything so incredible in his life. Even Dunstable was spellbound, his eyes as wide as saucers and his mouth agape.

'It's Mimir's Lake!' he whispered, as if fearful of disturbing the glorious display by making too much noise. 'No one has seen it for hundreds of years because of Ironwood and the Frost Giants. Goodness gracious! They don't know what they're missing!'

'I have heard my mother speak of it,' said the Princess. 'But I never thought it would be so beautiful!'

For almost a minute they stared at the frozen lake in awed silence. Finally the Princess spoke again.

'We will have to cross the ice somehow.'

At that moment, the peaceful silence was suddenly shattered. A rock the size of a fridge crashed down behind Peter, missing him by inches. They had no time to react before another fell just behind Dunstable, at least as large as the first, shaking the ground with its impact. For a second they simply stared at one another in wide-eyed astonishment, unsure what was going on. Then the Princess cried out in alarm.

'*Quick!* Take cover! We are being attacked!'

As Dunstable froze in shock, Peter spun around and stared into the gloom behind them. At first he could see nothing as his eyes, which a moment before had been staring at the bright lights of the frozen lake, struggled to pierce the darkness. Then their attackers became horribly clear.

Half a mile away, a dozen shaggy giants were racing towards them at terrifying speed. Even from a distance, Peter could tell they were truly massive, maybe five times the size of a man. As they ran, they used their long arms to pull themselves forward like gorillas. Peter watched in horror as one of them paused to pick up a gigantic rock from one of the boulder piles as if it was no heavier than a tennis ball, then rose to his full colossal height. For a moment the giant's black eyes regarded Peter and his mouth broke into a cruel smile, then he hurled the rock. Transfixed, Peter watched as it flew high into the air then fell towards him in a perfect arc, dropping rapidly as it got closer and closer. At the last moment the Princess shouted a warning and he finally reacted. Diving just in time, the rock struck the ground where he'd stood a fraction of a second earlier, shattering into a hundred pieces.

'Quick! We must run!' screamed the Princess, grabbing Dunstable who was still rooted to the spot in terror.

Peter leapt to his feet, his head darting from side to side, searching for a means of escape.

'Where? We're trapped!'

On either side of them, the craggy landscape stretched for miles. But they could not flee there. The Frost Giants with their huge lumbering strides would overtake them in seconds. Going back was obviously out of the question. There was only one choice left.

'Across the ice! It is our only hope!' cried the Princess.

There was no time to debate whether the ice would support them, or to worry that their progress across such a slippery surface would inevitably be slow and they would be sitting ducks for their fast approaching attackers. There was simply no other option. Instantly they sprinted towards the frozen lake and leapt onto its sparkling surface.

Peter ran behind the Princess and Dunstable, hoping his old trainers would find some grip. To his relief, he seemed to be making good speed. But his luck didn't last long. He hadn't run fifty yards when suddenly his left foot shot out from under him and he crashed onto the ice, his forehead striking the rock hard surface with a painful thump. Searing pain shot through his head as he frantically tried to get to his feet, but immediately he slipped down again, the ice allowing him no foothold. His heart pounding, he steadied himself with his hands then brought up his feet to raise himself off the ground. But as soon as he took a step forward, his back foot slipped and he crashed onto the ice again, twisting his ankle painfully.

Panic threatened to overwhelm him. He tried to rise again, but his ankle wouldn't take his weight and he immediately fell back down, twisting it still further. He didn't dare turn around as he knew the Frost Giants must almost be upon him. At any moment he expected to be crushed by an enormous rock.

He raised his head to see the others, hoping they at least would make it to safety. Dunstable was fifty yards ahead, showing surprising agility as he sped across the frozen lake. Instead of running, he was sliding like a skater, his feet never leaving the surface of the ice. He looked ungainly, but he was making good progress. With luck, he might even escape. But where was the Princess? He couldn't see her anywhere. Had she fallen too? His head throbbing with pain, he swallowed his fear and swivelled awkwardly on the ice so he could see behind him. Then he held his breath. No more than two hundred yards away, the Princess was fighting an aerial dual with the Frost Giants.

A dozen giants were there. Standing over thirty feet tall, they were bellowing with rage and pain as the Princess darted between them, stinging them with red bolts of energy that shot from her fingertips. The giants were flailing with their enormous fists, trying to swat her as if she was an irritating fly, but somehow she managed to avoid them as she weaved through the air, spinning and twisting.

Then, as Peter watched in horror, one of the largest giants took aim with a rock the size of a garage and hurled it into the air just as she was diving towards him. For a second Peter thought it would surely hit her, but at the last moment she darted out of the way. The rock crashed to the ground behind her, striking the leg of another Frost Giant who screamed in agony. Peter almost cheered, feeling like a football supporter whose team had just scored a goal.

Suddenly another giant appeared from a deep ravine directly behind her and hurled a much smaller rock. She hadn't seen him! The rock raced through the air towards her like a missile closing in on its target. Peter screamed a desperate warning, but she didn't see it until it was almost too late. Just in time she dived, but not quickly enough. As the rock sped past her, it brushed her head, stunning her instantly. Spiralling out of the air, she crashed to the ground. Immediately the giants raced towards her, leaping over the rocks to where she lay, screaming their terrifying cries of victory.

Peter froze as he stared at the terrible scene, unable even to breathe. Then anger rose within him.

'NO!' he yelled. '*Leave her alone!*'

He felt angrier than he'd ever felt in his life! In an instant he was on his feet, barely noticing the stabbing pain in his ankle as adrenaline pumped through his veins. Without thinking, he willed himself into the air and quickly picked up speed as he raced across the frozen lake towards the Princess, determined to get there before the Frost Giants. Faster and faster he flew, the freezing wind biting his face and ears. Within seconds he had passed the top of the ravine where they had gazed down at the lake minutes before. The first giant turned to swipe at him with his enormous fist, but he was much too slow. By the time he had swung, Peter was already out of reach, accelerating still faster to where the Princess lay on the ground.

Closer and closer, faster and faster. He was almost there! Desperately he stared ahead to where she lay, barely able to focus he was moving so fast. A giant was standing over her. In horror, Peter watched as he raised a huge rock above his head to crush her. In a moment it would be too late! Peter willed himself to fly even faster.

Speeding as fast as an arrow, he darted between the giant's enormous legs and reached down to lift the Princess. But he was travelling so quickly he couldn't get a proper hold. He had to slow to an agonising stop in order to gather her safely in his arms.

Above him, the giant paused for a second, his dark bearded face registering his surprise. Then, with all his mighty strength, he hurled the rock, seeking to crush them both together.

Peter could feel the shadow cast by the rock growing as it raced towards them. Then, with the Princess secured in his arms, he was away. The giant screamed in frustration and raced after him. But within seconds Peter was beyond the reach of even a giant's missile as he climbed high into the air, holding the Princess firmly. Somehow he had done it!

When he was finally convinced that he was at a safe enough height, he hung in the air so he could check on the Princess. She was breathing lightly, though she showed no sign of regaining consciousness. Relieved, he paused to consider his options. Directly beneath him, the Frost Giants were bellowing in rage, occasionally throwing rocks that arced briefly towards him before falling back down to earth, posing more risk to the other giants than to himself. He glanced across the frozen lake. In the distance he could see Dunstable highlighted against the dazzling light as he raced across the ice towards the opposite bank, oblivious to everything else in his desperation to escape. But he was not moving fast enough. He was still within range of the giants' missiles.

As if reading his mind, one of the giants turned towards Dunstable and grunted to the others. Immediately they ignored Peter and began to pick up smaller rocks which they could hurl further, then jogged to the edge of the lake. Instantly Peter's panic returned. He had to get to Dunstable before it was too late!

With his arms aching under the weight of the Princess, he dived back down again, speeding over the heads of the Frost Giants as he raced towards the distant figure of Dunstable. In a moment he was over the ice, the wind screaming in his ears as he dipped down to ground level. He was now flying so low he could see his blurred reflection on the surface of the ice.

He heard a grunt from the shore of the lake behind him and knew that the first rock had been thrown and was shooting towards its target. His body aching with the strain, he flew even faster, watching Dunstable grow larger and larger as he streaked towards him.

Closer and closer – faster and faster. He was almost there!

Then, with a painful thud, he crashed into the back of Dunstable. Together, all three of them were thrown across the ice by the momentum of his flight. A fraction of a second later there was an ear splitting crunching noise behind them as the rock struck the ice where Dunstable had been a moment earlier. But Peter had been flying so fast that they were already thirty yards across the frozen lake, skidding towards the far shore.

Finally they came to a painful halt, striking a rock on the opposite bank.

'*Ouch!*' cried Dunstable furiously, rubbing his back. 'Goodness gracious! Why on earth did you run into me? It's quite enough to be attacked by Frost Giants without having to put up with mad City Dwellers running you over! You should jolly well look where you're going, you know!'

Peter was too distracted to argue. He had only managed to keep the Princess safely cradled in his arms by dragging his elbows and knees painfully across the ice. But it was not just his elbows and knees that hurt; his whole body was shrieking in pain.

Finally, the tightly clenched muscles in his arms gave way and the Princess fell lightly onto the ice. Immediately her eyes popped open.

'Where are we? I think something hit me!'

In a moment she was on her feet, looking bright and alert once more as she stared across the frozen lake to the Frost Giants on the opposite shore. But they were now beyond the reach of even the furthest flung missile. For the giants to reach them, they would have to cross the ice themselves. But, as they watched, a great crack appeared where the rock had pierced the ice. Like a snake, it zigzagged its way towards them as cold water coursed through. There was no way anyone could cross the lake now. If the giants wanted to pursue them, they would have to make their way around the shore of the vast lake, and that would take them over an hour, even with their great speed. For the moment at least, they were safe.

The Princess relaxed and stared at Peter.

'What happened?'

Peter rose gingerly to his feet, his whole body aching.

'I...errr...' He tried to find the words to explain how he had saved her from the giants.

'He ran into the back of me, *that's* what jolly well happened!' interrupted Dunstable as he staggered onto the rocky bank. 'Almost killed me, he did! I was trying to get away from those dreadful Frost Giants when *bang!* - I was sent spinning across the ice by Peter! You really should look where you're going, you know!'

But the Princess was ignoring him and staring at Peter, her eyes burrowing into his. She glanced back across the glittering lake to the Frost Giants, who were still screaming furiously and hurling rocks that fell harmlessly short into the broken ice.

'You came back for me. You must have come back for me.'

'Well, I suppose I ...'

'You saved my life.'

Slowly, a smile formed on the Princess's face that Peter couldn't quite read. Fortunately, just when he was beginning to feel distinctly uneasy, Dunstable saved him.

'Come *on* you two! There's no time for idle chit-chat, you know! We've only just escaped from the Frost Giants! I think we should be trying to find Mimir's Cavern, don't you? I don't want to hang around here any longer than is strictly necessary, thank you very much!'

The Princess turned and stared daggers at him. Dunstable gazed back at her innocently, his eyes wide with anxiety, then turned and scurried up the rocky bank.

'I suppose he's right,' said Peter, eager to turn her attention back to the Quest. 'We'd better find Mimir's Cavern before the Frost Giants attack us again. We might not be so lucky next time.'

The Princess glared at him, her eyes flashing.

'Well! *Of course* we must go! We do have a Quest to complete after all!'

Tossing her long blonde hair, she pushed him aside and stomped after Dunstable.

Peter breathed a sigh of relief. She sounded exactly like her old self again.

*

An hour later, they were scrambling over the rocky mound, searching for the way into Mimir's Cavern. Between the three of them, they had explored every nook and cranny, investigating anything that even vaguely resembled a possible entrance, but they had found nothing. It was freezing cold and pitch black, and they were getting increasingly anxious. The Frost Giants could return at any moment and this time there was nowhere left for them to run.

'Oh dear! This really is no good, you know! No good at all!' moaned Dunstable, as he struggled up the rocky slopes behind the Princess. 'We're *never* going to find the entrance!' He glanced nervously at the sparkling lake two hundred feet below them, its vivid light reflecting on his glasses. 'I think we should give up! Let's head back to York before the giants come back!'

'Oh shut up!' barked the Princess in her most irritatingly arrogant voice. She had been in a bad mood with Dunstable in particular for the past hour now. 'If you have nothing constructive to say, then do not say anything at all!'

'But we've been looking for hours!' Dunstable exaggerated, pulling his blazer more tightly around him and hopping from one foot to the other to keep warm. 'I'm *freezing!* My fingers have turned blue, you know! And as for my toes – I can't even *feel* my toes!'

'Then go back across the lake and wait for the Frost Giants if that is what you would prefer!' retorted the Princess, glaring down at him from further up the rocky mound.

Peter ignored them. He was trying to concentrate. For some time now he had been experiencing a peculiar sensation. He had the distinct impression that someone was trying to show him something desperately important - something that was within his reach if only he could solve the riddle he had been set.

As was now his habit in times of trouble, he reached into his pocket and grasped Sigurd's talisman. The moment he touched it, the world around him changed. It was not an earth shattering, swept-off-into-another-world, kind of change. It was as if the world had blinked and re-appeared just slightly different than it was before. The rocks, the night sky, Dunstable and the Princess arguing just a few yards away from him – they all looked exactly the same. Yet he instinctively knew that something was different. He could feel it, though he could not immediately see it.

For a few seconds he simply gazed blankly around him, taking in the strange new sensation. Then something caught his eye. A few yards from where he was standing, a thread of light weaved its way across the rocks. Bright gold in colour, it was pulsating faintly in the darkness. At first he simply stared at it. Had it always been there, or had it appeared when he'd touched the talisman? He contemplated letting the talisman go to see if it disappeared, but then decided against it. Whatever it was, it was worth investigating.

Bending down, he examined the light more closely. Then he saw why it was pulsating. It was not a single thread at all but consisted of numerous tiny golden strands of light packed closely together, each so thin he could barely distinguish them. Then, as he looked more closely, he made another remarkable discovery. The tiny strands were not confined within the golden thread of light - they flowed into the outside world like trickles of water from a river. The air around him was absolutely full of them!

As he followed them, he suddenly realised what he was seeing. The strands of light were connected to things in the outside world all around him. The rocks, the frozen blades of grass at his feet, the lake below – all of them had tiny golden lines of light connected to them! The Princess had a bright strand connected to her stomach. Just below her, another one was connected to Dunstable. Hardly believing his eyes, he examined himself. Sure enough, a tiny strand of light was connected to his mid-riff. He tried to touch it but his hand passed through as if it wasn't there.

He forced himself to think, calming his racing mind. Clearly he had made an important discovery, but what was it? What did it mean? As he pondered, he took his hand off Sigurd's talisman. Immediately the golden lines disappeared.

Finding himself unexpectedly back in the same dark night he had left behind, it took him a moment to regain his bearings. The Princess and Dunstable were still standing close by, both looking thoroughly down-hearted. Needless to say, they were still arguing.

'I *knew* we'd never find it!' moaned Dunstable. 'And even if we do, we'll never pass the test, you know. Not in a hundred years! It's hopeless! Utterly hopeless! Why don't we head back down, *mmm?* Before the Frost Giants arrive and start throwing rocks at us?'

'Oh shut up!' snapped the Princess. She sat on a large boulder and crossed her arms in frustration, shivering in the cold. 'I need to think – and you are not helping!'

Fortunately they were both ignoring Peter, which was probably just as well as he was still gaping in surprise at what he'd just seen. Quickly controlling himself, he stepped carefully down the rocky slope towards them.

'What do you mean by *test*? What test?'

The Princess sighed her familiar impatient '*City Dwellers are so stupid!*' sigh.

'According to the legend, Mimir set a test long ago. He wanted to ensure that only Vikings who were 'worthy' could look into the magic water drawn from his Well.'

Standing up again, she resumed her searching, turning her back on them both. Dunstable shuffled towards Peter and stared at him nervously.

'It's meant to be very difficult you know! Very, *very* difficult! No one has ever passed it!'

Behind them, the Princess snorted, clearly in the belief that all that was about to change now she was here.

'What is the test?' asked Peter, ignoring her.

'No one knows!' said Dunstable, gazing anxiously at the Princess. 'No one has ever found Mimir to ask him! In fact, most Vikings think that *is* the test! To find Mimir! That's why no one has ever passed it – no one knows where he is! He must have a very good hiding place!' He leant forward and whispered behind his hand so the Princess wouldn't hear him. 'Assuming he even exists, of course!'

'Of course he exists!' snapped the Princess without turning around, her sharp ears catching his every word. 'It is just that no one has been clever enough to find him, that is all! Up until now, of course.'

'But we've been here for ages and we haven't found *anything!* Not a single thing!' whined Dunstable, slightly shocked that she had overheard him. 'And the Frost Giants will be here at any moment! I think we should go. I think we should go now whilst we still can!'

The Princess turned and glared at him, her hands wedged into her hips.

'Well, if you would kindly *shut up* for a few minutes and stop *blubbering*, I *might* be able to concentrate properly!'

Leaving them to their endless arguments, Peter crept away and clasped Sigurd's talisman in his right hand again. Immediately the voices of Dunstable and the Princess receded into the background and the fantastic world of light re-appeared around him. Once again, the rocks, the ice and the distant mountains all looked the same, but superimposed upon them were countless golden strands of light. They spread out in a vast network which stretched as far as he could see, all leading off from the bright concentrated thread that snaked up the rock-face just a few feet away from him. Cautiously he followed it, scrambling up the slippery rocks away from the Princess and Dunstable. Then he stopped.

About ten yards above him, a small waterfall was gushing out of a hole in the rock-face into a clear pool. A tiny stream was flowing from the pool down to the frozen lake below, weaving its way through the rocks. But it was the waterfall that captured his attention. Behind the falling water was a bright light – so bright he couldn't stare at it directly. The golden thread led directly to it.

Climbing higher, he tip-toed around the edge of the pool. Out of the corner of his eye, he was vaguely aware that the Princess and Dunstable had stopped arguing and were watching him from below, but he ignored them. Standing in front of the waterfall, he instinctively reached out his left hand to touch the falling water.

Instantly everything changed. He found himself standing on a narrow ledge above a cavern, the walls of which were sparkling in a hundred different brilliant colours. A narrow stone stairway led down from the ledge to a wide sandstone floor forty feet below. At the centre of the floor was a small well. Suddenly his heart stopped. A well! The Well of Wisdom! He had found it! He had found Mimir's Well!

In his excitement and surprise, he stepped backwards and lost contact with the falling water. Immediately the scene changed. He was back in the cold grey night again with the waterfall tumbling innocuously in front of him. The Princess and Dunstable were standing at the edge of the pool, staring at him in surprise.

He turned towards them.

'I think I've found it! I think I've found Mimir's Well!'

The Princess regarded him sceptically.

'Where? I cannot see anything.'

'Look!'

He grabbed her hand and pulled her towards him. She pulled back, furious that he'd laid hands on her, but he was too strong. He hauled her towards the waterfall then pushed her forwards until she touched the water.

For a moment, he wasn't sure whether she'd seen anything as she continued to struggle. Then she stood very still and her eyes grew wide in astonishment.

'It *is* the Well! I do not believe it! You *have* found it!'

Dunstable, out of curiosity rather than boldness, poked a finger into the water and immediately leapt back in shock.

'Goodness gracious! What was *that?* It's not magic, is it? I do hope it's not magic!'

But the Princess had already decided that there was no time to waste. The search had taken longer than she had anticipated, and the night was wearing on. The Frost Giants could still be looking for them and they might be attacked at any moment. Grabbing Dunstable by the considerable collar of his blazer, she stepped through the falling water, pulling him in after her.

With a final glance over his shoulder to the sparkling lake below, Peter darted after them.

Chapter 11

Mimir's Well

The first thing Peter noticed upon stepping into the cavern was that there was not a drop of water on him, despite passing through the waterfall. But before he had time to consider this puzzle, his senses were overwhelmed by the incredible sight before him. The cavern was ablaze with light! Every inch of its walls was glowing vibrantly.

Curious to find what caused the incredible display, he studied the walls more closely. The same thought had clearly occurred to the Princess and Dunstable as all three of them leaned forward to examine the cavern wall beside them. Embedded in the rock were what appeared to be countless shards of glass. Each about the size of a finger-nail, they sparkled vividly as if a nugget of pure light had been trapped inside.

'Is there glass in the walls?' asked Peter to no one in particular.

Suddenly the Princess gasped.

'Not glass…*diamonds!* Look!'

For a moment Peter stared at the wall in bemusement as the Princess's words slowly sunk in, then his jaw dropped in shock. There was no doubt about it. Only the purest diamonds could create such a display. And the cavern walls were packed full of them! Thousands and thousands of glittering diamonds, setting the cavern aflame with blazing light!

'Goodness gracious!' whispered Dunstable in astonishment, frantically cleaning his glasses with his handkerchief before throwing them back onto his nose. 'This place must be worth an absolute fortune!'

Hardly believing what they were seeing, they descended the stone stairway, unable to take their eyes off the diamond encrusted walls. Dunstable, in particular, was fascinated by them. Halfway down, he suddenly stopped. A particularly large diamond was embedded low in the wall just in front of him. Letting Peter and the Princess pass him by, he glanced around the cavern furtively to make sure they were alone, then bent down and began scratching furiously at the wall around the enormous diamond with his fingernails, desperately trying to edge it out.

Meanwhile, Peter and the Princess had almost reached the bottom of the stairway. Standing on the final step, the Princess paused and stared up at Dunstable. She was about to rebuke him when her eyes fell upon the glittering diamond he was attempting to remove from the wall. Instantly her expression changed and her eyes lit up with desire, reflecting the diamond's sparkling light. For a moment she hesitated, biting her bottom lip in agonised temptation.

'We should not take anything,' she whispered, as much to herself as to Dunstable. 'Mimir must be around here somewhere. We do not want him to catch us taking anything from the walls.'

But Dunstable didn't stop.

'Just *look* at all the diamonds! There are thousands and thousands of them! Do you think he would notice if we took one? Just *one* little diamond?' His eyes were wide with desire as he pulled on the stone with renewed vigour. It was already half way out of the wall, shining like a Christmas star.

'But we came here to get answers from Mimir's Well, not to steal diamonds,' said the Princess quietly to remind herself.

Dunstable tore his eyes away from the stone for a moment to glare at her, his face set with stubborn determination.

'Look. Since I left York, I've been attacked by wolves and had big rocks thrown at me by Frost Giants! I've jolly well earned a diamond I'd say!'

Still the Princess hesitated as she stared at the diamond, wavering between her determination to complete the Quest as quickly as possible and her desire for the glittering stone.

But the Princess had a love for precious stones and all beautiful things. The way they sparkled! The way they shone! She was totally intoxicated by them. For the past few days, all her attention had been taken up by the Quest. But now that they had found Mimir's Cavern and had almost succeeded, why shouldn't she allow herself a small treat? After all, she told herself, for once Dunstable was right. There must be thousands of the precious stones in the cavern walls. Nobody seemed to want them. Would anyone *really* notice if they took one? *Just one?*

That was it. She had all the justification she needed. Her eyes wide with longing, she raced back up the steps towards Dunstable.

Peter alone resisted the lure of the diamonds. He too was distracted, but not by the sparkling stones. He had ceased to even notice them the moment he'd set foot on the cavern floor. All his attention was focused on something entirely different - a strange tingling sensation he felt in the pit of his stomach. It has been steadily growing from the moment he'd stepped through the waterfall. It was the same feeling he'd experienced outside when he'd seen the golden lines. But now it was stronger – much, much stronger. There was some energy source in the cavern – something incredibly powerful. He could feel it vibrating through his body. And he was almost positive it was coming from the Well.

Standing at the bottom of the stairway, he instinctively reached into his pocket and clutched Sigurd's talisman once more.

At first, it seemed as if nothing had happened. No strange threads of light appeared, and the cavern looked just the same as it had before. But then he noticed that the Well in the centre of the cavern floor was pulsating faintly with a hazy red glow as if a light was hidden inside it. He approached it cautiously, studying it in earnest for the first time. Compared to the shining diamonds in the walls, it was plain – not at all what he was expecting. About five feet high, it was made out of dull grey stone. Above it, a simple rope pulley system was suspended from a wooden bracket. At the end of the long looped rope was a grey wooden pan, no larger than a small saucepan.

Releasing the talisman, he stood on the tips of his toes and leant forward to peer over the stone rim of the Well. But it was so dark, he couldn't see a thing. Could the Well really be so special? He remembered what the Princess had said at the Council - that Mimir had put an enchantment on the water drawn from the Well. But there was no sign of Mimir. Peter wondered at this. Where was the Well-keeper whose wisdom was so renowned? Surely he should be here guarding his Well? Perhaps he had left the cavern long ago and it was only his legend that remained?

But, with or without Mimir, the time had come to fulfil the

MIMIR'S CAVERN

Quest. Taking hold of the rope, he began to lower the pan into the dark Well. It was deeper than he thought, and he had almost run out of rope by the time he heard a faint splash of water far below. He waited a few moments, his heart beating with excitement, then gently pulled on the rope to raise the pan, which judging by its extra weight was now full of water.

It took several agonising minutes before it re-appeared above the rim of the Well. Immediately he grasped it with one hand whilst keeping the rope steady with the other, taking special care not to spill a drop of the precious water.

For a moment he hesitated as something held him back from the next momentous step. The Princess had said that all he needed to do was look into the water drawn from the Well and the answer to any question would be given to him. He wondered if he needed to actually speak the question out loud or whether the water would somehow 'know' what he had in mind. For a few seconds he waited, nervous and unsure, then he gazed into the pan.

At first he could see almost nothing. The water was cloudy from the long journey up the Well shaft, and all he could see was swirling grey sediment that seemed to glow faintly with a pale red light. But as he cradled the pan in his arms, the water began to clear. Slowly a shape formed - circular but long. What was it? He could feel his heart pounding in his chest in anticipation. Was it a building? No, it was too uneven for that. Frustrated, he waited for the water to clear. Was it a face? Yes! He could see what looked like someone's ears and hair. But who was it? He ran through the possibilities in his mind. Maledict? Sigurd? The Queen? Then he jumped in shock as he finally recognised who it was. There was no doubt about it. It was a face he knew better than any. Staring down at the water, his reflection was staring back up at him.

A hundred different emotions surged through him at once. Frustration, anger, amusement, embarrassment. All the effort it had taken to come here! All the tension he'd felt when he'd stared into the supposedly enchanted water! And what did he see? His own reflection! His emotional whirlwind finally settled. Now all he felt was incredibly stupid.

Fortunately, no one had witnessed his foolishness. Half way up the stairway behind him, the Princess and Dunstable were totally absorbed in their task. The Princess had retrieved a small knife from her rucksack which she was using to dig around the stone, whilst Dunstable was pulling on it frantically with his fingernails. But though the diamond looked as if it just needed the slightest tug for it to fall, still they couldn't quite release it no matter how hard they pulled and twisted. Undeterred, they renewed their efforts, their eyes bright with desire as they stared at the prize that was so nearly theirs.

Returning his attention to the water, Peter thought for a moment. Surely something was wrong? What was he missing? He had filled the pan with water from the Well and gazed into it. He had done everything right! Why then could he only see a reflection of himself?

Perhaps he should ask the Princess. He glanced at her again, trying to catch her eye, but she was still completely captivated by the diamond in the cavern wall, oblivious to everything else. Should he wait for Mimir? But he was beginning to wonder whether Mimir actually existed. He was meant to be the guardian of the Well after all, making sure that only those who were 'worthy' could use its waters, but he was nowhere to be seen! Was the whole legend of Mimir's Well just a myth? Some of the Vikings had said as much at the Council. Perhaps it was all just some far-fetched tale Vikings told their children to amuse them. And if Mimir's Well was a myth, what else was untrue? Then he remembered what the Queen had said about the Well. He knew that she wouldn't lie and couldn't easily be misled. Also, he had seen too many fantastic things in the past few days not to believe in the Well's much vaunted powers. No, he had to be missing something!

Gazing down at the water again, he asked a silent question: *How can Maledict be defeated?* Once more his reflection stared back at him impassively.

He was just about to lower the pan into the Well and try again, when suddenly the cavern disappeared and he found himself standing in a dark chamber. Gazing out of a narrow window a few feet away from him was a tall figure. He was dressed in a long brown wax coat with his features hidden behind the folds of its hood. Peter knew immediately who he was, though he'd never seen him before. Standing just in front of him was Maledict the Necromancer.

For a moment, Peter was so shocked he almost dropped the pan and ran. But something held him back and he remained rooted to the spot. Fortunately Maledict hadn't noticed him, though he was now looking straight at him, or maybe he couldn't see him. In any case, he seemed distracted, as if considering a difficult choice. He turned to look through the narrow window again. Standing behind him, Peter followed his gaze. Outside the chamber it was night-time. Once again it was raining heavily. Then Peter saw what he was looking at. In a wide courtyard below, a great army was gathered - an army of trolls. Perhaps two thousand of them were there, hemmed in by the tall stone wall of an old fortress. Faint light was glinting off their armour as they waited for the command to march to war.

Suddenly Peter's heart missed a beat. In the distance, a graceful ancient building was looming on the horizon. High above the roof-tops of a city it rose, unmistakable in its grandeur. He recognised it instantly. The ancient building was the Minster. Maledict was in York!

A cold dread fell over him. *Maledict was in York!* They were too late! Then his attention was drawn into the dark chamber again. Something was glinting in the darkness. Just beneath the rim of Maledict's hood was a steel crown. A large stone was held in a clasp at its centre. As Maledict gazed down at his great army it glowed faintly. Peter immediately knew what it was. Directly in front of him was the Viking Stone - the seed of Yggdrasil - which Maledict had cut from the tree over a thousand years ago.

The moment he recognised it, the scene changed. Suddenly he was outside in the cold air. It was night-time again. He was standing on a cliff with the wind gusting around him, almost lifting him off his feet. Below him, the sea was crashing against a rocky shore. A storm was brewing, worse than any he'd ever known. He gazed up and saw clouds hurled across the sky. But it was no ordinary sky. Beyond the clouds it was bright red, as if the heavens had been set on fire. Then he saw something. High in the air, several dark shapes were circling as if looking for something. They were so high up they looked tiny, but he somehow knew they were truly massive.

As he held his breath in horror, one of them spotted him. It stopped circling and launched into a dive. As fast as a lightning bolt, the creature sped towards him, growing larger and larger. In a moment he recognised what it was, and his heart raced even faster in excitement and terror. The creature was a dragon! There was no doubt about it! Its sinewy wings, its cold lizard eyes, its outstretched talons like an eagle's, ready to rip and tear. On its back sat an enormous man-like figure, his face burnt black and his eyes bright red as he glared down at him. Suddenly Peter knew that he had to do something incredibly important, and that if he didn't act now, everything would be lost. A distant memory came back to him fleetingly. But before he could grasp it, the dragon was upon him. With a horrifyingly bloodthirsty cry and a rush of wings, the dragon's talons reached out to take him. In terror, he covered his head with his arms, waiting helplessly for the fatal impact. But before it came, the scene changed once more.

He was back in the same chamber as before. Maledict was sitting on a stone throne in the centre of the room, his back towards him. This time, he wasn't alone. A grey figure was standing in front of Maledict, cowering in fear. Peter couldn't see him clearly as he was obscured by Maledict's body but, as he strained his ears, he could just make out a small timid voice.

'They're in the secret entrance, your majesty. I've done what you asked. Please don't punish me!'

When Maledict replied, his voice was deep and full of menace.

'You have done well. However, there is one more task I will ask of you…'

Before Peter could hear any more, the scene changed and he was back in the sparkling cavern again, gazing at his worried looking reflection in the water.

He drew back from the Well as he contemplated what he had seen. A thousand questions remained unanswered. In the last vision, who was the other person and what was he doing? It sounded like treachery. In the second vision, what was the significance of the scene he had witnessed? Had he really seen a dragon? What was the strange creature on its back? Finally and most urgently, what was happening in York? Was the city already taken? Would they return to find it swarming with trolls?

It was the first vision that worried him the most. Whereas the other two were short and hazy as if their outcomes were unclear, it was longer and horrifyingly vivid. He felt sure he'd been shown something vitally important – something that was crucial to their Quest. He remembered the silent question he had asked when he first peered into the water: *How can Maledict be defeated?* The answer had somehow been revealed to him.

He replayed it again in his mind. There was no doubt that the person he'd seen was Maledict and that he'd been in York. But he was sure there was something else – something essential that he was missing. Suddenly he thought of the Viking Stone. He remembered Sigurd telling him that it was the only seed of Yggdrasil, and that Maledict had stolen it and used its power to do many unspeakable things. Even now, he was using it to help him in his assault on York. There was something about the way he'd been shown it. The vision had ended the moment he'd recognised it, almost as if that had been its purpose.

Then he had it! It came to him in a terrifying flash. They had to *steal* the Viking Stone! There was no other way to defeat Maledict! Without the stone, his powers were weakened and he was vulnerable. With it he was almost invincible! A cold sweat broke out on Peter's forehead and a deep nausea rose in his stomach. How were they going to steal the stone when it was embedded in Maledict's crown? How do you steal the crown from the head of the most powerful sorcerer that ever lived and escape alive?

Troubled, he gazed at the water in the wooden pan again. For a moment he wondered what he should do with it, but some instinct told him he should return it to the Well. Holding the pan carefully, he gently poured it back. After a long silent pause, it splashed faintly far below. Then something startling happened. As the last drop of water descended into the Well, a piercing cracking noise shook the cavern as if the mountains were splitting around them. At the same time, all the light from the diamonds in the walls focused like an intense spotlight on the Well, leaving the rest of the cavern in complete darkness. Hidden on the stairs above, Peter heard the Princess and Dunstable gasp in surprise.

Just in front of the Well, the shape of a man began to form. First there was little more than a hazy outline of swirling light, then his features began to emerge. Within seconds an old man appeared, seemingly made of nothing more than sparkling light. He stared at Peter with large unblinking eyes, a slight smile on his wrinkled face, then inclined his head in a small bow.

'I am Mimir, keeper of the Well. You alone have passed all the tests I have laid before you. You have overcome the mighty Frost

Giants that guard my cavern, you have found the hidden entrance and you have resisted the treasures that are held within the cavern walls. Now you have found the answer you have been looking for. Here you have found yourself. In Mimir's Cavern, wisdom is found not only in the waters, it is found in the hearts of those who seek it.

'Now you must go. A new Quest is before you and your path is clearer. Be wary who you tell what you have seen, for you have not yet understood all that has been revealed to you and all may not be what it seems. The roots of the mountains run deep and little is what it first appears to be. Beware he who opposes you! He knows you and why you have come here. He will try to stop you. Trust no one until you are back within the Walls of York, and even then you must be cautious as danger surrounds you. Go now and tell no other the secrets of Mimir's Well!'

Once more the old man bowed. Then, as he smiled one final time, he began to disintegrate. In a blinding flash, the light that had formed his body shot out in all directions. When Peter opened his eyes again, Mimir was gone. Once again the cavern was ablaze with light as the diamonds sparkled in the walls.

Peter glanced at the Princess and Dunstable. They were staring down at him, their faces white with shock. The diamond they had tried so hard to remove - which a moment before had looked as if it was finally about to come loose - was firmly embedded in the wall again.

Chapter 12

Fast Flight Back Home

They made their way down the rocks in silence, each of them lost in thought.

Peter, in particular, had a lot on his mind. Haunted by the first vision he'd seen in the water, he was desperate to return to York as quickly as possible. He wondered if the city was already taken or whether he'd seen something that would happen in the future (and if so, could it be stopped?). Every moment they delayed was a moment lost. But there was something more immediate that worried him almost as much. Sooner or later he would have to tell the Princess that the only way to defeat Maledict was to steal the Viking Stone from his crown. That would have been hard enough at the best of times, but since they had left the cavern, she had been in a truly foul mood.

Peter was right. The Princess was indeed in an incredible strop. In fact, she was absolutely furious! She was furious that Peter had drawn the water from the Well when it clearly should have been her, furious that Mimir had shown him reverence (even bowed!) but had barely even noticed that she was standing just a few feet away (didn't he realise she was a Princess?), and *especially* furious that Peter hadn't told her what he'd seen in the enchanted water! Most of all though, she was just plain furious with Peter. He was simply being far too...*confident* all of a sudden! After all, *she* was the leader of the Quest – *not* him - and it was about time he realised it too!

Dunstable was also in a bad mood. Like the Princess, several things were irritating him. He was angry that Mimir had appeared just when he'd almost released the enormous diamond from the wall, he was angry that both the Princess and Peter had ignored his pleas for *'just one more go'* at trying to remove it, and he was *particularly* angry that they were outside in the freezing night again when they could be inside the lovely bright cavern surrounded by diamonds. He nibbled on one of the Princess's Viking biscuits moodily then threw it away. There were two more things he was angry about, he decided. He'd had quite enough of eating nothing but biscuits, and quite enough of walking through mountains and woods in the night, expecting to be attacked by enormous rock-hurling Frost Giants or ferocious wolves at any moment!

For several minutes they moodily made their way down the rocky mound, the Princess leading with Dunstable sulking close behind and Peter lagging some yards further back as he wrestled with his dilemma. Not a word was spoken. During that time, the Princess made an unpleasant discovery: the biscuits were almost gone. They had almost nothing left to eat.

That was the last straw. Suddenly her anger and resentment boiled over. Now she wanted an argument – an excuse to unload her frustration on somebody. She turned around and glared at Peter. Silhouetted against the night sky by the light of the lake below them, his ragged dark hair flopped over his forehead as he bowed his head, clearly deep in thought. For a moment she hesitated. She found him both irritating and fascinating at the same time. Part of her admired him – his strange powers, how he had learnt to fly so quickly, and the fact that he seemed so different from other City Dwellers. But another part of her found him nauseating to the core. Why did he not understand that she was a Princess and he was only a City Boy? Why, despite this obvious fact, had both the Queen and now Mimir shown him such respect? And, most importantly, why was he completely ignoring her!

The time had come, she decided, to make a few things clear to him. The lack of food was the perfect opportunity! Deciding that she couldn't wait for him to catch up to her, she marched past Dunstable, pushing him out of her way. Bristling with indignation, she stood directly in front of Peter, her legs slightly apart and her hands on her hips.

'So, *Mr Know-It-All*, when do you intend to tell us what you saw at Mimir's Well then? Perhaps you are planning to wait until we have all starved to death before you let us in on your little secret?'

Rudely awakened from his musing, Peter was taken back by the vehemence of her voice and was momentarily lost for words. Even Dunstable jumped in surprise, his daydream about shining diamonds rudely disturbed. But the Princess didn't wait for Peter to regain his wits.

'So! You did not know that we have almost run out of food? Typical! I always knew we should not have brought a *City Boy* on a Quest! Perhaps, *Mr All-Knowing-One*, you might like to tell *me* what you saw in Mimir's Well so someone better qualified than you can make a decision? I am, after all, the leader around here, in case you had forgotten!'

Her voice was so arrogant and condescending that it took Peter some time to compose himself. He was about to retaliate, but perhaps due to the gravity of what he had to say, he just managed to restrain himself.

'I saw…some sort of vision. We have to return to York as quickly as possible. I think Maledict has broken through the Walls – or is about to anyway. It's all very confusing! When we get back to York – to defeat him - we have to…'

'We have to *what* precisely? Come on, we have not got all night, you know!'

Peter finally snapped.

'We have to steal the Viking Stone, that's what! We have to steal it from Maledict's crown. That's the only way to defeat him! Is *that* clear enough for you?'

The Princess was momentarily stunned. She'd rehearsed her next cutting line in her head before Peter had even replied, but now she was completely lost for words. Behind her, Dunstable was staring at Peter in absolute horror.

'*Steal* the Viking Stone? From Maledict's Crown? While it's still *on his head??*'

'That's not all,' continued Peter, ignoring Dunstable as his eyes bore into the Princess's. He was now so angry he wanted to shock her and gain his revenge for her being so rude to him. 'Remember what Mimir said about Maledict knowing what we are doing? I think he has known all along and has been trying to stop us! That's why the wolves attacked us in Ironwood. I think we might have trouble getting back to York.'

Despite his anger, Peter just retained enough self-control to remain silent about the second and third visions he had seen. The first one was significant enough for the time being and, recalling Mimir's warning, he wanted time to consider what the other two might mean before he told anyone.

The Princess's surprise lasted only a few seconds before her face set with grim determination. Now, at last, she had a clear purpose – a goal to aim for. The fact that it seemed almost impossible to achieve didn't worry her in the slightest, and she immediately began imagining the glory she would receive if she succeeded. For a moment, she forgot about how angry she was.

'I *knew* he was up to something when the wolves attacked! I *knew* it! Still, he will not find us easy to stop! We will get back to York even if his whole army is after us! Then we can go for the Viking Stone!' She glanced at Peter and some of her anger and resentment crept back as she remembered that Mimir had shown him the answer and not her. 'Of course, *I* could have told you back in York that the best way to defeat Maledict was to steal the Viking Stone! Not that anyone bothered to ask me, of course! I do not think Mimir is so clever. In fact, I think he is rather dull!'

'I wish you *had* told us back in York!' said Dunstable sulkily. 'Then I could have stayed there where it is nice and safe and warm, instead of being almost killed by giants and wolves - and almost freezing to death!'

The Princess ignored him.

'We need to return to York quickly! I must speak with the Queen!'

'Should we… *fly?*' suggested Peter, hopefully.

Dunstable shrieked in protest and started shaking his head vigorously.

'*Hmm*. It *would* be the quickest way,' pondered the Princess. 'But if Maledict is looking for us, he will certainly see us if we fly. We need to get back without being seen.'

'But it could take days otherwise!' insisted Peter. 'And what if we're attacked by Frost Giants again, or by wolves? By the time we get there, it could be too late!'

The Princess folded her arms and rested her chin on her fist to think.

'Most of his army will probably be close to York by now. We should be okay until we get close to the city. And it is a dark enough night for us not to be seen by any children. We could fly to about five or six miles from the Walls then walk from there. That way, we could be back in York within a few hours if we hurry!'

Dunstable, who had been glancing from the Princess to Peter in an increasing state of agitation, suddenly started jumping up and down in front of them.

'*Excuse me!!* Haven't you forgotten something? I *can't fly!* I don't want to fly either, thank you very much! You can't leave me here! I'll get squashed by Frost Giants! Or eaten by wolves! Or…'

'We could, maybe, carry him?' ventured Peter.

Dunstable gaped in horror at the suggestion.

'No. He is so terrified of flying he would not keep still. We would drop him for sure,' replied the Princess, managing to increase Dunstable's terror still further. 'I *could* put a sleeping spell on him, but they are not very reliable and he could wake up at any time. If he woke up when we were in the air, I dread to think what would happen!'

Suddenly Peter had an idea. He took the Princess's arm and led her away from Dunstable, who stared at them plaintively, like a condemned man awaiting his fate.

'What about the Queen's gift – the happiness chocolate? Do you think it would calm him down a little?'

The Princess's eyes widened.

'That is not a bad idea! It might just work! I do not know how long the spell will last though. Still, it has to be worth a try!'

Turning his back on Dunstable, Peter reached under his jumper and shirt and opened the brown pouch that contained the Queen's gifts. Inside he found the tiny bar of magical chocolate wrapped in silver foil.

'Now we've just got to fool him into eating it! It's not very big. I hope we've got enough!'

'Leave it to me,' said the Princess. 'I will make sure he eats it all!'

Turning around, they approached Dunstable. He gazed at them warily.

'Dunstable. We have decided to walk after all,' announced the Princess. 'But we need to build our strength up as it is such a long way. Fortunately, Peter has brought some chocolate for us. We saved the last bit for you!'

Quickly removing the foil, Peter held out the chocolate and gave it to Dunstable, trying to look as casual as possible.

'It's a special City Dweller variety. One of my favourites!' he said quickly, noticing Dunstable's puzzled expression as he took the strange looking bar and sniffed it suspiciously.

But Peter didn't know about Dunstable's love of chocolate, or the fact that chocolate was the only City Dwellers' food Vikings craved for as they hadn't mastered the art of making it themselves. As a result, it was considered a rare delicacy. And Dunstable, who liked it more than most, was very, *very* hungry!

For several seconds, Dunstable stared at the chocolate. Peter and the Princess tried to appear unconcerned, pretending to discuss the best route back to York. Then, as they watched him out of the corners of their eyes, he took a tiny nibble out of the bar. Immediately his eyes lit up with pleasure. In two large bites, the chocolate was gone.

'I say!' he exclaimed, licking his lips. 'That was really *jolly* nice, you know! I *do* like a nice bit of chocolate every now and then! I'm so glad you've dropped that nasty flying idea! Did I tell you how much I dislike heights? It sounded far too scary for…'

Suddenly his eyes bulged with surprise, as if something he'd never experienced before had just happened.

'Oh dear…I feel rather…'

Within a second, though, he recovered from whatever had caused his discomfort and a miraculous change came over him. Rubbing his hands together in excitement, he beamed up at them, his smile stretching from ear to ear. He looked like a child who had just arrived at a fairground, bubbling with anticipation.

'My! My! Oh what fun! What joy! That chocolate – it must have been even better than I thought! I feel like a new Viking, you know! What are we going to do now, *mmm?* Shall we play with the Frost Giants again? I feel in the mood for adventure!'

Peter and the Princess gazed at each other in astonishment.

'We thought we might, err, try a bit of *flying?*' proposed Peter speculatively.

'Flying? What an absolutely *splendid* idea! I've never been flying, you know. Always wanted to of course, but something always held me back. Can't remember what it was…' For a second his smile faded, but then it bounced back even broader than before. 'Still, no matter! When do we start? I'm so excited I can hardly wait!'

'We could start now if you like?' suggested Peter.

'Sounds jolly good to me! No time like the present I always say!

Strike whilst the iron's hot! He who waits is lost! A stitch in time saves nine!' He laughed so loudly you would have thought he'd just told the world's funniest joke. 'Come on then! Who's going to carry me?'

He held up his arms in eager expectation of being carried and gazed at them enquiringly, a broad grin fixed on his face. This new, super cheerful Dunstable could easily get irritating, Peter thought.

'I think we will carry you between us, just to be on the safe side,' declared the Princess sharply, flicking her hair back in irritation.

Together they stood on either side of Dunstable and wrapped his arms around their shoulders.

'Don't drop me!' he giggled. 'Though I'm sure I'd bounce straight back up again! I feel as light as a feather!'

Exchanging a brief wishful glance over Dunstable's shoulder, Peter and the Princess pushed off from the ground and rose jerkily into the air. He was heavier than they were expecting, and it was difficult to fly side by side whilst ensuring they kept a firm grip on his arms.

'Weeeeeeee!' cried Dunstable, oblivious to their discomfort as he kicked his legs playfully, obviously having the time of his life. 'Oh my! This is simply *wonderful!!* I never realised what I was missing!'

The world slowly fell away beneath them. Higher and higher they rose, soaring into the night sky, then they began to make their way forward, battling against the freezing wind that gusted around them. Gradually they began to pick up speed.

'Come on! We're hardly moving!' Dunstable protested. 'This won't do at all! I want to go *really* fast! Come on you two! Let's have some fun!'

Peter and the Princess ignored him. Their attention was focused on the ground. Beneath them, the frozen lake was glittering in the darkness, the only highlight on the bleak grey landscape. On its shore they could see tiny figures.

'Frost Giants!' said the Princess.

At first, Peter couldn't believe that the tiny figures below them could possibly be enormous Frost Giants. But as he watched them move, loping along the ground using their arms to pull themselves forward, he was in no doubt that the Princess was right. He shivered, glad they were out of range of any rock missiles. But Dunstable's attention was focused on something else.

'Goodness gracious! Look at that! It looks like a big fluffy blanket! Can we take a closer look? Can we? *Pleeeease?'*

Up ahead were low-lying white clouds, stretching to the distant horizon. Peter stared at them uneasily. He had forgotten how high up they were. Immediately he felt giddy and wobbled in the air before recovering himself.

'Keep steady!' shouted the Princess, throwing him an irritated glance.

'Wow! You almost dropped me there!' giggled Dunstable.

It wasn't long before they reached the clouds. As Peter gazed down, he began to feel uneasy again. The clouds looked so thick and impenetrable. What would happen when they were inside them? Would they fall out the other side? Suddenly he began to doubt his ability to fly. But the Princess was eager to press on.

'Hold him tight,' she yelled. 'We are going in!'

Peter closed his eyes and tried to calm himself. When he opened them again, the dark night sky had been replaced by dense white mist. It swirled around them, so thick he couldn't see more than a few feet in any direction. They were effectively flying blind. Instinctively he pulled on Dunstable's arm to slow down. Then, just as he was beginning to panic, they shot out into the dark sky beneath. It happened so quickly he didn't have time to prepare. He had no choice but to look down, and when he did, his heart leapt into his mouth.

They were terrifyingly high – far higher than he had ever flown before. Below them, the rocky ground sloped downwards towards Ironwood. They were so high up that the distant wood looked like a tiny dark mat dropped onto the vast landscape.

Peter closed his eyes as his stomach spun inside him.

'I didn't realise we were so high up!' he mumbled, forcing down his mounting nausea.

'Do not worry!' shouted the Princess above the blasting wind. 'We can dive down now we can see where we are going! Hold tight!'

'*Dive! Dive!*' squealed Dunstable in delight, sounding like a mad submarine captain. 'Oh this is such jolly good fun! Look how small everything looks from up here! We must be on top of the world! I can see for miles and miles!'

Peter tried to ignore him. His stomach was churning ominously and his head was dizzy. He longed to be back on the ground again. Squeezing his eyes shut, he clung onto Dunstable as they dropped down from the clouds.

They picked up speed quickly, the freezing wind roaring around them. Dunstable wobbled in their arms in his excitement, making them sway precariously from side to side. That was more than Peter could take. The horrible taste of panic began to rise from his stomach. He felt like he was going to be sick at any moment. He simply *had* to get back down to the ground - back to where it was safe!

Ducking his head, he increased their speed, dragging the Princess and Dunstable behind him, until they were falling out of the sky like a stone.

'*Weeeeeeeeeeeee!*' whooped Dunstable. 'Look how fast we're flying now! *Woooow!* Faster! Faster!'

'Slow down Peter!' warned the Princess, her voice barely rising above the wind screaming in their ears. She risked a frantic glance at him over Dunstable's shoulder. 'It is too dangerous at this speed!'

'*Faster! Faster!*' urged Dunstable.

But Peter was gripped by a desperation to reach the ground as quickly as possible. With his eyes still tightly shut, he put in another spurt until they were falling out of the sky faster than a falcon. The wind blasted around them, buffeting them from side to side. Down they fell, far out-pacing the falling rain.

'Peter! We are going too fast!' shrieked the Princess, her hair trailing vertically behind her as she desperately tried to pull him back.

Peter couldn't hear her above the roar of the rushing wind; not that he would have taken any notice anyway. All his attention was focused on getting back to solid ground as quickly as possible.

Down, down they fell, streaking out of the sky like a lightning bolt.

'*We are going too fast!*' screamed the Princess, beginning to panic also. 'We must pull up! *We must pull up!!*'

'*Woooooooo!*' shouted Dunstable in delight.

'*PETER!!!*' screeched the Princess.

'*Weeeeee…!* Oh…! Dear me, I suddenly feel a little odd!'

Dunstable jolted in their arms as if he had just woken up.

'Oh no! *Ohhhhhhh noooooooooooo!!*' he squealed in absolute

horror. 'Weeeee'rree *flyinnnnnngggg!'*

The happiness chocolate had worn off!

Dunstable screamed in terror and jumped so hard in their arms they almost dropped him. Then, as if Dunstable's panic had somehow cured his own, Peter finally opened his eyes. Suddenly he realised the terrible danger they were in. The ground was racing towards them at an alarming rate. But it was no longer a distant obscure landscape miles below. Now he could clearly see individual trees, houses and even a car, its headlamps lighting up a grey winding road like twin torches. They were only a few hundred feet above it - and they were travelling much too fast!

His heart in his mouth, Peter pulled on Dunstable's arm as hard as he could to slow them down before it was too late. But, such was the momentum they'd built up, they scarcely slowed. The Princess realised he'd finally come to his senses and together they strained, frantically trying to pull up in time. Out of the corner of his eye Peter saw a field full of cows lazily munching on the grass. They were racing towards it at horrifying speed. It was too late. They were going to crash!

'*Ohhhhhhhhh noooooooooooooooooo!'* screamed Dunstable, as he covered his head with his hands.

With a final agonising effort, Peter and the Princess strained with all their strength. Then, with a fantastic *whoosh!* and a sharp intake of breath from the Princess, they sped inches above the ground for a terrifying moment before racing back up into the sky in a perfect arc. Below them, Peter heard a cow's startled moo as they dashed over her.

Finally slowing, they came to a halt in mid-air, thirty feet above the ground.

'*Let me down! Let me down!'* squealed Dunstable, fighting and kicking in their arms.

Slowly, they flew back down until, with enormous relief, they landed in the middle of the dark field. Bending over, Peter fought to regain his breath, relishing the solid feel of the earth beneath his feet. When he stood upright again, he noticed that the Princess and Dunstable were glaring at him, their faces cringing with disgust. He gazed down and realised why. Whilst he had landed on muddy grass, they were both standing in a freshly laid cow-pat, which was steaming in the freezing air around their feet.

Feeling decidedly awkward, Peter grinned at them apologetically.

'Well, we were in a hurry, and we got here pretty quick, didn't we?' He nodded towards the cows which were gathering around them, sniffing them curiously. 'Don't reckon much about the smell round here though!'

Chapter 13

The Last Chance Café

'So, where are we then?' asked Peter, putting on his best cheerful voice.

It was now about an hour since they had almost crash-landed into the cow field. In that time, no one had said a word, though several dark looks had been exchanged. They were walking along a narrow country lane lined by hedgerows. It was dark and raining heavily. On either side of the lane, wide fields stretched to the grey horizon, broken only by shadowy clusters of trees.

Other than the occasional distant farmhouse, there was no sign of any people. Since they had found the lane, only two cars had passed them, their headlamps briefly lighting up the dark landscape before they disappeared into the distance. They were cold, wet and miserable. And they had eaten the last of the Viking biscuits.

Peter wondered what time it was – late certainly, probably almost midnight.

'Are we near York?' he asked when no one replied to his earlier question, his breath forming a wispy cloud that hung in the air in front of him. He desperately wanted to break the ominous silence, even if it meant risking an argument. 'Bit damp, isn't it?'

The Princess and Dunstable stopped in the middle of the lane and regarded him sullenly. Neither had forgiven him. The sudden excitement the Princess had felt when he'd told her about stealing the Viking Stone had long since faded in the freezing night. To make matters worse, his antics in the air had reminded her of the events at Mimir's Well and why she'd been so angry with him earlier. Meanwhile, Dunstable was angry with both of them for 'tricking' him into eating the happiness chocolate which, judging by his dark expression, had now most definitely worn off.

'Well, let me see...' said the Princess in answer to Peter's original question, her sarcastic tone making him cringe. She crossed her arms and tapped the side of her face with her fingers in mock concentration. 'As I was hurtling down to earth, wondering whether I was about to die thanks to you, I thought I had better check where we were going, just in case by some miracle we actually managed to survive diving out of the sky at a hundred miles an hour!'

Peter winced.

'I just want to know whether we're going in the right direction, that's all.'

'Of course we are! You do not think we are walking down this road in the middle of the night in the pouring rain just for the fun of it, do you? We are heading south which, I believe, is where York is. I would guess we are probably a few hours walk from the Walls. Too close to fly without running the risk of being spotted. Not that we would want to go through *that* again!'

'No thank you!' said Dunstable sulkily.

'Right then,' continued Peter, trying not to let the Princess's tone annoy him but failing miserably. Couldn't she just forget about his little mistake? It wasn't as if anyone had been hurt after all. 'We can't afford to get lost, that's all.'

'I *beg* your pardon? *'We can't afford to get lost'*? You should have thought about that before you made us drop out of the sky into the middle of nowhere!'

'It's just that we haven't got any food left now all the biscuits have gone,' continued Peter heedlessly.

The Princess took an ominous step towards him and placed her hands on her hips, her eyes boring into his.

'Oh *really*? And that is *my* fault, is it? My fault that we had to eat what was left of the food after the shock of your little stunt in the air?'

'I didn't say it was anyone's fault!' said Peter, standing his ground, beginning to get angry now himself.

'I'm hungry,' complained Dunstable unhelpfully.

The Princess jabbed her finger into Peter's stomach.

'See what you have done to Dunstable? He is a nervous wreck, thanks to you! What a stupid idea to use the happiness chocolate! The Queen should have given her magical gifts to someone intelligent – not a stupid City Boy like you!'

That was it. Up until then Peter had been patient with her,

embarrassed that he'd panicked when they had flown down from the mountain. But now she had pushed him too far.

'Someone *intelligent?* Weren't *you* the one who spent all her time in Mimir's Cavern trying to steal a diamond from the wall? Or have you conveniently forgotten about that little fact?'

The Princess glared at him, so angry she couldn't immediately speak. All the resentment she'd been feeling over the past hour rose to eruption point. Here he was, a City Boy – *a mere City Boy* – daring to criticise *her* – the Princess! Who did he think he was?

'How *dare* you speak to me like that? When were *you* planning to tell us what you saw at Mimir's Well? I had to practically *drag* it out of you!'

'I would have told you when I was ready!' replied Peter stubbornly.

'When you were ready! And what were you waiting for? Until Maledict had captured York? Until trolls were standing on every street corner? Or are we not worthy enough for you, is that it? Do you want us to follow you and obey your orders, whenever you see fit to tell us what they are?'

Peter couldn't believe it! The Princess, of all people, was implying that *he* was arrogant! Standing toe to toe in the middle of the lane, the gap between their faces narrowed to barely an inch as they glowered at each other. Beside them, Dunstable gazed from one to the other, not quite sure what to do with himself. His own anger with them both was forgotten in his curiosity to see what would happen next and who would be the victor.

'So, you want us to follow *you* and do whatever *you* say, is that it, *your Highness?*' yelled Peter, spitting the words out in his fury. 'You are '*The Princess*' after all! And when were *you* going to tell us we'd run out of food? When we were eating grass for dinner?'

The Princess looked ready to explode.

'How dare…'

She didn't finish the sentence. Suddenly she stood perfectly still with her mouth open, forming a word that never came. Distracted by something, she slowly turned her head from side to side and sniffed the night air. For a second, Peter stared at her in disbelief, wondering what she was doing. Then he smelt it too.

Beside him, Dunstable had also noticed it. His eyes grew wide behind his glasses as his head darted in every direction, desperate to find the source.

'I say! Can you smell that?' he whispered.

'*Mmmmmm!*' replied Peter and the Princess in unison.

For the moment, their argument was forgotten as a greater need demanded their attention - hunger. Coming from somewhere hidden in the darkness close by was the most mouth-watering aroma of cooked food any of them had ever smelt. Almost immediately their stomachs rumbled in protest.

'Goodness me! Where on earth is it coming from?' said Dunstable, spinning around frantically, thrusting out his nose as he peered into the dark fields around them.

But the Princess, whose senses were the keenest, was already jogging away from the road across a muddy field. Peter and Dunstable raced after her, desperate to find the source of the wonderful smell.

They hadn't gone far when she stopped. Her sharp eyes searched the open farmland ahead as Peter and Dunstable waited impatiently beside her. The rain continued to fall almost silently around them, the combined rumble of their stomachs the loudest sound in the night.

'We are close!' she whispered, after a pause of several long seconds. 'The smell is stronger here. We should be able to see something! Wait a minute, what is that?'

'What is what?' demanded Dunstable instantly, squinting into the distance in the direction the Princess was looking. 'Can you see the food? *Can* you?'

'There is a house on the hill over there by the trees. It does not look like a City Dweller's house. I think the smell must be coming from there!'

Peter and Dunstable followed her gaze, their eyes straining to see what she was looking at. Seeing nothing, they jogged eagerly behind her as she set off across the field again. A few agonising seconds later they finally saw the grey shape of a small hill emerge out of the darkness. On top of it was a battered looking wooden shack. It was nestled beside a dense thicket.

'Who would want to live there?' pondered Peter, studying it curiously.

They crept closer, their stomachs protesting ever more loudly in response to the mouth-watering smell, which was now so delicious they could almost taste it. When they were about twenty yards away, they stopped and peered out from behind the trees at the edge of the thicket. The house looked even more battered close up. Above the front door was a rickety wooden sign. It was swinging gently, though there was hardly any wind. On it was written '*The Last Chance Café*' in faded red ink.

'Strange place for a café!' puzzled Peter. 'It must be deserted. No one would run a café in the middle of a field, miles away from anywhere.'

'Someone is home. Look! They have lit a fire!' said the Princess.

Sure enough, a warm orange light was glowing through the house's only window, inviting them in from the cold. The delicious smell was now stronger than ever.

Curiosity and hunger overcame their caution. They crept closer still, the seductive glow beckoning them forward, until they were standing next to the window. Wiping circular holes on the damp glass with the sleeves of their coats, they peered inside.

The interior of the strange café was in complete contrast to the grubby looking exterior. Warm and enticing, it looked like an old fashioned country cottage. The first thing they noticed was a log fire in the centre of the room, its flames swaying contentedly. The whole room was glowing with its homely warmth. Above the fire on a black tripod was a large copper kettle, which was merrily whistling its readiness to serve a warming drink. Beside the fireplace was a large cushioned rocking chair and a tall Welsh dresser with countless white tea-cups hanging from its hooks. At the far end of the room beyond the dresser was an old fashioned kitchen. Numerous pans were sitting upon an enormous black stove, full no doubt of delicious food simmering to perfection.

As they pressed their faces against the window pane, their eyes finally rested upon the dining table at the back of the room. Even the delicious smell had not prepared them for what they saw there. The enormous table was laden with the most mouth-watering food they had ever seen in their lives! It was difficult to know where to look first! Everything they loved to eat was laid before them! In the centre of the table were the main courses: freshly cooked leg of lamb with mint sauce dripping off it, a joint of succulent beef surrounded by plump Yorkshire puddings, pork with apple and chestnut stuffing, a pure white chicken breast with lemon and bread sauce, steam rising from it! There was almost too much to take in! Beside them were countless accompanying dishes - golden roast potatoes, creamy buttered mash, thick juicy sausages, crispy bacon! Even the vegetables looked delicious! And there were puddings too - lots and lots of puddings! Hot syrup sponge, sticky toffee pudding, jam roly-poly, bread and butter pudding, treacle tarts - all accompanied by piping hot custard or vanilla ice-cream. Finally, there were the cakes - mountains of jam tarts, mince pies, chocolate sundaes, blueberry muffins, cheesecakes and dozens of other varieties they couldn't name but longed to taste.

For perhaps a minute, they simply stared at the glorious sight in front of them, their empty stomachs screaming for attention. Then it became too much for Dunstable. Suddenly he raced from the window to the door, his usual timidity forgotten. Before Peter and the Princess could react, he banged on it furiously.

'Let me in! Let me in! I'm *sooo* hungry!'

Peter and the Princess were about to whisk him away when the door opened and the glorious smell became so strong they stopped dead in their tracks. An elderly lady appeared on the doorstep. She was dressed in a long blue apron and was wearing thick silver rimmed glasses that were perched on the end of her nose. In fact, she looked very much like Peter's grandmother, though plumper and softer in the face. Bending down, she greeted Dunstable with a kindly smile such as only grandmothers can give, and opened the door wider to let him in.

Dunstable needed no further invitation. He darted inside. The sweet looking old lady turned and, without appearing to notice Peter or the Princess, closed the door behind her.

There was a moment of stunned silence before either of them could speak.

'Dunstable!' cried Peter in shock. 'She's taken Dunstable!'

'And he is inside with all that wonderful food!' protested the Princess.

Unsure what they should do, they raced back to the window and pressed their noses against the glass once more to see what was going on inside.

Dunstable was sitting at the end of the table closest to the fire. In front of him was a large plate, already piled high with delicious looking food, which the sweet old lady was adding to even as he ate. After a few seconds the plate was too full to add anything more and the old lady stood beside him, pouring him a steaming cup of tea from a large brown tea-pot.

Peter and the Princess moaned in unison, their stomachs screaming in protest.

'What should we do?' asked Peter. 'Should we go in?' His mouth was watering so much he could hardly speak. 'It wouldn't hurt to get something to eat, would it?'

'We need to keep our strength up,' agreed the Princess, nodding vigorously.

'Mind, I suppose we should be careful,' said Peter, without sounding very convincing. 'Remember what Mimir said about Maledict? It could be a trap?'

'I am hungry.'

'Me too. She's just a nice old granny after all. There couldn't possibly be any danger, could there?'

'Absolutely not. I say we knock on the door and invite ourselves in for dinner.'

There was no need for further debate. They dashed to the door and knocked loudly three times. Almost immediately it swung open in front of them. Once again they were engulfed by the glorious smell.

'Come in! Come in, me dears! It's much too cold to be standin' on er *door*-step!' said a croaky but kindly voice from inside. 'I've been waitin' fer you, I have. Dinner's ready – get it whyle it's hot! I do hope you're hungry, me dears. There's so much to eat!'

They didn't need a second invitation. Darting inside, they raced through the kitchen to the dining-room table as if their lives depended on it and sat down beside Dunstable, who barely looked up he was eating so ravenously. Grabbing two plates, they immediately began helping themselves to the delicious food in front of them.

They were so busy eating that it was several minutes before they paused long enough to study their host. The old lady was sat watching them from the rocking chair beside the fire with two enormous pampered cats squashed together on her lap. One of them was pure white and the other jet black, and both were purring loudly as she scratched behind their ears. Beneath her apron, she was dressed in a large green cardigan and an old-fashioned tweed skirt, with pink bunny slippers on her feet. Her wrinkled face was full of warmth as she smiled at them in a kindly granny kind of way.

For a moment they all stared at her, unsure what to say. She smiled back at them reassuringly.

'Well, you look lyike you could all do with er nice cup o' tea, I'd say me dears! I've put er kettle back on! Can't beat tea, I say. Best drink of er day and all thyat sort o' thing! Do you take milk and suger? One lump or two? *Shocking* weather we've been having, isn't it me dears?'

She stopped scratching the ears of the cats on her lap long enough to pour some milk from a white jug into two large white tea-cups that seemed to suddenly appear in her hands.

'Excuse me. Who *are* you?' asked the Princess, a little rudely, as she bit into a large slice of blackberry pie (she had decided that, as the puddings looked so delicious, she would eat them first before progressing onto a main course).

'Me name's Betty, me dear. I'm er witch. I live 'ere alone – 'cept fer me cats thyat is. Slasher and Mauler keep me company, don't you me dears.' She tickled the ample chins of the two fat cats on her lap, who almost seemed to be grinning as they gazed up at her, their enormous green eyes glinting.

All three of them almost choked on their food.

'Excuse me. Did you say that you are a *witch?*' asked Dunstable tentatively, a sausage wrapped in bacon and cheese suspended from the end of his fork.

'Thyat's rite me dear. But don't you let thyat worry you none. You don't want to go believin' everything you hear 'bout witches, now do you? Been er witch since I was er little girl, even younger than you are, me dear!' She nodded towards the Princess. 'You don't think I *cooked* all this food now do you? I ain't got time fer thyat sort o' mularky. I just put me witch's hat on, waved me wand, said er few magic words and thyat was thyat!' She picked up a black pointed hat and a long thin stick, which was presumably her wand, from behind the dresser and waved them in evidence. ''cept fer er cakes, of course. They're me special-itee, you see. Made with me own secret ingredients in faact.' She tapped the side of her nose with a bony finger and winked mysteriously. 'There ain't no cakes like Betty's cakes, me dears!'

BETTY AND HER PETS

Peter, the Princess and Dunstable exchanged worried glances. They'd heard of secretive old witches living with just their cats for company before, but this was the last place they expected to find one. The fact that witches were renowned for their powerful magic and evil ways didn't make them feel any easier. But Betty looked so sweet and was so welcoming that, after a few more mouthfuls of her delicious food, they quickly put aside their suspicions.

Meanwhile, Betty was busy with the tea.

'So, was thyat one lump or two me dears?'

'One please,' replied the Princess, without looking up from her food.

Betty passed the Princess her tea-cup.

'Is thyat one lump fer you too, me dear?'

Peter nodded, his mouth too full to speak.

'*Do* have a Lemon Tart! Me own recipe, you see! Take two! There's plent-ee to go round, me dears!'

Stretching over the two fat cats, she passed Peter a plate full of sumptuous looking tarts.

There was silence again for several minutes as they ate Betty's delicious tarts.

'Betty,' said Peter finally, holding a tart in one hand and a pork pie in the other. 'When we came in, you said you had been waiting for us. How did you know we were coming?'

Betty looked momentarily uncertain.

'Did I? Did I really, me dear?'

Peter and the Princess nodded, their mouths full of Lemon Tart.

'Well, I am er witch. I must 'ave looked in me crystal ball or sommert, I expect. Would you lyike any more tea, me dears?'

They shook their heads in unison. They were all so busy eating they hadn't had time to drink their tea yet and their cups were still full.

'Now, eat up me dears! I do lyike to see young-uns with healthy apper-tites, I do!'

Immediately all of their concerns disappeared again and they thought only of food. For the next twenty minutes not a word was spoken as they ate as if they hadn't eaten in a week. Meanwhile, Betty leant back on her rocking chair, watching them intently as she stroked the enormous fat cats that were somehow squeezed onto her lap.

Finally, when they had almost eaten their full, Peter spoke again.

'Betty?'

'Yes, me dear?'

'Why is this place called *'The Last Chance Café'*?'

Again, for a fraction of a second, Betty looked uncertain.

'Why…? Well, you know how it is, me dear. It's so *hard* to think of er good name, isn't it? I mean, all er good-uns are taken, aren't they?'

Before Peter could question her further, the Princess spoke.

'Why do you live here? Do you not know that Maledict's troll army is attacking York? They could come here at any minute.'

'Oh, I don't reckon they'd be much worried about an old witch lyike me, do you? Not much of er threat to them, am I me dear?' As if to emphasise her words, one of her bunny slippers fell off her foot and struck the floor. 'Anyway, where else are people going to get er nice bite to eat round here?'

'But aren't you afraid of trolls?' asked Peter.

Betty laughed – a strange cackling noise that rose from the back of her throat. 'Trolls? Afraid o' trolls? No, me dear. I ain't afraid o' no trolls.'

Her words had a strange effect on the cats. They almost appeared to be laughing and winking at one another as if they had just heard an extremely funny joke which only they understood. The black cat, who was even bigger and fatter than the white one, was so amused he almost fell off her lap, his chubby paws clawing the air frantically for a moment before he caught hold of Betty's skirt and hauled himself back up. Betty gave their ears a sharp tug and they immediately started purring and acting more cat-like again.

'Besides,' continued Betty. 'You'd be sur-prised how many people come through 'ere, me dears. Vikings on Quests, frightened children, lost explorers – all sorts! An' what they all *really* need is er nice place to come fer er bite to eat!' She gave them a familiar wink. 'Would you lyike some jam on your muffin, me dear?'

Dunstable paused as he was about to bite into the muffin he'd just put on his plate and gaped at Betty, his mouth wide-open. The Princess gave him a nudge.

'Goodness! Er, no…thank you.'

Now that their stomachs were full, all three of them were feeling uneasy. They suddenly felt decidedly uncomfortable in the presence of a witch, and there was something about Betty that gave them the impression that she was not quite what she seemed.

'Vanilla slice anyone? *Do* try one of me straw-berry scones! No one makes scones lyike I do, me dears,' said Betty amiably, smiling broadly as if nothing in the world would make her happier than watching them eat one of her wonderful buns.

They shook their heads. They were all eager to leave. The Princess stood up purposefully.

'We had better be going now. We have a long journey ahead of us, I am afraid.' She kicked Dunstable and Peter under the table to get them to stand up also. 'We are all extremely grateful for your hospitality.'

Peter and Dunstable nodded as they rose awkwardly to their feet and shuffled towards the door.

Betty smiled at them as they retreated, but this time her smile was sinister, as if she was hiding some dark intent. Slasher and Mauler jumped off her lap and ambled towards them, licking their lips and looking strangely pleased with themselves.

Peter, the Princess and Dunstable retreated towards the door, walking backwards.

'Thank you for the meal! Sorry we have to go, but we are in a bit of a hur…'

The Princess's words were cut abruptly short as all three of them gasped in horror. Slasher and Mauler were changing shape right in front of them! Suddenly they were growing upwards and outwards, getting larger and larger. Their front paws changed into huge hands, their whiskers withdrew into their noses and their cat-like expressions turned into hideous sneering faces. At the same time, their fur disappeared and was replaced by coarse hairy skin. Then, as they watched in horror, they slowly rose up on their hind legs, which had now grown thick and muscular. In a matter of seconds the transformation was complete and they had gone from overweight cats to eight feet tall muscle-bound creatures that towered above them, grinning hideously. There was no doubting what they were.

'*T-T-T-TROLLS!!*' squealed Dunstable, shaking from head to foot.

In a mad panic, they sprinted for the door.

The door refused to open.

Desperate to escape, all three of them pushed it with all their strength, then pulled so hard they almost fell over. Still the door didn't budge an inch.

Trapped, they turned around to face the trolls, who were now smirking at them, licking their lips and sharp teeth.

'Leavin' so soon, me dears?' said Betty the Witch, walking calmly between Slasher and Mauler. She was now wearing her witch's hat and her wand was raised in her hand, sparks flying from its tip. 'But we ain't even had any crump-pets yet!'

Chapter 14

After Dinner Surprises

Peter woke suddenly, a sharp pain in his arms bringing him abruptly back to consciousness. Blinking in shock, he quickly gathered his senses. The reason for his pain was immediately clear. He was hanging from a chain attached to the ceiling, its steel manacles biting into his wrists.

Forcing himself to remain calm, he closed his eyes and swallowed, then opened them again and gazed around him. He was clearly in some kind of cellar, though it was so dark he could barely see a thing.

'*Hello?*' he called out hesitantly. 'Is anybody there?'

The only response was a slight echo as his frightened voice bounced off the cellar walls.

Closing his eyes again to calm his mounting fear, he tried to remember what had happened, but his mind was strangely dimmed and he could barely think. The last thing he could remember was the ugly sneering faces of the trolls that had been cats moments earlier as they reached out to grab him, whilst Betty stood behind them with her wand in her hand, muttering strange words. He could clearly remember her triumphant expression and her eyes glinting maliciously behind her silver glasses. Then he had lost consciousness. He had no idea what had happened next, but the thought of Slasher or Mauler carrying him down to the cellar and chaining him to the ceiling made him shiver with disgust.

Shivering involuntarily, he stared into the darkness. It was his worst fear – to be alone and forgotten in a cold dark place, unable even to move. He would rather face the Frost Giants again, or even Maledict himself - anything was better than this! Straining his head back, he stared up at his manacled hands as he swung aimlessly from side to side. He'd never felt so totally helpless! Chained to the ceiling in a cellar in a witch's haunt. He remembered Mimir's warning. How could they have been so stupid?

He wondered where the others were and how they were faring. No doubt they were as helpless as he, chained in another dark cellar close by. Or maybe they had escaped and were looking for him? But would they find him here? Would they leave without him? He recalled his first vision in Mimir's Cavern: Maledict's troll army with the Minster in the background. He had to escape quickly to warn the Queen and the other Vikings! But how?

Suddenly the image of the Queen flashed across his mind and he remembered her gifts. His mind was still hazy, either from the pain in his arms or whatever it was that had knocked him out. He forced himself to think. What were they? Happiness chocolate! But what use would that be, other than allowing him to enjoy his captivity? In any case, he had given it all to Dunstable. What were the others? His mind was agonisingly slow! He shook his head to clear it, the chain clinking mockingly above him. The speed potion! Again though, what use would it be whilst he was still chained? But what about the last gift – the transformation mask? Surely that had possibilities?

There was no time to waste. He pushed his head painfully forward and stared down his body to see if the pouch was still attached to his belt, praying that the trolls hadn't taken it. But his baggy jumper was so long it hung over the top of his jeans. His arms screaming in pain, he pulled on the chain and raised his legs so that his jumper fell away from his trousers, then stretched his head forward again. He breathed a sigh of relief. It was still there, tied to his belt. Now all he had to do was somehow reach into it, remove the mask and put it on his face - all with his arms chained above his head!

Flopping back down again, he took a moment to prepare himself. Then, summoning all his strength, he raised his legs and hips as high as he could. The sharp edges of the manacles of the chain dug into his wrists, but he ignored the pain, concentrating only on what he was doing. If he could raise his legs high enough, he could loosen the string that tied the pouch to his belt with his mouth! Then all he would have to do is grab the transformation mask with his teeth and put it on!

For almost a minute, he strained in agony as he tried to force his legs higher. But he couldn't raise them enough. The highest he could manage was level with his chest, but even when he thrust his neck as far forward as he could, his mouth was still over a foot short of the pouch. Finally the strain became too much and he dropped his legs again, breathing heavily. He decided to try a different approach.

Pausing just long enough to get his strength back, he began to swing on the chain like a trapeze artist, slowly building up speed until his legs were swinging out in front of him. He waited until he'd reached the highest point then twisted his hips and head in a desperate attempt to reach the pouch with his mouth. He was glad no one could see him as he must have looked very peculiar indeed as he swung back and forth, straining his neck to reach the pouch.

For several minutes he swung and twisted until the manacles dug so painfully into his wrists that tears of pain clouded his eyes. But still he couldn't reach it. No matter how high he swung or how far he stretched his neck, the pouch was always just beyond reach. Exhausted, he dropped down again and simply dangled without moving like a fish on a hook. He had no idea that being unable to use his hands could be so frustrating!

As he hung, he tried to think clearly. There must be a better way! Perhaps he could swing high enough to hook his legs on the chain above his head? No, only a gymnast could raise his legs so high. Suddenly he had a better idea. What if he tried to fly? Even though his hands were chained, he still might be able to raise the bottom half of his body high enough to reach the pouch. If he could manoeuvre well enough, he might be able to untie the knot with his teeth and take out the mask. Then all he would have to do is somehow put it on his face. Easy!

Clearing his mind, he imagined his legs and hips flying. This proved to be difficult from a chained position, particularly as he could barely move the top half of his body. Eventually though, his legs began to lift into the air, rising above his stomach until they were floating in front of him. It was a strange sensation seeing his legs suspended in the air above him with almost no effort on his part! The pain in his wrists had lessened too. Why hadn't he thought of this before? He could have saved himself a lot of excruciating straining and twisting!

Now came the tricky part! With his chin pressed against his

chest so tightly he could barely breathe, he swung back on the chain and brought his knees up close to his body so he could reach the pouch with his teeth. He worked almost blindly, desperately pulling on the string that tied the pouch to his belt to undo the knot, cursing himself for tying it so tightly. It didn't help that he was beginning to feel dizzy from hanging practically upside-down for so long. Forcing himself to concentrate just a little longer, he finally undid the knot and used his nose and chin to nuzzle his way inside.

Then disaster struck. Just as he felt something cold and hard against his nose and stretched forward to grab the mask with his teeth, the pouch came loose and dropped infuriatingly onto the floor.

He couldn't believe it! He'd been so close! In despair, he quickly lowered his legs, fighting the horrible feeling that he was going to be sick at any moment. Stretching out to ease his aching muscles, he felt the blood flowing through his body again as sensation slowly returned. Finally his nausea passed and he gazed down to the floor to see where the pouch had landed. Fortunately it was just beneath him. He could clearly see the mask inside, its edges glowing faintly in the darkness. All he had to do was somehow reach it. He wondered how far off the ground he was. Surely it wasn't far? There was only one way to find out.

Trying to relax his shoulders and legs to make his body as long as possible, he pointed his feet and stretched as far as he could. To his relief, his toes just brushed the floor. Inch by inch, he reached out with his left foot and managed to hook the mask by placing the toe of his shoe in the gap for the left eye. His heart began to race with excitement. So far, so good. Now all he had to do was lift it and somehow put it on his face!

He took a deep breath then slowly raised his leg inch by inch, horribly aware that the mask was dangling precariously on the tip of his shoe. When it was high enough he swept his other foot across and clamped the mask firmly between his feet. He breathed a sigh of relief. The next stage, though, was likely to be the hardest. Taking deep breaths to psyche himself up, he swung with his hips and raised his feet as high as he could, gritting his teeth as his muscles screamed in protest.

But, once again, he couldn't raise them high enough! The highest he could lift them was level with his waist, and there was no way he could put the mask on his face from there, no matter how far he stretched his neck forward. The pain of even lifting it that high was almost unbearable! This time 'flying' with the lower half of his body wasn't going to help. He simply couldn't move his feet far enough to allow him to put the mask on his face.

He tried again, screaming out loud as he tried to force his legs higher. But after a minute of agonising stretching, his grip slipped and he dropped the mask onto the floor again. He stared at it in frustration. He was still no nearer to using its magic.

Magic? Could he somehow 'do' something magical? But, other than flying, he'd only ever managed it once when they had been attacked by wolves, and he didn't even know how he'd done it then! He tried to recall what the Princess had told him about magic when she'd been showing off, cursing himself for not listening properly. All he could remember was something about using his mind to connect with whatever it was he wanted to do. That didn't sound too difficult!

Hanging perfectly still, he stared at the mask on the floor, trying to reach out to it with his mind and will it to move.

Nothing happened.

He tried again. But still the mask didn't move an inch. After about five minutes and a dozen or so unsuccessful attempts, he had developed an enormous headache. Clearly he was doing something wrong. How on earth had he done it before?

He began to despair again. What made things even worse was that he had the means to escape right in front of him, if only he could use it! If he could just reach the mask, he could be free! He stared at it angrily, blaming it for refusing to co-operate.

It moved half an inch, then lay perfectly still again as if nothing had happened.

His jaw dropped in shock! Had he made it move? If so, how had he done it? He focused again and commanded it to move. But the mask remained resolutely on the ground as if mocking him.

Suddenly he heard a scream – a heart-piercing scream of fear and anger from somewhere nearby. It lasted for several seconds then stopped abruptly.

For a moment, Peter hung on the chain as still as stone, then his mind began to race. Who had screamed? Was it the Princess? Was it Dunstable? Were they being tortured somewhere nearby whilst he hung here, completely helpless?

Then, just as frustration welled up inside him and he reached his lowest point, his mind suddenly became clear. He knew exactly what to do. He stared at the mask, feeling his mind connect with it. Then he willed it to move.

Instantly the mask flew up from the ground and landed squarely on his face.

A wave of elation flooded through him, but he held it back. He didn't have time to reflect on how he'd done what he'd just done. He hadn't freed himself from the chain yet. The only way to do so would be to turn himself into something very small. In his mind's eye, he pictured what he wanted and sent a silent command to the mask pressed against his face. Then he waited, hardly daring to believe it would work.

Slowly, dramatically, the cellar and everything around him began to grow in size. At the same time, the manacles around his wrists seemed to widen until his hands slipped easily through. As the cellar expanded, his eye-level dropped lower. When his feet touched the floor he felt an irresistible urge to lean forward and rest on his hands. In just a few seconds, he was crouching on the ground on all fours, completely free at last. He had turned into a mouse.

For a moment he paused. The world had become a vastly different place. Everything was absolutely gigantic! He stared at the manacles that had previously bound him. They looked as if they were miles above him and appeared big enough to chain a giant! But, moments earlier, they had been quite tight on his wrists.

It wasn't just the size of everything that was different - his sight had also changed. The cellar had become much brighter, as if someone had turned on a light. His other senses were also enhanced. Coming from somewhere above him, he could hear a voice he hadn't heard before, though he couldn't catch the words. And he could distinctly smell a dirty, sweaty smell which he was sure must have been troll. Worryingly, he could neither hear nor smell the Princess or Dunstable.

There was no time to waste. Cautiously but quickly, he trotted across the stone floor, pleasantly surprised by how easy it was to run on all fours and how agile he felt. At the far end of the cellar was a bolted wooden door that would have presented a considerable problem if he had still been in human form, but as a mouse he simply slipped underneath it.

He found himself at the bottom of a stone stairway which led seemingly endlessly up. Here the relative advantages and disadvantages of being a mouse were reversed. To a human, the steps would have been no problem and he would have raced up them in no time at all. But to a tiny mouse, each step was as tall as a house.

Gathering himself, he took a running jump and landed in the middle of the first step. He was then presented with a difficulty he hadn't anticipated: there was much less room to run to give him the momentum he needed to leap onto the second step. To make the most of what little space there was, he positioned himself at the corner of the step and ran diagonally. With a great bound, he landed on the second step.

He took a moment to regain his breath. Climbing the stairway was clearly going to be difficult. There were at least a dozen more steps and already he was tired. For a moment he contemplated changing himself back into a human, but then thought better of it. What if he was disturbed? A mouse would be easy to miss, but a human? He could find himself straight back in the cellar, chained to the ceiling again. No, it was better to continue as a mouse, at least for the time being.

Retreating into the corner, he leapt onto the next step and then the next. Either he was getting used to being a mouse or his urgency was driving him on as he was beginning to find it slightly easier to make the jumps. He decided to allow himself half a minute rest for every three steps and, after ten more leaps, he was finally at the top of the stairs. He gave himself a full minute to recover before going on.

He was now in a long corridor. At its far end was another door. Beneath it a strong light was shining. He scampered towards it and slipped underneath.

Blinking in the sudden brightness, he found himself in a large room, the air of which was full of intriguing smells. He recognised it instantly. It was Betty's dining room where the sumptuous feast had been laid. All the food was still on the table, though there were also several empty plates. In the middle of the room, the fire was burning low.

Suddenly he froze. At the far end of the dining table, almost out of view, Betty was lounging on her rocking chair. She was still wearing her witch's hat and her wand was laid across her lap. Crouched on the table in front of her was Mauler, back in his white cat form. He was gazing at her with green malevolent eyes, licking his lips with his long pink tongue.

'Quite er suc-cessful night I reckon, me boy!' said Betty, sounding immensely pleased with herself. 'And to think thyat they came rite to *us*! Walked rite through er door they did! Who'd have thought thyat, eh? Never underestimate er power of good food, me pet!'

The cat made a strange hissing, meowing sort of noise that might have been laughter.

Peter, still in mouse form, decided to take a closer look. He crept around the edge of the wall then darted behind the Welsh dresser, before ducking behind a chair leg at the opposite end of the table.

Betty took several long gulps from the large beaker of foaming beer she was clutching in her left hand. Like Slasher and Mauler, she too had transformed. No longer did she look like a kindly old granny. Now no one could possibly mistake her for anything other than a witch. It wasn't just the black pointed hat she was wearing - it was the enormous hairy warts on her chin, her crooked nose and the grating, high-pitched cackle of her voice. Even her silver glasses somehow looked sinister as she peered through them, her eyes glinting.

On the table in front of her, Mauler was now rolling on his back with laughter, hardly able to keep himself from falling onto the floor.

'They walked straight in they did me pet!' screeched Betty, beside herself in amusement. She paused briefly to take another large swig from the beaker. 'All I had to do was put on me best granny rout-ine, magic up er bit of cookin' and they was putty in me hands they was! And *you*! Such er *sweet-lookin' pussy-cat*!' She prodded Mauler with a bony finger as he rolled on the table and put on his best cute cat expression. '*Lovely* little pussy-cat! You shall be dinin' on Viking to-nite, me dear!'

Mauler licked his lips wickedly.

'Course, you can't eat *all* of 'em!' added Betty, much to Mauler's obvious disappointment. 'Thyat Princess, she'll be worth er bob or two to er rite people, I reckon. Can't eat her, me dear! And thyat City

Dweller – his *Lordship* wants 'im, though I can't imag-gin why. You can eat er other one, er stupid lookin' little un. But only if you're good thyat is. No more sneakin' down to er basement and pokin' thyat Princess to find her juiciest bits, or we'll be havin' words we will me pet!'

She wagged her finger at Mauler, who turned his pink nose up in protest and tried (unsuccessfully) to look innocent. Sulking, he waddled to the edge of the table and sat with his back to the witch. Clearly the Princess was his favoured menu option.

Huddled behind the chair leg at the opposite side of the table, Peter listened in disgust. The scream he'd heard earlier must have been either Slasher or Mauler, presumably in troll form, trying to find the Princess's 'juiciest bits'. At least he knew for certain that she and Dunstable were alive, and that she was a prisoner somewhere in the basement. All he needed to know now was where she was and hope that Dunstable was with her. He briefly wondered who 'his Lordship' was, and why he should be wanted by him, but then dismissed the thought. There were more important things to worry about.

Whilst he was wondering what he should do next, Betty started cackling again.

'*Er Special* One! Ain't thyat what he said? Who'd er thought thyat, eh? He didn't look lyike much special to me! Still, if he wants 'im and is prepared to pay, thyat's just fine by me, I reckon!' She turned to Mauler, who was still sulking with his back turned to her, and poked him in the ribs. 'Talkin' of which, we're expectin' visit-ers! We need to make er necessary prepar-rations! Where's Slasher?'

Turning around, Mauler looked at her blankly, shrugging his cat shoulders.

'I bet he's downstairs torturin' thyat Princess again!' Betty rose awkwardly to her feet, looking like she'd drunk a little too much beer. '*Slasher! Slasher!* Get back in 'ere rite this minute, me boy, before I turn you into an insect!'

Hearing no reply, she shuffled into the kitchen then bent down and opened a trap-door in the floor that Peter hadn't noticed before.

'*Slasher!* You leave thyat Princess alone! There'll be plent-ee of time fer fun and frolics layter. We've got visit-ors to prepare fer! Slasher! You *listenin'* to me?'

There was a deep-throated groaning noise from somewhere below followed by the sound of heavy foot-steps getting closer and closer. A few seconds later, the enormous head of Slasher, in troll form, appeared through the trap-door, looking extremely disgruntled.

'Come on out rite this minute!' growled Betty, standing aside to give him room, her arms crossed sternly in front of her. 'What did I say to you not half-hour ago? You'd better not 'ave hurt her, or they'll be er price to pay there will! She's precious goods, she is! If I find thyat you've taken er bite out of 'er when I wasn't lookin', you'll be in serious trouble young troll!'

By now Slasher had squeezed through the trap-door. He stood in front of Betty with his head slightly bowed like a naughty schoolboy, despite being almost twice her height. Betty looked him up and down in disgust.

'You trolls – you ain't half ugly! Think I'll 'ave you as er cat again fer er time being, I reckon! Though it might be tradition-null fer er witch to keep er cat or two, I ain't never heard of one keepin' no trolls!'

She picked up her wand which she had left on the table and pointed it at Slasher. Instantly he started shrinking. In a moment, the ugly great troll was replaced by an irritated looking black cat. Meanwhile, Mauler laughed so much he rolled off the edge of the table and landed with a painful thump on the floor.

'Much better! Now, we're expectin' visit-ers. I want you two out of er way sharpish. Is thyat clear?'

Slasher and Mauler looked at her blankly, unwilling to be anywhere other than where the food was.

'I *said*,' repeated Betty, her eyes flashing behind her silver rimmed glasses as she folded her arms and tapped her wand against her shoulder in menacing fashion, 'I want you two out of er way. *Understand?* Or would you be wantin' a little reminder?'

She raised her wand threateningly and Slasher and Mauler immediately dashed under the table like startled rabbits, then slunk away with their heads bowed low. If expressions could speak, theirs would clearly say *'you spoil all our fun!'* Together, they pulled the front door open with their paws and went outside to sulk.

'Rite! Let's make this place good and tyidy!' croaked Betty to herself as she slammed the door shut behind them. She took a long swig of beer, then dropped the empty beaker onto the table. 'Arhhh! Finest brew this side of er Pennines thyat is! Now, where shall I start?'

Turning around sharply, she walked towards the far end of the kitchen and out of Peter's view. As quickly as he dared, Peter crept to the other side of the table and rose on his hind legs to see what was happening. Betty was busy. Waving her magic wand, she muttered a few words he didn't understand and suddenly all the plates, cups and saucers on the table lifted into the air and floated towards the kitchen. At the same time, the tap came on and started to fill the sink with soapy water. Piece by piece, the crockery plopped in, splashing water onto the floor. Then a washing brush appeared and started frantically scrubbing the dishes. When they were clean, they rose out of the water and floated towards a towel that was patiently hanging in mid-air for them. Finally, after being wiped dry, they drifted over to the welsh dresser and piled themselves into neat stacks.

Betty waved her wand again and a dust-pan and brush raced out of a cupboard and started rapidly brushing the floor. Every few seconds, the brush paused whilst the dust-pan flew towards a pedal bin, which obligingly opened its lid to allow the dust-pan to drop its contents inside, and raced back to join the brush again and continue where they had left off.

Peter realised that this was his chance. The trap-door was still open in the kitchen, Slasher and Mauler were out of the way and Betty was pre-occupied preparing for her visitors. Waiting until her back was turned, he raced across the kitchen floor to the trap-door as fast as his four legs would carry him, then leapt onto the first step below.

Just in time! He was barely inside when he heard Betty's command: 'Trap-door shut!' and the heavy wooden door crashed down behind him.

Catching his breath, he paused for a moment. It only took his mouse-eyes a second to adjust to the sudden darkness. He knew he had no time to waste. Betty's sinister sounding visitors were clearly expected at any moment, and he definitely didn't want to be around when they arrived. He must find the others and escape quickly!

He raced down the stairs as quickly as he could. When he reached the bottom, he ducked underneath another thick wooden door. Once again, he found himself in a dark cellar. It was similar to the one in which he'd been chained, only much larger.

Raising himself on his hind legs, his mouse eyes pierced the darkness as he searched for the Princess and Dunstable. For several seconds he looked back and forth, surveying each corner of the cellar. But all he could see was the empty stone floor stretching to the distant brick walls. Where were they? There was nothing else for it but to try to find the entrance to wherever the Princess and Dunstable were being kept. It surely couldn't be far!

He scampered to the other side of the cellar as fast as he could. But when he got there, he couldn't see a door. Confused, he raced around the four walls, desperately looking for the entrance to another room. But the only door was the one he'd come in through. He trotted to the middle of the room to collect his thoughts. Surely he had missed something?

He had just sat back on his hind paws to contemplate the puzzle when a moaning noise made him jump in shock. It was coming from somewhere above him. Leaning back on his tail, he stared upwards and almost fell over in joy! There, high above him, the Princess and Dunstable were hanging upside-down from the ceiling! Suddenly he realised what a fool he'd been. He had forgotten how small he was! Though they were only six or seven feet off the ground, in his mouse form that seemed like miles. It hadn't occurred to him to look that far up!

He breathed a sigh of relief. He had found them! Now all he had to do was figure out how to get them down and escape before it was too late!

Chapter 15

After Dinner Guests

The Princess and Dunstable were hanging upside-down from two long chains attached to the ceiling, the Princess's long hair dangling down towards Peter as he crouched beneath her. She had sore looking red marks all over her face and body, whilst Dunstable had turned a worrying shade of green. Due to the darkness and Peter's small size, neither of them had seen him.

It was time for Peter to change back into his human form. But how? Suddenly he wasn't so sure anymore. Since he'd put the mask on, he'd been unaware of it on his face. It had simply melted onto him when he'd changed into a mouse. But how would he change back again? For a moment, he panicked. What if he couldn't do it? Would he stay as a mouse forever? With a great effort, he managed to calm down. Clearing his mind, he visualised changing back. Immediately he felt himself stretching. He watched in bemusement as the world around him began to shrink. At the same time, he rose up on his back legs and stood up straight. A few seconds later the transformation was complete and he was back in his familiar human form, standing on two legs again.

Ignoring a brief temptation to go down on all fours and twitch his whiskers, he shook his arms and legs in relief, then reached up to his face. The mask fell easily into his hands. He dropped it into his pouch and peered into the darkness, missing the keenness of his mouse eyes. To his surprise, he realised that the cellar, which a moment before he'd thought gigantic, was actually no larger than his mother's living room.

Suddenly he heard a sharp intake of breath above him.

'Finally! You certainly took your time!' said the Princess irritably. 'Come on then! What are you waiting for? Get us down! *Quickly!*'

Peter turned around and almost bumped heads with the Princess, who was glaring at him impatiently. Clearly hanging upside down for hours had not adversely affected her and she was her usual abrupt self. Just behind her, though, Dunstable didn't look well. His face was green and his tongue was lolling out of the side of his mouth as he swung gently from side to side.

The Princess, upside-down, crossed her arms in impatience over the delay.

'What are you waiting for? I do not want to be hanging here all night! You had better wake up Dunstable and get him down first. I think he is feeling rather sick.'

As if to prove her point, Dunstable moaned and shuddered.

Peter paused a moment longer to consider his options. Getting them down was going to be difficult. They were hanging several feet up in the air. How on earth was he going to break the chain?

'Fly up and un-hook the chain from the ceiling?' suggested the Princess icily, reading his mind.

'Oh. Right!'

Feeling a little uncomfortable with the Princess's upside-down head glaring at him from just a few inches away, Peter stared up at the ceiling. Both of their chains were suspended from an enormous black hook. All he had to do was lift the chains over it and lower them onto the floor. But would he have the strength? His arms were still numb from his own ordeal.

'Hurry up!' urged the Princess impatiently.

There was no alternative. He leapt up and rose into the air past the Princess and Dunstable. Taking hold of Dunstable's chain first, he wrapped his legs around the hook to help support the weight, then, with a mighty heave, he pulled on the chain.

To his surprise and relief, he managed to lift it over the hook quite easily. But his elation was short lived. As soon as he cleared the hook, Dunstable became very heavy indeed. Though Peter tried to lower him gently, his feet were slipping and he could barely support Dunstable's weight. Suddenly the chain slipped through his hands and Dunstable fell three feet onto the stone floor, striking it with a painful thump. That was enough to wake him. Moaning in pain, he rolled on the ground, clutching his head.

'*Shush!*' whispered the Princess loudly, making almost as much noise as Dunstable. 'Hurry up Peter! Get me down!'

Ignoring Dunstable for the moment, Peter returned to the hook. Hoping the Princess would be lighter, he took hold of her chain and heaved on it with all his strength. But the effort of lifting Dunstable had weakened him. With a tremendous effort, he just managed to force it over the hook, but then, just as before, he couldn't hold on. Despite all he could do, the chain slipped through his hands and the Princess fell to the floor. Fortunately, unlike Dunstable, she was both agile and alert. With no effort at all, she spun in mid-air and landed gently on her feet like a gymnast completing a perfect vault. Peter followed her down.

When he reached the ground, Dunstable was sitting up next to the Princess, looking a slightly healthier shade of greenish pink as he rubbed his head.

'You could have been a little more careful, you know!' he whimpered, looking daggers at Peter. 'I've got a big lump on my head thanks to you!'

Peter and the Princess helped him to his feet and removed the chain from his ankles. As the Princess brushed herself down, frowning at the numerous stains on her once perfect clothes, Peter couldn't help staring at the red marks on her face and neck. Feeling his eyes upon her, she touched the sores tentatively and winced in disgust.

'Those horrible trolls!' she shuddered, looking almost as ill as Dunstable. 'They kept coming down and pinching me! *Ugh!!*'

'Come on! We'd better go!' said Peter. If he had not been so anxious to leave, he might have found the thought of a troll pinching the Princess to '*find her juiciest bits*' amusing, but now all he wanted to do was get out of Betty's house as quickly as possible. 'We'll have to be careful. The only way outside leads through the kitchen, and I don't want to bump into Betty again!'

'You leave her to me!' said the Princess, her eyes flashing. 'I have a score to settle with that witch! She is going to really regret ever daring to chain *me* up! Her *and* her pet trolls!'

Peter regarded her curiously.

'Couldn't you have freed yourself? I mean, *magically?*' He made a vague circular gesture with his hands.

'No - not whilst I was hanging upside-down! That is why she did it, the old hag! You cannot cast spells when you are hanging upside-down! *Everybody* knows that!'

Peter considered continuing the conversation, but then changed his mind. There wasn't time to argue. Betty's guests could arrive at any moment. He pointed to the stairs at the end of the cellar.

'They lead to the kitchen. Betty's up there. She's expecting visitors. I think she's planning on selling you…' he nodded towards the Princess, who immediately jumped in red-faced outrage, looking as if she'd never been so insulted in her life. Dunstable, clearly feeling better now he was the right way up, started to chuckle under his breath '…and she was going to feed Dunstable to her trolls.' Dunstable's smile evaporated as the Princess regarded him smugly. 'I think we need to leave before they arrive.'

'I think so too,' agreed Dunstable, suddenly looking very ill again.

'We need to escape without Betty realising,' continued Peter, thinking out loud. 'That way we'll get a head-start at least. We don't want to have to fight our way out. Not with a powerful witch and two hungry trolls about.'

'And how do you propose we do that if she is in the kitchen and that is the only way out?' asked the Princess sceptically. 'Actually, I think we should make *sure* we find that…that *witch*… and her pet trolls!'

There was fire and a lust for revenge in her eyes. Tiptoeing around the guilty parties was definitely *not* her preferred means of escape! Anyone who had hung her upside-down for hours on end and threatened to sell her was clearly asking for trouble! Fortunately, Dunstable was on Peter's side. The prospect of being eaten by trolls was not a pleasant one, and he wanted to be as far away as possible when they came downstairs for breakfast.

Realising she was outnumbered, the Princess crossed her arms and put on her *spoilt – Princess – not – getting – her – own – way – and – not – happy – about - it* expression. She turned to Peter and fixed him with a frosty glare.

'So. What is *your* great plan then?'

Peter thought for a moment.

'I'm going to use the mask to change myself into one of her trolls – Mauler, I think. Then I'm going to take you two upstairs. If Betty sees us, I'll pretend I'm taking you somewhere for safe keeping or something ready for her guests.'

'Great plan!' said the Princess cynically, rolling her eyes. 'And what if the *real* Mauler turns up? We will look pretty silly then!'

'We'll just have to take that chance. You agree Dunstable?'

Dunstable was looking worried and confused. Peter had completely forgotten about his fear of magic. The Princess raised an eyebrow as if to say *'and what shall we do about him?'*

'Dunstable,' said Peter, coming quickly to a decision. 'I'm going to blindfold you. That way you won't see me change into a ...into something else.'

Dunstable looked even more confused than before.

'Look, I'm going to put a blindfold on you and when I take it off, we'll be outside and safe again. All you have to do is walk where we lead you. Ok?'

'You will have to block his ears too, otherwise he will hear you as a troll,' pointed out the Princess.

Peter shot her a warning glance designed to stop her mentioning the word *'troll'* again.

'And block his nose, otherwise he will smell you as a troll,' added the Princess unhelpfully.

Dunstable was now looking more confused than ever. Peter was about to attempt an explanation when the Princess pounced on Dunstable and yanked on his tie, removing it in one neat movement as it snapped through the air like a whip. Before he could react, she reached up behind him and tied it around his head, completely covering both his eyes and ears. She pulled it tight.

'Ouch! My lovely tie! Oh dear! I can't see anything at all!'

'If you take it off, Dunstable, you will see the ugliest, nastiest troll you have ever seen in your life,' warned the Princess. 'You might want to hold your nose too.'

'Er...pardon?'

'I said: *IF YOU TAKE OFF THE BLINDFOLD YOU WILL SEE AN UGLY TROLL GRINNING AT YOU! IF YOU DO NOT HOLD YOUR NOSE TIGHTLY, YOU WILL SMELL A HORRIBLE SMELLY TROLL! GOT THAT??'*

Dunstable was silent behind the tie for a moment.

'I'll definitely keep it on in that case then.'

'Good. Right! I think we can finally go now, assuming everyone is ready of course?'

Suppressing a momentary regret that he hadn't left her dangling from the ceiling, Peter put the mask on his face again and pictured Mauler in his mind's eye. Immediately he began to grow. He felt a strange tingling sensation as coarse hair sprouted all over his body. His front teeth turned into sharp fangs and enormous muscles bulged on his arms and legs. Within a few seconds, he was a hideous eight-foot troll.

The Princess looked shocked by the transformation.

'You are ugly! You are *really* ugly! Your normal face is quite good-looking by comparison!'

'Thanks,' said Peter dryly, his voice sounding startlingly deep and troll-like. He felt dirty and ungainly and was in no mood for her humour. 'Let's go then shall we?'

He trudged up the stairs, finding it difficult to walk properly as a troll. The Princess carefully steered Dunstable behind him, his blindfold firmly in place. When Peter got to the top of the staircase, he stopped and shuffled awkwardly around to face them.

'Follow behind me. If we meet Betty, look like you're prisoners!'

'Really? And what *exactly* do prisoners look like?' asked the Princess.

'I don't know – glum, sad, tortured - that kind of thing.'

The Princess raised a cynical eyebrow. Without waiting for the inevitable sarcastic comment, Peter pushed the trap-door open a few inches and peered through the gap. His troll eyes were weak and blurry, and he had to squint to focus properly. Fortunately, there was no sign of Betty. As nimbly as his ponderous troll form would allow, he climbed into the kitchen, with the Princess leading Dunstable just behind him.

The kitchen appeared to be deserted. As quickly as they could without making a noise, they crept towards the front door. They were nearly there when it suddenly swung open and Betty walked in. She stared at Peter / Mauler in surprise.

'What you doin' 'ere with them prison-ers? Didn't I tell you to clear off outsyde 'til er visit-ors arrived?'

Straining to hold back the Princess as she tried to push past him to confront the witch, Peter tried to remain calm and look and sound like a troll.

'I fought I'd bring 'em to you,' he replied, as stupidly as possible.

Betty regarded him curiously.

'You *thought? I* do er thinkin' round 'ere, remember? *I'm* er wicked witch and *you're* er hired muscle. Got it? Why 'as thyat one got er tie wrapped round his 'ead?'

Peter hadn't anticipated the question. He stood dumbly for a moment, trying to think of a good reason, until the Princess, who was still trying to push him out of the way, kicked him from behind.

'Errr,' he stuttered, unintentionally sounding just like a dim-witted troll. 'I told him I was gonner eat him and he said he wanted blind-foldin' first. It was his last request like.' It was a poor answer but all he could think of at the spur of the moment.

Betty, though, seemed satisfied with the explanation.

'So, you thought thyat you'd sneak 'im and er Princess out-syide and have yourself er little picnic, did you? Didn't I tell you thyat er Princess is not fer eatin'?'

Peter nodded stupidly. Shrugging his troll shoulders, he bowed his head meekly. Betty reached up and patted him as if he was a naughty but loveable dog.

'You're er *bad* troll! Still, it saves me er job! Take 'em out-syide – they'll be 'ere any min-it I reckon! I'll get er other one.'

She turned sharply on her heels and walked towards the door in the dining room that led down to the first cellar.

Peter couldn't believe his luck! As soon as Betty disappeared down the stairs he raced towards the front-door, pulling the Princess and Dunstable behind him.

'Quick! It'll only take her a second to realise I've escaped!'

Outside, it was still dark and raining heavily. Peter raced towards the small thicket a stone's throw from the house, hoping the trees would hide them from Betty when she discovered she'd been tricked. They hadn't gone far when Dunstable, who was still blindfolded and holding his nose, ran straight into a tree stump and crashed to the ground on top of the Princess. Peter dashed back to pick them up, then skidded to a stop. It was too late! Betty was framed in the doorway behind them, her face bright red with fury. In her hand, the tip of her wand was glowing ominously.

'Think you can escape from me, do you me dears? Think you can blind me with cheap Viking mar-gic and run away rite under me nose, do you? Well, we'll see about thyat won't we? We'll soon see about thyat!' She approached them menacingly, sparks flying from her wand.

As Dunstable struggled to rise to his feet, his blindfold came loose. He took one look at Betty on one side and another at Peter in troll form on the other, and shrieked in terror.

'Oh no!' he squealed. '*Please* don't squash me or turn me into anything unpleasant!'

Throwing himself face down onto the ground, he pulled his jumper over his head.

Meanwhile, the Princess faced the witch. She had twisted her ankle painfully in the fall and was now very, *very* angry indeed.

'So, old hag! You were going to *sell* me were you? *Me! A Princess!!*'

Betty stopped. She raised her wand and began muttering a spell. But she was much too slow. Before she could complete the incantation, her skin suddenly broke out in dozens of enormous red spots. Dropping her wand, she screamed in horror and began frantically scratching herself, her arms a-blur they were moving so fast. In a few seconds, every inch of her skin was covered in spots that were clearly itching like crazy. She didn't know where to scratch next! The Princess glared at her.

'That should keep you busy for a while, witch! Do not worry. They will disappear in a couple of days, if you are lucky. Of course, you may not have any skin left by then!'

Tossing her hair in satisfaction, she turned around and walked calmly towards Peter. Though she looked nonchalant, Peter was sure he could see a little self-satisfied smile appear at the corner of her mouth.

'You had better change back now,' she said matter-of-factly as she passed him. 'Otherwise we will never get Dunstable to come out.'

Peter nodded and changed back into his human form. He made a mental note to never upset the Princess again.

As soon as his transformation was complete, he helped Dunstable to his feet and pulled his jumper away from his face. Dunstable peered up at him for a moment to make absolutely sure he wasn't a troll, then turned and stared at Betty, watching her in wide-eyed astonishment as she hopped and scratched.

They were about to follow the Princess when suddenly they froze in fear. Coming from somewhere hidden in the thicket ahead, they could hear trolls' voices. Peter recovered just fast enough to muffle Dunstable's terrified cry. He turned to the Princess and was about to suggest they go by another route when an unbridled smile of anticipation spread across her face. Barely able to contain her glee, she jogged towards the trees.

Just a few yards inside the dense thicket, Slasher and Mauler were bent over an enormous pot suspended above a fire. Floating in the simmering water inside the pot were several lumps of earth that may have contained recently dug up vegetables. They were arguing over what to put in next, each trying to wrestle the pot off the other.

'I reckon it needs some spinach!' insisted Slasher, heaving the pot out of Mauler's hands. 'It says in me cook book: *'Take Viking, put in pot with fresh spinach. Season to taste. Boil till Viking stops screaming.'*

'Blah! You're always spoilin' good grub with spinach! I hates spinach!' replied Mauler pulling the pot back.

'You're just common you are. Surprised you want to cook 'em at all. No sophistication.'

'Hark at you! The *sophisticated* troll! Think you're gettin' too big for your boot you are! Be reading poetry next, I shouldn't wonder!'

'How dare you! I'm a Wood Troll! I don't read poetry!'

'Or filing your nails, I expect…'

'You better watch your mouth!'

'…or wearing a frilly hat!'

'Right! You've asked for it!'

'Or…*umph!* Awww!! That hurt that did! Nobody punches me on the nose and gets away with it!'

As they grappled with each other, boiling water spilling everywhere, they suddenly noticed the Princess standing a few yards away, staring at them calmly.

'Oye! That's that Princess, that is,' said Mauler. He let go of Slasher's throat and licked his lips. 'She'd be a lot better eatin' than that little Viking, I reckon! Girl humans – they're much tastier!'

'You're not wrong there mate!' said Slasher. 'I was nibblin' her earlier when she were tied up. The tastiest human you ever did nibble she is! Just needs a little spinach, that's all.'

Mauler looked at Slasher in disgust. He was about to speak when Slasher's right hand rose up all by itself and punched him in the face.

''*Ere!* What did you do that for?'

But Slasher was staring at his foot in amazement as it swung out and kicked Mauler hard in the shins.

'*Ouch!* You're askin' for a knuckle sandwich you a….*ouch*!' said Mauler, cut short by Slasher's fist striking him full on the nose again.

'Right!' said Mauler, blood pouring from his face. 'That's twice you've punched me, and you ain't going to punch me a third time!'

Slasher, to his complete astonishment, punched him a third time.

'It's not my fault!' protested Slasher, staring at his guilty fists in disbelief. 'I don't know what's happnin' to me. I'm possessed!'

Mauler wiped his bleeding nose on his hairy arm and walked towards Slasher menacingly, smiling evilly.

'Look! It's *her* that's doin' it!' squealed Slasher, backing away quickly. 'That Princess! Look! She's grinnin' and doin' funny things with her hands!'

Mauler was too angry to listen. He took another step forward then leapt on him. Together, they rolled on the ground, Slasher desperately trying to remove Mauler's teeth from his ear whilst pummelling his head with the side of his fist.

The Princess gave them one final satisfied glance then dusted her hands in satisfaction.

'I think that will keep them busy for a while! We can go now!'

Reminding himself to be nice to the Princess for the time being, Peter tip-toed past the rolling trolls. Gently pulling the Princess behind him, he ran deeper into the thicket. Fortunately Dunstable needed no such urging. As soon as they passed the trolls, he sprinted past Peter as fast as his legs would carry him and waited just ahead, crouching behind two large oak trees, his eyes blinking nervously through his glasses.

But before they could reach him, the ground suddenly began to shake and a thunderous pounding noise arose from the field behind Betty's house. Peter and the Princess turned to see what could possibly be making such an uproar, but whatever was approaching was hidden behind the house and the dip in the hill beyond it. The sound quickly grew louder. In moments it was accompanied by the sharp clinking of metal upon metal. Realising the danger at the last moment, they threw themselves onto the ground next to Dunstable and stared through the trees towards Betty's house.

Out of the darkness, a column of perhaps fifty trolls appeared, marching three a-breast in perfect order. Dressed in bright silver armour, each held a long spear rigidly upright in front of him and wore a short stabbing sword by his side. But what shocked Peter most was their size. The trolls were all well over nine feet tall, far taller even than Slasher and Mauler! But terrifying though they were, his attention was immediately drawn to the man riding a black horse behind them. Slightly bowed as if through age or weariness, he was dressed in a long brown wax coat. His face was hidden behind a black hood, though Peter could clearly see his shining eyes behind its folds. Though dwarfed by the trolls, there was something about him that conveyed a power far greater than the mere physical presence of any troll. As Peter stared at him, he felt a cold shiver run down his spine.

Moving with alarming speed, the trolls came to a halt in the field outside Betty's house, no more than fifty yards from the thicket. They stood perfectly still and expressionless as the man slowly drew his horse up to the house.

Framed in the light from the open kitchen door, Betty was still leaping up and down as she frantically scratched herself, oblivious to everything else. The man came to a halt in front of her, his black horse tossing its head in temper. With a wave of his hand, she suddenly stopped scratching and stood perfectly still. She stared in surprise at her ominous visitor and shuddered in fear.

'They have escaped then, I take it?' the man asked simply. He spoke with a quiet voice, its calm authority making it even more menacing. If a deadly snake could speak before striking the victim it had cornered with no hope of escape, it would surely sound like he.

The effect on Dunstable was devastating. Turning white, he began to shake uncontrollably, whimpering quietly as if he was in pain. He buried his head in the mud and grass and clamped his hands over his ears.

'I…I didn't realyse thyat you would be comin' your-self, *M-Marster!*' Betty squirmed, shaking in fear as she repeatedly bowed before him. 'She…she fooled me she did! Thyat Princess fooled me – with her rotten sp-spell!'

'And the boy? He is gone too, I suppose?'

MALEDICT

'I had 'im Marster! I had 'im chained in er cellar, I did! He-He somehow escaped. He must 'ave freed er Princess and er other one. He c-changed into one of me trolls. I would 'ave stopped 'em otherwise. Honest I would!'

Even from a distance, they could see how truly terrified Betty was. The dark figure had never raised his voice and appeared completely calm, but there was no doubting his tone, subtle though it was.

'I don't suppose you noticed which direction they went, did you?'

Betty turned even paler.

'N...N...No Marster! I was...pre-occupied, s-so to speak...'

'Yes, I saw that.'

'Thank you fer, er, stoppin' thyat nasty spell.'

'Don't mention it.'

Slowly, ominously, the man dismounted from his horse and casually walked towards her. Betty shrank away, twitching in horrified contemplation of what he was about to do. For a moment, he simply gazed at her without speaking, the silence even more terrifying.

'So. Let me get this straight. I like to understand things clearly. I've come all this way to pick up some prisoners, and when I get here, you tell me that they've escaped and you do not know where they have gone. Does that about sum the situation up?'

Bowing her head, Betty shook with terror.

'And these three prisoners that you let slip through your fingers so easily consisted of, let me see...a spoilt brat of a Princess, a useless City Dweller and a pathetic snivelling Viking who is terrified of magic?'

Betty briefly nodded, not daring to raise her head.

'I see. That is rather...*disappointing*.'

Again, there was deadly silence. Peter felt sure that something terrible was about to happen, such was the menace behind the man's words. He appeared to be merely pausing for a moment to contemplate what terrible punishment to inflict upon the witch. Betty was now shaking so much she could barely stand. Peter almost felt sorry for her.

'I suppose I might as well be off then in that case,' said the man after a pause of several agonising seconds, still speaking as calmly as if he was discussing the weather. 'There is no point in me being here, after all, with no prisoners to collect?'

'Um, no, I sup-hose not M-Marster,' mumbled Betty, clearly thinking he couldn't leave quickly enough.

He walked slowly back to his horse. Then he paused for a moment and gazed towards the thicket. Peter's heart froze in terror. The man appeared to be staring right at him! For perhaps ten seconds the man's eyes bore into him, though it seemed to last a lifetime. Then, as if satisfied, he mounted his horse and steered it to the front of the line of trolls, who were standing perfectly still, awaiting his command. As he urged his horse into a trot, they fell in behind him. Betty breathed a gigantic sigh of relief.

'Oh Betty?' he called out suddenly, coming to an abrupt stop. He didn't turn around. The impassive trolls ground to a halt behind him. Betty almost jumped out of her skin.

'Awww! Er, yes Marster???'

'You won't disappoint me again, will you?'

'N – N No Marster!'

'Only, I do so hate being disappointed. You wouldn't want to upset me, would you?'

Betty's voice sounded so terrified, Peter could barely catch her words.

'No-o – I w-wouldn't. I c-certainly w-wouldn't...M-Marster!'

'Good. I feel so much better now.'

Once again he urged his horse forwards, quickly breaking into a trot. Behind him, the trolls immediately began a fast march across the fields and down the slope behind Betty's house. In seconds they had disappeared into the darkness, though it took almost a minute before the sound of their marching feet finally faded.

It was some time before any of them stirred. Dunstable, in particular, was shaking and blubbering, and try as they might, they couldn't get him to move. After about half an hour, during which they repeatedly tried, but failed, to bring him to his senses, the Princess took Peter's arm and urged him aside, out of Dunstable's earshot.

'That was too close! *He* has come! Do you understand what this means? The siege of York must have already started! This is bad, very bad! We have to get back quickly!'

Peter didn't need to ask who 'He' was. He knew the answer already.

'I think Mimir was right,' she continued, speaking so quickly in her agitation he could barely follow her. 'I think he knows about the Quest and used the witch to try to stop us.' She paused and stared into the distance in the direction the trolls had disappeared. 'York cannot be more than a few miles away. We must leave! We may already be too late!'

A few minutes later, through a mixture of persuasion, sympathising and references to the proximity of Betty and her pet trolls, they managed to persuade Dunstable they would be much safer once they were back in the Viking Halls in York. Then they began the race home, hoping they still had a home to return to.

Chapter 16

The Race to the City Walls

It was a dangerous journey back to York. The whole countryside was crawling with trolls. Some were marching across fields or along winding country roads, whilst others were camped on hilltops or were simply lying nonchalantly in grassy fields, watching the sun rise above the horizon as the day began. The closer they got to the city, the more trolls they encountered, and the more eager they became to get back to York as quickly as possible. The Princess urged them on, leading them across fields and roads, occasionally pausing just long enough to allow them to gasp for breath before driving them on again.

Despite the trolls, they made good progress. The one advantage they had was stealth. The three of them could move quietly, whereas it was impossible for even one troll to move without making a noise, and when they were gathered together the racket they made could be heard for miles around. Also they were wary, whereas the trolls clearly had no fear of being discovered and did nothing to hide their presence.

Helped by the trolls' clamour and the Princess's acute senses, they finally reached the first streets of York an hour after dawn.

As they feared, troll battalions were patrolling the outskirts of the city. Their progress slowed dramatically as they were forced to creep from street to street, ducking behind houses and garden walls whenever they saw trolls approaching. They hadn't gone far when they turned a corner and saw the City Walls looming tall and proud less than two miles in the distance. Beyond them soared the Minster, its twin-towers rising majestically above the city. Immediately their spirits were lifted. They were almost home at last! Then they froze. Between them and the city lay the vast expanse of a horse racecourse. Over a mile long and half a mile wide, it stretched towards the distant Walls. Swarming across its muddy fields was a vast army of trolls.

The Princess was the first to react. In a flash, she grabbed their coats and hauled them behind the wall of a house before they were spotted. For a moment they gasped for breath, their hearts pounding, hardly believing the number of trolls they had seen. But the Princess didn't allow them to rest for long. Almost immediately, she led them into a back-alley that was hidden from the trolls on the racecourse by the tall houses enclosing it on either side. They sprinted down the alley until they reached a narrow street at its far end, then came to a sudden stop. They had now gone as far as they dared.

Crouching behind the garden wall of a large Victorian house at the end of the street, they peered nervously ahead. The racecourse spread into the distance towards the city, its green puddle-strewn field marked by white railings that guided the horses on race days and a tall, empty, spectator stand. At its centre was the troll encampment. An enormous black tent was raised there and hundreds of armoured Mountain Trolls were sitting on the grass outside it, sharpening their spears and axes. Strewn across the rest of the field were countless Wood Trolls. They were marching back and forth in tight battalions led by ferocious Mountain Trolls, their whips dangling from their hands as they barked endless insults.

It was a terrifying sight. It wasn't just the number of trolls that was so frightening, it was their boldness - setting up their camp so close to the city in broad daylight as if they didn't care whether City Dwellers could see them. No longer were they content with hiding in the mountains or forests of the far desolate north, occasionally attacking unfortunate passers-by. Now, for the first time, the Wood and Mountain Trolls had gathered together to form one terrifying army and had stepped out into the open.

Unsure what to do next, the three of them knelt on the pavement behind the garden wall. Mixed with his fear, Peter felt a nagging sense of disbelief. He still hadn't got used to the fact that Vikings and trolls, and the other magical creatures he had seen, lived in the same world as City Dwellers but couldn't be seen by them. Within a few yards of the nearest trolls on the edge of the racecourse, people were walking along the pavement and cars were racing along the busy road, all completely unaware of the terrifying creatures that stood just a short distance away from them. Like the City Dwellers,

Peter had lived all his life in ignorance, unaware of the strange magical world entwined with his own and the wonders and horrors that lay within it. He wondered whether *he* had ever walked blindly past a troll, and felt a cold shiver run down his spine.

The Princess had other matters on her mind. After her initial shock at the boldness of the trolls, she was concentrating on how to get back to the Viking Halls as quickly as possible. After surveying the troll army for almost a minute, she ducked beneath the garden wall and squatted on the pavement beside them, bristling with frustration.

'This is no good! We simply *must* get past the trolls! I have to see the Queen immediately!'

Crouched beside her, Dunstable's eyes were wide open behind his glasses as he shook his head in terror.

'This is hopeless! Utterly hopeless! I've never *seen* so many trolls! We'll never get back now! Never! Might as well wait here until they catch us and squash us!' He pressed himself against the wall and shrank beneath his blazer, shaking with fear.

'Could we fly over them?' suggested Peter, ignoring the look of alarm that spread over Dunstable's face. 'If Maledict knows we're here anyway, we'd have nothing to lose, would we?'

'Of course we cannot fly over them!' replied the Princess sharply, glaring at him in irritation that her train of thought had been interrupted by such a stupid suggestion. 'The trolls *do* have archers you know. In any case, it is broad daylight and there are City Dwellers around. We might be spotted by children.'

'But there are thousands of trolls here!' protested Peter incredulously. 'Children can see *them*, can't they? They're hardly going to be worried about us!'

'I do not care! We can*not* fly over the city in daylight! Those are the rules!' insisted the Princess defiantly, refusing to give in to his logic.

'What about waiting for darkness then? There'd be less children around then.'

The Princess threw Peter a withering look, as if she was being forced to explain something completely obvious to someone very stupid indeed.

'Trolls can see perfectly well in the dark, remember? That is when they hunt, jumping out on people in the middle of the night.

We would be shot down before we got within fifty yards of the Walls! Anyway, we cannot wait that long.'

'Then we should walk around the Walls then, and get into the city somewhere where there are less trolls,' continued Peter stubbornly.

'We have not got time! Anyway, I want to see what they are up to before I talk to the Queen! This is the perfect opportunity!'

'So, what do *you* suggest then, assuming you've got any suggestions at all?' said Peter icily, annoyed by her instant dismissal of his ideas and doubting whether she had any better ones.

She glanced across the racecourse again, her eyes narrowing in concentration.

'I *do* have one actually! A much better one than yours too! Stay here!'

Before Peter could say another word, she darted out from behind the garden wall and sprinted towards the busy road that bordered the racecourse. She was in full view of the trolls! She ran about twenty yards, then leapt behind a house halfway to the road.

Startled, Peter urgently scoured the troll army. Fortunately, none of them appeared to have seen her.

'What *are* you doing?' he whispered as loudly as he dared.

The Princess turned around and gestured to him.

'Wait there! I will not be long!'

Beside Peter, Dunstable rose to his knees and peered over the garden wall, his curiosity to see what the Princess was doing overcoming his fear of the trolls.

'What on earth is she up to? She's going to get herself squashed if she's not careful, you know!'

Peter shrugged his shoulders. He had absolutely no idea.

As they watched, the Princess darted from cover. Leaping over a wall, she sprinted across a garden, then rolled onto the ground behind an old red car. She was now just ten yards from the busy road that ran alongside the racecourse. So far she hadn't been seen, mainly because the trolls were not expecting any Vikings to try to get into the city and hadn't set any guards. But Peter couldn't see how she could possibly go any further without being spotted. More importantly, he couldn't understand why she apparently wanted to walk straight into the troll camp in the first place. Had she gone completely bonkers?

Hidden behind the parked car, the Princess paused as if undecided what to do next. Then disaster struck. A man in a dull grey suit walked down the street just in front of her. He went straight to the car, completely oblivious to the Princess, and pulled out a key from his pocket. Unlocking the driver's door, he sat inside and turned on the engine, reviving it loudly into life.

Peter and Dunstable barely dared watch as several trolls, alerted by the noise, strolled to the edge of the racecourse across the main road to take a closer look. The only thing keeping the Princess from being seen was the car! Then, to their horror, the car began to move.

'Oh dear!' whimpered Dunstable. 'I can't watch!'

He dived back under the garden wall and covered his eyes with his hands. Peter continued to stare at the Princess as the car pulled away from the curb towards the main road. But the Princess didn't stand still. As the car moved, so did she, running crouched behind it, careful to keep it between her and the watching trolls.

Fortunately for her, the main road junction was only a short distance away and the car moved slowly. With the Princess still concealed, it eased to a stop as the driver waited for a break in the traffic.

Meanwhile, just a few yards across the road, the trolls were losing interest. One by one, they turned back towards the centre of the racecourse. If the car could remain stationary just a little longer, the Princess might still be safe!

But before the last of the trolls had turned away, the car suddenly pulled out into the main road and turned sharply to the left, its tyres screeching. Still hidden behind it, the Princess immediately broke into a run, ducking as low as she could to avoid being seen whilst struggling to keep up with the car. It accelerated slowly due to its age and the wet road, but soon even the fast sprinting Princess was struggling to remain concealed. Just as the car was beginning to pull away from her, she dived out from behind it, narrowly avoiding another car that was coming from the opposite direction, dashed across the road and threw herself behind some trees on the edge of the racecourse.

Hardly daring to breathe, Peter studied the trolls to see if she'd been spotted. Fortunately they were staring hungrily at a group of students who were walking past them on the pavement. Somehow, she had managed to get onto the racecourse without being seen.

She was now opposite a grey tent Peter hadn't noticed before. Though much smaller than the enormous black tent in the centre of the racecourse, it was still the size of a small house. Twenty or more Mountain Trolls were sitting on the grass outside it, idly sharpening their spears and swords.

Pausing for a few seconds to regain her breath, the Princess dashed out from behind the trees. Fast as an arrow, she sprinted across the grass towards the tent then leapt behind it, still unseen by any of the trolls.

Hidden behind the tent she was relatively safe, until she decided to move again. As Peter watched her, she started doing something peculiar with her hands, though he was too far away to tell what it was. Then, as she ducked down and disappeared, he suddenly understood. She had cut a hole in the fabric of the tent and crawled inside!

'Oh dear!' whispered Dunstable, peering bravely over the garden wall once more to see how she was getting on. 'That'll be where they keep their weapons, you know! Lots and lots of sharp swords, nasty pointy spears and all sorts of unpleasant things! Why on earth does she want to go there?'

Peter glanced at him blankly and shrugged his shoulders. He was as baffled as Dunstable.

Together, they stared at the hole in the tent the Princess had crawled through, expecting her to be discovered at any moment. Several minutes passed without anything appearing to happen. Then, just when Peter was contemplating whether he should try to help her, the small flap of tent fabric she had cut opened and the Princess popped out, dragging a large bundle behind her. She paused for a moment to ensure no trolls were watching, then raced back towards the road with the bundle slung over her shoulder, before diving behind the trees on the edge of the racecourse again. Peter and Dunstable searched the faces of the trolls beside the tent. Somehow she had made it without being seen.

For the moment, she was hidden. This time though, it would be much more difficult to repeat her trick of running behind a car carrying such a heavy looking load. To make matters worse, the trolls that had so nearly spotted her before had returned and were now standing just twenty yards away from her, leaning on their spears as they stared across the road. As soon as she stepped out, she would be seen. His heart thumping in apprehension, Peter wondered what she would do next.

For a long minute she waited, squatting perfectly still. Then, to his horror, the trolls at the edge of the road began to amble towards the trees where she was hiding. In a moment, they would surely see her!

The Princess knew it too. Peter could clearly see her as she ducked lower, her eyes fixed on the trolls. What was she doing? Then, just when she was about to be discovered, an open-topped double-decker bus appeared on the busy road behind her. It was clearly a tourist bus. The words *'The York Horror Tour Bus – Are You Brave Enough To Take Our Ride?'* were emblazoned in blood-red paint along its length beside a picture of someone being tortured. It came to a stop just in front of the trees behind which the Princess was hiding. A small group of tourists were waiting on the pavement there, dressed in bright coats and scarves, all with enormous cameras draped around their necks.

As quick as a flash, the Princess leapt the low perimeter rail of the racecourse and darted behind the bus, completely unseen by the trolls and the tourists. She was only just in time! The trolls had made their way to the trees and were now studying the bus, taking obvious delight in the gruesome picture on its side. Then, as Peter and Dunstable watched in terrified fascination, the bus began to pull away. Fortunately it was slow to accelerate, and the Princess was able to run beside it hidden from the trolls, though perilously close to the traffic racing by in the opposite direction.

Soon, however, the ponderous bus began to pick up speed. Slowly she fell back, desperately holding onto her heavy load, until she was level with the back wheels. She was seconds away from being seen! At the last moment, she dashed between two cars travelling in the opposite direction, hurdled the garden wall of a hotel on the other side of the road and threw herself onto the grass, the bundle still held tightly in her arms.

Tearing their eyes away from her for a moment, Peter and Dunstable stared at the trolls. Fortunately all their attention was still focused on the bus and they showed no sign of having seen her. Meanwhile, the Princess darted behind the hotel. She was now completely hidden from the trolls behind the row of houses which faced the road. Somehow, she had made it.

A few minutes later, she jogged around the corner of the street in which they were hiding, a triumphant smile on her face as she carried the enormous bundle over her back.

'That was…*really stupid!*' exclaimed Peter furiously as she dashed across the street towards them and ducked under the wall. 'What were you doing?'

The Princess's smug smile was instantly replaced by an offended frown.

'Working on getting us home, that is what! What do you think I was doing?'

Peter glanced at the bundle she had dumped on the pavement in front of them. Inside were dirty looking clothes.

'What's that?'

'It is our ticket back into the city! You do not think I dragged it all the way here just for fun, do you?'

Peter gritted his teeth.

'Are you going to tell us what you've got in mind then, or are we supposed to guess?'

With a petulant toss of her long hair, the Princess unwrapped the bundle and emptied its contents onto the pavement, revealing two black troll tunics and cloaks complete with helmets and breastplates.

'We are going to put these on! I will cut them down to our size. Trolls do not see very well in the daylight. If they do not look too closely, we might just…'

'Goodness gracious! They're *troll* clothes!' snorted Dunstable, shrinking away from them in disgust. 'Trolls wear them! *And* they're smelly! I don't want to look like a smelly troll, thank you very much!'

Peter was equally unenthusiastic as he gingerly picked up a cloak. It stank of stale sweat and was covered in coarse troll hairs.

'So this is your wonderful idea, is it? The one you almost got killed for? We'll be spotted a mile off! We're much too small to pass as trolls! Why are there only two uniforms anyway?'

'If you two will *kindly* let me finish! As I was *going* to say… Dunstable is so short no one could possibly mistake him for a troll, no matter what he was wearing or how bad their eyesight. That is why you are going to have to carry him on your shoulders Peter.'

'Oh really?' said Peter scathingly. 'That's a wonderful idea! And what am I supposed to do if we have to make a run for it?'

The Princess ignored him. Kneeling on the pavement, she began cutting the uniforms with her knife. In moments she was done. She handed Peter a roughly cut troll tunic and cloak.

'This is what we are going to do,' she announced, the tone of her voice indicating that the matter was not subject to debate. 'We are going to walk across the racecourse through the troll army into the city. It is almost mid-day, the worst time of day for trolls, and the sun will be behind us. With luck, they will not be able to see us well enough to realise who we are.'

Dunstable, who had been looking increasingly tortured whilst she spoke, finally lost all restraint.

'*WALK THROUGH THE TROLL ARMY!!?* Are you *absolutely mad?* You want to *walk* through the *hundreds* of nasty, smelly trolls that are on that field, sharpening their spears and swords? Oh no! I don't like this idea at all! I don't like it one little bit! We'll be *squashed*, I tell you! We'll all be sq...'

'Shut up Dunstable!' interrupted the Princess, staring at him menacingly.

'*But...!*'

'Has either of you got any better ideas? Or do you want to hide here forever?'

Peter was tempted to mention his previous suggestions that they either fly over the trolls or simply find somewhere where there were not so many of them and enter the city from there, but something about the Princess's expression told him that they were unlikely to meet with her approval. He glanced at Dunstable, but he was staring wide-eyed at the troll uniforms laid out on the pavement looking absolutely petrified.

'Right!' continued the Princess. 'If there are no more objections, then perhaps we can get a move on?'

Retreating behind a house further down the street where there was more cover, they gingerly began to put on the troll clothes. They turned out to be even more revolting than they first thought, and absolutely stank of sweat and something even more unpleasant that they dared not guess. Still, for Peter at least, there was one small compensation: he got to see the Princess's face as she dressed herself. He knew that however disgusting it was for him to put on the stinking clothes, it was ten times worse for her, obsessed as she was with the way she looked. As he watched her, he couldn't help grinning. She looked a million miles from her usual immaculate appearance. The troll breast-plate, which covered almost her entire body, was wonky and dull, her helmet was sitting precariously on her head with her long blonde hair bundled up inside and, despite her rapid alterations, the troll tunic and cloak were still far too big for her.

'What is so funny?' she demanded, turning around sharply and staring daggers at him.

'You look…*different*, that's all.'

'Really? That is because I am wearing a horrible smelly troll uniform! You look a bit 'different' yourself!'

Peter chose not to argue and busied himself with the gruesome task of dressing. But he couldn't resist an occasional glance at the Princess or suppress the smile that forced its way onto his lips.

Finally they were done and Dunstable reluctantly climbed onto Peter's shoulders as he bent down on one knee. To improve their disguises, the Princess and Dunstable tied the troll cloaks around their necks, letting them drape around them, completely covering their bodies. Unfortunately, the cloaks were the most revolting of all, absolutely reeking of stale body odour and whatever hideous things trolls got up to.

'Better to wear a troll's cloak than have one squashing you!' advised the Princess curtly in response to Dunstable's disgusted expression.

'Why *do* trolls squash people anyway?' asked Peter, rising unsteadily to his feet as he peered through the tiny gaps in the black cloak Dunstable had tied around them. 'Why don't they just bash them over the head or force them to smell their arm-pits or something?'

'To break all their bones of course!' replied the Princess irritably. 'Then they can eat them without damaging their teeth! Trolls only have little teeth and they certainly do not use knives and forks! There is nothing a troll hates more than breaking his teeth against bone!'

'Oh,' said Peter, wishing he hadn't asked the question. Perched on his shoulders, Dunstable made a strange choking noise.

With their disguises complete, they were finally ready to

attempt the dangerous journey through the troll army. However, they couldn't cross onto the racecourse at the same place the Princess had earlier. Several trolls were standing there and they didn't want to risk being questioned, no matter how good their disguises or bad the trolls' eyesight. They therefore decided to make their way down another back-alley until they reached a position opposite the far corner of the field, where there were fewer trolls. But, as soon as they got there, the downside became apparent. They would now have to walk diagonally across almost the entire racecourse and through the heart of the troll army in order to reach the safety of the city on the other side.

Without being noticed, they crossed onto the racecourse and stepped onto the grass. Hundreds and hundreds of trolls were scattered across the huge field in front of them. Some were on guard duty (though they paid little attention to anything other than the sharpness of their spears and the contents of their noses), some were resting, others were eating unidentifiable animals which they were roasting on spits and still others were marching back and forth. The whole camp was alive with activity; a hive of gigantic ants crowded together, waiting for the command to fight.

Nervously, they began their journey across the field, Peter and the Princess mimicking a troll's lazy stride as best they could, whilst skirting around the most congested areas. But though they chose their path carefully, it was impossible to avoid the trolls completely, and several times Peter cringed as a troll stopped to squint at them, clearly wondering why they were so small. At one point, a particularly large Mountain Troll bumped into him and stopped to glare at Dunstable as he wobbled in terror on Peter's shoulders.

"*Ere!* Watch it shorty! Why don't you look where you're goin'?'

Fortunately, the Princess rapidly intervened, ushering them away from the belligerent troll as quickly as possible.

Slowly they made their way towards the enormous black tent in the middle of the racecourse. Hundreds of trolls were lounging in front of it, though there were almost none behind. If they could just get past it without being seen, they would almost be safe. It would then be just a short sprint to the City Walls, which were looming invitingly in the distance. But Peter was beginning to tire. The weight of Dunstable on his shoulders and the troll armour he was wearing were beginning to take their toll. It didn't help that Dunstable was clinging onto his neck so tightly he could barely breathe.

'We...must...stop...for...a...few...seconds,' he panted after about five minutes. He was feeling so tired he could barely walk.

'Just a bit further until we are past the main tent, then we will stop!' whispered the Princess, glancing at him anxiously. Seeing him wobble, she took hold of his arm and steered him urgently forward.

Through the tiny gaps in the troll cloak, Peter could clearly see the tent about forty yards ahead. But between it and them were at least a hundred trolls. Hardly able to breathe, he tried to loosen Dunstable's grip on his neck, but he couldn't reach around his legs. The closer they got to the tent, the tighter Dunstable pulled. Feeling weaker by the second, Peter fought desperately for breath. He felt himself stagger and almost fainted. He was already falling when the Princess caught him. A few seconds later he heard her faint voice beside him.

'We can wait here! Sit down for a minute. Then we must move again!'

Peter collapsed in a crumpled heap on the grass, sending Dunstable sliding awkwardly over his head and shoulders. Gasping for breath, he peered across the field. They were lying just behind the enormous black tent in the centre of the racecourse, hidden from most of the trolls around them. Less than twenty yards away, a dozen Mountain Trolls were sitting around a fire sharpening their weapons. However, the bulk of the troll army was on the side of the field away from the city - the side through which they had just passed. He glanced over his shoulder and was relieved to see that they were much closer to the Walls. A five minute run or a half minute flight and they would be safe.

Beside him, Dunstable rose unsteadily to his feet. The black troll cloak was wrapped around him like an enormous blanket and the troll helmet was perched on his head, covering his eyes and most of his face.

'Are we there yet?' he squeaked blindly. 'Are all the nasty trolls behind us?'

'*Shush!*' whispered the Princess as she leant over Peter, keeping guard. 'We have just got a little further to go. We are taking a break so Peter can get his breath back! I will let you know when it is safe!'

Peter gazed up at the Princess wearily.

'What's the plan then?'

'We have done the hard part! We have passed through most of the troll army. Now all we have to do is pretend we are patrolling as close to the city as we can get away with without any trolls getting suspicious. Then we will make a run for the Walls.'

Peter nodded. He was too tired to think and was more than happy to be led by the Princess, as long as he could rest at the end of it. Taking a deep breath, he bent down so that Dunstable could climb back onto his shoulders then rose awkwardly to his feet. He had only just followed the Princess beyond the cover of the tent, though, when a dark shadow fell across him.

'Oye! What you doin' 'ere, you 'orrible little troll?'

Peter froze, unsure what to do next. On his shoulders he could feel Dunstable go rigid with fear. Towering above them was a giant Mountain Troll. He was holding a spear twice Peter's height in his enormous right hand and a gleaming sword was sheathed at his side. Snarling, he squinted down at Dunstable's helmeted face, his eyes struggling to focus.

'Can't you 'ear me soldier? I said, *what-are-you-doin'-'ere?* You pathetic little trolls shouldn't be wanderin' down 'ere close to the Walls. You should be at the back of the field like the rest of your snivellin' little kind.' Suddenly he bent over and thrust his head towards them. Pressing his ugly squashed up nose against Dunstable's helmet, he began to sniff loudly, sounding like a frenzied vacuum cleaner. ''*Ere!* Summut's up! You smell funny!'

Dunstable couldn't take any more.

'*Pleassseee* don't squash me!' he squeaked, shaking so violently on Peter's shoulders he almost fell off.

'Eh? What did you say? 'Ere! I don't think you're a troll at all! I think you're a Viking or summut! Guards! I've found some spies! Guards! *Gua...ooomph!*'

Stealing up unseen behind him, the Princess had flown up and struck him as hard as she could with the hilt of his own sword. But it was too late. Already the Mountain Trolls who were sat nearby were leaping to their feet, enraged at the sight of the Princess felling their comrade.

'*Run!*' yelled the Princess.

They didn't need to be told. With surprisingly agility, Dunstable leapt off Peter's shoulders and sprinted towards the City Walls, with

Peter and the Princess close behind. As he ran, Peter glanced over his shoulder. The whole troll army was now aware of their presence and was converging on them from all directions. It was fortunate they had made it past the black tent as, for the moment at least, the pursuing trolls were all behind them. If they could just stay ahead for long enough, they might still make it!

Sprinting as fast as his tired legs would allow, Peter cast off the cumbersome troll breastplate as he drew level with Dunstable, the Princess right beside him. They had now reached the edge of the racecourse. Side by side, they sped across a road, dodging several cars, and raced down a narrow side-street. Up ahead, the Walls were getting closer, no more than a few hundred yards away.

'How…will…we…get…through…the…Walls?' gasped Peter, his lungs burning as he strained every muscle to run faster. 'Are … we…heading…in…the… right…direction?'

The Princess pointed towards a small turret on the Walls almost directly ahead of them.

'*There!* We can get in through there! I know the password!'

With renewed vigour, they dashed along the pavement in the direction the Princess had indicated. Peter risked another quick glance over his shoulder. At least twenty Mountain Trolls were racing out of the racecourse behind them, but they had a reasonable head start and were only slowly being caught. With a bit of luck, they would reach the Walls in time!

Then, as they sprinted across another road, disaster struck. As Dunstable was looking for a gap between the speeding cars, he tripped down the curb and fell heavily to the ground. Before he could react, Peter crashed over him, scraping his knees and arms painfully on the tarmac.

'Oh no! I think I've twisted my ankle!' squealed Dunstable in absolute panic, his face turning white as he cringed in pain.

Peter leapt to his feet as the Princess came to an abrupt halt beside him. Together they raced over to Dunstable and grabbed him beneath each arm. But Peter's legs were badly bruised and, with the added weight of Dunstable, he could barely hobble. Agonised, he gazed ahead. The Walls were less than a hundred yards away. They were so close!

But not close enough. They had barely staggered to the other side of the road when the sound of pounding feet behind them became rapidly louder. Before Peter could turn, he felt heavy hands on his shoulders.

'Stop right there! I've got you now!'

It was the same troll the Princess had struck. A large red sword handle imprint was clearly visible on his forehead.

'No where to run now, you filthy scum! I'll show you what happens to anyone who bashes me over the 'ead!'

Peter and the Princess spun around with Dunstable still suspended between them, his eyes firmly shut as he froze in terror. There was no hope of escape this time. They were confronted by at least twenty enormous Mountain Trolls. Side by side, they backed down a narrow alleyway between two houses, passing two elderly women chatting in a doorway, completely unaware of what was going on around them. But the alleyway was a dead-end. There was no where left for them to go! Bravely, the Princess stood her ground and faced the trolls, her expression determined. But they simply laughed at her, their ugly faces leering in pleasure. Then the troll with the sword imprint on his head stepped forward.

'So, what do we have 'ere then lads? A ponsy girl-Viking, a pathetic little maggot and a City Dweller? What did 'is Highness say? *Look out for a City Dweller travellin' with a Viking Princess and a snivellin' little rat!* I think we're in luck lads. I think we've hit the jackpot! He's going to be *very* pleased when he hears the news, very pleased indeed! Still, doesn't mean we can't have a bit of fun with 'em first, eh lads?'

The troll soldiers, who had now completely surrounded Peter and the Princess, laughed as they stroked their swords in anticipation of the 'fun' they would shortly be having.

'You will never take us alive!' hissed the Princess, standing tall and defiant.

But before the troll could reply, several things happened at once. First, the Princess struck out with a spell that flung him violently backwards, his already bruised head striking a car with a painful crunch. At the same time, another troll thrust his spear at Peter, who just managed to dodge out of the way, crashing into Dunstable in the process. Then, as Peter rolled on the ground trying to evade several clutching troll hands, he heard the sound of racing feet and a vaguely familiar voice shouting wildly.

'*Attack! Attack!* Take the prisoners! *Take the prisoners!*'

But the last thing that happened was the worst. One of the trolls reaching down to grab him suddenly fell crashing forward, crushing Peter under his enormous weight. For a moment, Peter was vaguely aware of a scuffle taking place around him as the breath went out of his lungs. Then everything went ominously quiet. He descended into darkness and was aware no more.

Book2

The Return of Sigurd the Dragon Slayer

In Book 2 - The Return of Sigurd the Dragon Slayer.....

York is under siege as Maledict unleashes his army against the Vikings.

As the Prince battles the trolls on the city streets, a desperate plan is hatched to steal the Viking Stone from Maledict's crown. But as the final devastating battle is about to be fought, the meaning of Peter's visions at Mimir's Well becomes clear and the Vikings realise that Maledict has a still more sinister purpose in mind.

As the skies burn red and creatures from legend awake, the Princess and her companions must stop the most terrifying Viking prophecy from being fulfilled.

You can order further copies of this book direct from Hall Publishing.

FREE UK DELIVERY!

To order further copies of *The Last Vikings*
please send a copy of the coupon below to:

Hall Publishing Company
25 Windmill Rise
York
YO26 4TU

I enclose a UK bank cheque or postal order, payable to
Hall Publishing, for £_____, at £6.99 per book.

NAME: _____

ADDRESS: _____

_____

_____

_____ POSTCODE: _____

Please allow up to 28 days for delivery. Do not send cash. We will not share your details with any other firm or person.

Please tick the box if you do not want to receive further information from Hall Publishing about further books from S.P.Grey ☐